"Let's get airborne,

we can all get better acquainted once we're safely out of here," Amundson said.

But just as Amundson finished speaking, a loud explosion shook the clearing. They looked up in time to see the escort gunship erupt into a ball of fire. Simultaneously, automatic-weapons fire from the surrounding woods raked Dean and his men, leaving them all either dead or wounded.

"Goddamn!" Amundson cried. "They've been following us the whole time." He pushed the President-elect and Ellen toward the second chopper, their only hope of escape.

As the three neared the helicopter door, the President-elect cried out, then stumbled and fell to the ground from the impact of three bullets in his back. He lay facedown, his blood staining the snow.

THE ODYSSEY PROJECT

THE ODYSSEY PROJECT

LAWRENCE DE MARINO

PAGEANT BOOKS

PAGEANT BOOKS
225 Park Avenue South
New York, New York 10003

Cover artwork by Alan Ayers

Printed in the U.S.A.

First Pageant Books printing: March, 1989

10 9 8 7 6 5 4 3 2 1

Chapter One

IIII IIII IIII IIII IIII

The long black limousine moved along Pennsylvania Avenue, then slowed and pulled into the White House driveway, up to the guard shack. The driver and lone passenger were eyeballed by the guard, then waved on.

The limousine continued on to the entrance, where two marines snapped to attention. The driver hopped out to open the door for his passenger, while a Secret Service tail car pulled up behind the limo. Even though they were on White House grounds, four agents got out of the tail car and formed a protective wall for the limousine's occupant.

Waiting patiently was Alex Harris, chief of staff to the outgoing, lame-duck President of the United States.

Harris walked forward to greet the limousine's passenger, Adam Porter, who stepped out of the car onto a carpet of frost-covered leaves. Porter removed a glove, and they shook hands warmly.

"Good morning, Alex," Porter said.

"Good morning, sir."

"A little chilly to be standing out here without a topcoat, isn't it?"

Harris shrugged, and motioned for Porter to enter the White House. "The others have already arrived, so if you'll follow me," he said.

They entered the White House, pausing briefly while Porter handed his topcoat to a waiting servant.

"Congratulations," Harris said, as they walked down the corridor toward the West Wing and the Oval Office.

"Pardon?"

"On your victory last week."

"Why, thank you, Alex."

"When the campaign began, I didn't think you had a prayer of winning."

After a pause, Harris spoke more softly. "If I can be of any help to you during the transition, just let me know."

"I'm sure we can find some common ground, Alex," Porter replied. "In fact, there is something you can help me with right now."

"What's that?"

"What's your boss up to with this emergency meeting on national security?"

Harris shrugged. "You've got me. All I can tell

you is there are two CIA guys in there with him."

Porter could not conceal his irritation. "I've been trying to reach him all week to arrange the first transition meeting. He hasn't returned any of my phone calls—then last night his secretary calls about this 'urgent' eight AM meeting. It better be important."

Their conversation ended abruptly as they reached the Oval Office. Harris opened the door and looked in. He spoke softly to the occupants, then beckoned Porter to enter.

Two men were seated in comfortable armchairs before the President's desk. Next to them stood an empty chair. The President took his pipe from his mouth and stood to greet Porter. The other two men also rose to greet the new arrival.

The President offered a hand. "Good morning, Senator."

"Good morning, Mr. President."

The President turned slightly, motioning toward the other two men. "I believe you already know Dr. Stanton, my director of the CIA, from the confirmation hearings four years ago."

"Yes, indeed I do. How are you, Doctor?"

"Just fine, Senator."

"The other gentleman must remain anonymous for security reasons, at least until you're the official tenant here. However, I can tell you he's the senior analyst for the CIA."

The President resumed his seat, and the other three men followed his lead. Before the President could continue, there was a soft knock at a side door.

"Come!" the President said loudly.

A steward entered, carrying an ornate serving set.

"Ah, good," the President said. "Gentlemen, how about some coffee to get the heart pumping?"

"Yes. I could use a cup," Porter said.

"How do you take it, sir?" the steward asked.

"Cream," Porter answered.

The steward served Porter first, then each of the other men in turn, then left through the same door. Making sure the steward was out of earshot, the President resumed his conversation.

"Before we begin, I want you to know that four years ago, as President-elect, I received the same briefing you're going to get today."

The President paused and fidgeted with his pipe, tapping the bowl on the edge of a large ashtray while his three guests waited for him to resume. Plainly, it was difficult for him to continue. "What do you know about the geological history of the planet?" he asked Porter.

Porter leaned back in his chair, a puzzled look on his face. "I know virtually nothing about geology, Mr. President, but—"

"Neither did I until four years ago. Do you know that huge land areas have periodically been covered with ice sheets?"

"Yes, I believe I read that somewhere," Porter said, irritation edging into his voice. "It's happened several times, as I recall."

"Four times, to be exact. Four ice ages."

"With all due respect, Mr. President, what the hell does an ice age have to do with national security?"

The President sighed. "History is about to repeat itself. Within our lifetimes, we will experience the beginning of the fifth ice age."

The room fell quiet. Porter was suddenly very aware of the tick-tocking of the grandfather clock to the left of the President's desk. The President-elect stared at the President, who chewed on the stem of his pipe and calmly returned Porter's gaze.

Porter looked at Stanton, who quickly averted his gaze, then turned to the elderly CIA analyst, whose reptilian smile did not waver.

Finally, Porter broke the silence. "Are you serious, Mr. President?"

"Dead serious."

"Someone must have made a mistake."

"There's no mistake, Senator. The possibility of a new ice age has been common knowledge in the scientific community for a long time."

"How long?"

"The original discovery was made in 1952 by a group of European scientists during an expedition to Antarctica."

The President paused again, this time to relight his pipe, while Porter fidgeted in his chair and glanced nervously at the two CIA men next to him.

With his pipe relit, the President continued, "They did some core drillings on the West Antarctic ice sheet and discovered a slushy layer along the interface where the ice meets the bedrock of the Antarctic continent.

"They hypothesized that the slushy layer would someday get so thick the entire ice sheet would slide off the continent into the sea, triggering a new ice age.

"The CIA, whose task it is to develop contingency plans for potential natural disasters, devised a plan to deal with a new ice age—Contingency Twelve.

"To monitor developments along the ice sheet, we established a string of stations across West Antarctica. During the fifties, sixties, and seventies, the slushy layer widened, eventually becoming a hundred feet thick in some places.

"At that point, the ice-age scenario began to look like more than just a scientific hypothesis, so we reviewed and updated Contingency Twelve."

"Mr. President," Porter interrupted, "I find this very difficult to believe."

"I'm not surprised. That was my first reaction, too. But if you'll just be patient, the director and the senior analyst will soon present more evidence than you will care to see."

The President blew a long smoke ring toward Porter, who studied the President intently as he spoke. "In January of this year," the President continued, "we received an urgent signal from our people at Byrd Station.

"Dr. Stanton has a tape recording of that message. Dr. Stanton, if you would..."

Stanton reached down and switched on a tape recorder. After five or ten seconds of static, an anxious voice came on. "Hello, Control? This is Iceman One. Do you read me? Over."

"Hello, Iceman, this is Control. We read you loud and clear. You're not scheduled to broadcast for another two hours. What's up? Over."

"We have final test results. All stations report the slushy zone is now present along the entire West Antarctic ice sheet. Please advise us of our next move. Over."

"Roger, Iceman, I understand. I mark the time as 0136, inclusive. Stay close to your radio. Out."

There was a silence, then Control's voice again. "This is Major Frank Simmons. I have just received a call from Iceman One at Byrd Station. Phase One of Contingency Twelve is indicated. Please confirm ..."

Stanton snapped off the recorder. "Major Simmons is a crisis manager at Langley. He phoned the assistant director, who immediately authorized the implementation of Phase One of Contingency Twelve."

"Just what the hell *is* Contingency Twelve?" Porter asked.

"In Phase One, we threw a secrecy net over Antarctica so that no one else could find out about what's going on," Stanton said.

"Actually, it wasn't difficult," the President added. "Luckily, they were able to pass the word to us in January, and we evacuated them to the Falkland Islands before the Antarctic winter set in. Once that hits, the whole continent is absolutely unreachable from the beginning of March until the end of October."

"If this had happened a few years ago," Stanton said, "we would have had a hell of a time keeping the lid on. Back then, Antarctica was populated like a mini United Nations—besides the British and ourselves, France, New Zealand, Australia, Chile, Argentina, Russia—even the Poles had a base. But they've all pulled out."

"Why?" Porter asked.

The CIA director smiled. "Antarctica is a rough place. There's at least one fatal accident every year. When we decided we wanted the place to ourselves, we...took certain steps to raise the accident level. Then we withdrew our support for the Antarctic Treaty. Without our participation, logistics became almost impossible for the Europeans.

"Meanwhile, Antarctica itself grew colder, making resupply during the short summer months very difficult and expensive. Finally, even the nations close to Antarctica pulled out —Chile, Argentina, New Zealand, and Australia. The British were able to hang on by resupplying from the Falklands—"

"That's why we supported the British against the Argentines," the President interrupted. "We needed the Falklands for this operation."

There was a long silence. Porter stared intently at the President, who sighed deeply again.

"Antarctica has been incommunicado since

the ice sheet slipped off the continent. Yesterday, our aircraft got their first look at the leading edge of the ice. Today, they will fly over the area again.

"That's why I've asked you to join us, Senator..." The President glanced at his watch. "In a few minutes, we'll be getting a live transmission from one of our planes."

The President stood up. "A TV monitor has been set up in my study," he said, pointing toward one of the side doors. He led the other three men to his study, where a communications officer was adjusting the picture on a huge projection screen. Four stiff-backed cane chairs had been set up for them, and they made themselves comfortable before the screen.

The screen was already on, and it showed the ocean from high above. The water was gray and very choppy. As they watched, a voice came over a loudspeaker. "Hello, Control, this is Bird's-eye One, do you read? Over."

"I read you loud and clear on audio, Bird's-eye, and the video is crystal clear. Over."

"We are about five minutes to target. Visibility is good in all directions. Over."

"Roger, Bird's-eye. Let us know when you see the ice. Over."

"Roger, Control. Out."

While the four men waited, Stanton identified the speakers in the radio transmission. "Control is the same Major Simmons you heard earlier on the tape. Bird's-eye is transmitting a scrambled signal to Simmons at Langley, and they're patching it through to us."

For what seemed like hours, the four of them sat intently watching the screen, which continued to show only the gray, angry sea. Then, the pilot's voice cut into the silence: "There it is! By God, I've never seen anything like it!"

The gray of the ocean suddenly gave way to the glistening whiteness of ice as the camera caught the towering cliffs that formed the edge of the ice sheet. The plane rose to climb above the mountainous ice peaks.

The four men stared in awe at the colossal expanse of ice. Finally, the President stood up. "I've seen enough. How about you, Porter?"

"Yes," he said softly.

They returned to the Oval Office and resumed their seats. The President relit his pipe nervously. "Up to this moment, I guess I didn't fully believe it all."

"Nor I," said Porter. "What happens now that the summer season is starting down there? Others are bound to find out."

"Uh-uh," the President said. "Dr. Stanton, would you explain Phase Two of Contingency Twelve."

"Certainly, Mr. President." Stanton glanced at his watch. "In about half an hour, the British defense minister will announce that a British frigate has been lost off East Falkland Island under suspicious circumstances, and that an Argentine submarine has been spotted in the area.

"The British will use this pretext to declare a

quarantine of the South Atlantic and South Pacific around Antarctica. This time, our support for them will include outright military assistance. In fact, naval units from the Virgin Islands are nearing the quarantine area even as we speak."

Stanton stopped, and again there was quiet in the room.

Finally, the President broke the silence. "The Canadians, Australians, and New Zealanders were told this morning. We expect them to help with certain military operations later.

"Absolutely none of this can be made public, Senator," the President emphasized. "Here's my directive." He matter-of-factly tossed a document in front of Porter.

The President-elect picked it up and read the first page:

TOP SECRET
FOR EYES ONLY

Porter swallowed nervously and hesitated.

"Go ahead, read it," the President said.

Still Porter hesitated, fingering the pages gingerly. The document was only two or three pages long. Finally, he turned the page and began to read while the others waited patiently.

When Porter was done, he handed the document back. "I never realized you had such powers of censorship," he said.

"It's not uncommon," the President said.

"The details of this crisis must not be made public until we are ready," Stanton insisted.

"Exactly how will this movement of the ice from Antarctica into the ocean cause an ice age?" Porter asked.

"The ice will cover some two million square miles of ocean," Stanton answered. "The white surface of the ice will reflect more sunlight than the water it covers. This will cause the temperatures to cool worldwide. Then the glaciers will start to form."

The President continued, "Of course, the advent of the glaciers themselves is a problem we won't face in our lifetimes. But the temperature drop will have an immediate impact."

Porter nodded as the implications became clearer to him. "Have you considered using nuclear weapons to break up the ice?"

"That was the first thing I thought of, too," the President said. "But the ice is fifteen thousand feet thick in some places, and hundreds of miles wide. Even if we explode enough nuclear devices to destroy the ice, we would contaminate the Earth for centuries.

"And the water from the melting ice would raise the level of the seas and flood our coastal cities. Even now, the oceans have begun to rise because the ice is displacing so much water."

"So what can we do about it?"

"The senior analyst will cover that portion of the briefing," the President said tersely.

The elderly man took his cue. "Senator," he began, "the first effects of the cool-down will be evident soon after you take office. We'll have a late spring, drought next summer in the Midwest, and then an early winter."

Porter did not like the man's smug, overbearing style and was annoyed the President still had not introduced him by name.

"Eventually, our climate zones will shift southward, degrading our ability to feed ourselves." The senior analyst paused to emphasize the importance of his words.

"Do you have a solution to propose?" Porter asked.

"The solution is not a proposal," the old man said. "It's been in effect since February, when we learned about the coming ice age. It's called Operation Migrant. Its ultimate goal is to resettle Americans into areas that will be free of the freezing weather."

"Exactly what areas are you talking about?"

"We're talking about the Yucatan in southern Mexico, the Caribbean, Venezuela, Brazil, Colombia, Central America, Surinam, and Guyana. We've coded them the Green Belt."

"But you're talking about crossing national boundaries. That's war!" Porter said excitedly.

"The nation must survive," the senior analyst said calmly.

Porter turned to the President in disbelief. The President nodded his head solemnly to confirm what the CIA man had said.

The senior analyst continued, "When you take office in January, we'll expect you to implement the rest of Contingency Twelve, including Operation Migrant."

His face was crinkled into a smug sneer as he spoke. He waited for a moment, daring Porter to register an objection. When Porter remained silent, the analyst continued, "Of course, everything we've discussed is top secret. I mention these programs now only so you won't be surprised when you're asked to authorize expenditures for them."

Porter felt a flash of anger at the man's arrogance. He was unable to restrain himself, and was about to jump out of his chair when the President stood up, preempting Porter.

"Gentlemen, I'm scheduled to brief the President-elect on domestic affairs this morning, and we're running late. If you'll excuse us ..."

The senior analyst rose reluctantly, plainly annoyed at the President's intervention. He and Stanton gathered their papers and prepared to leave.

"Good day, gentlemen," Porter said frostily. The two CIA men left the room.

When he was sure the other two men were out of earshot, Porter said angrily, "My God, Mr. President! What the hell is going on here? Who's running this country—you or that overbearing old bastard?"

"Easy, Senator. That old man has more power in one finger than I have in both hands. Old J. Edgar was a piker next to him."

"But who is he?"

"No one has been able to answer that question for me in four years of asking, Senator. Nobody knows he's alive—not the press, not Congress, not the public."

"Well, I know he's alive, and by God he'll answer to me—"

The President interrupted. "He's got a big jump on you. He probably has a file on you as thick as your fist. If you got a girl in trouble in high school, he knows about it. Did you park by a fire hydrant this morning? He knows about it. He probably knows your shoe size, your hat size, and the size of your bank account—and I hope you didn't take any illegal campaign contributions, Senator, because if you did, he knows about it."

"How could a man gain such power in this country and not be known?"

"He stays behind the scenes—always. He uses politicians for his own ends—we're all his chess pieces, so to speak. And you, Senator, are about to be promoted from pawn to queen. Through you, he plans to implement Operation Migrant, whether we want it or not."

"But surely, with the power of the Presidency—"

"I'm not getting through to you, am I, Senator?" the President interrupted. "What am I supposed to do, send the army after him? *He* controls the intelligence services, and the Secret Service has a hard time just keeping the *crackpots* from shooting me, much less dedicated professional killers in my own government. The damn Secret Service sure couldn't protect Kennedy, could they?"

There was a long silence. "Are you telling me that *he* assassinated Kennedy?" Porter asked softly.

"I'm telling you there's nothing to be done about him," the President said evasively. "Believe me, I tried—from the first day I sat in this chair. I was as incensed about him then, as you are now." The President suddenly stood up and leaned over his desk toward Porter.

"I'll never forget that first day. I tried to run an intelligence check through Stanton, my brand-new CIA director. He came back to me two hours later, wringing his hands. He'd gone to several department heads to request a file on the man. They all simply smiled and walked away." The President was close to losing control. To vent his anger, he began to pace back and forth behind his desk, gesturing wildly to make his points.

"I have to run the damn country, while he's running loose, answerable to no one, always solidifying his power. And believe me, he knows where all the bones are buried—who's screwing whom, who's got his hand in the cash drawer, and who's getting contributions from where."

The President stared out the window at the garden outside the Oval Office. The trees were mostly stripped of their leaves except for a few tenacious survivors still clinging to the bare branches; the flower beds were covered by protective plastic sheets; and the closely clipped lawn was white from the morning's hard frost.

With his back to Porter, he was framed between the American flag on his left and the presidential flag to his right.

"I'll tell you something I probably shouldn't," the President said in a calmer tone of voice. "He already disliked you even before today's meeting. He was pissed off because you won the election. He wanted me back in office. I'm a known quantity—easy to keep on a leash."

The President paused, then turned to face his successor.

"I'll bet he's really uptight about you now, Porter. He won't know what to expect. But I think he's also a little frightened of you."

The President sat down and became reflective again. He picked up his long-cold pipe and thrust it between his teeth.

"In fact, I'm sure of it. Things are getting close to crucial in this Operation Migrant. I think he's got you figured for a tough nut."

"You ought to know after three months of campaigning against me," Porter said.

"That's true! But I have to tell you, my heart wasn't in it for a second term. I felt like a eunuch guarding an empty harem. I made a lot of sacrifices and compromised most of my principles to become President—only to find the presidency stripped of its power by him and his people..."

The President's voice trailed off. "Needless to say, I dislike and distrust him. I'm sure he's using the ice-age problem to expand his own power. But he's no longer my problem—he's yours. But I'll tell you what I'd do if I were you."

"Yes, Mr. President?"

"Investigate Operation Migrant with your own agent. You've got almost three months before you're incarcerated here in the Big White Jail—that was Harry Truman's name for this place, and he was right. If you've got someone you can trust—someone close to the intelligence community—have him check it all out."

Porter nodded his agreement. "I think I know just the man."

"Good. But pay attention to what you're getting into. You've got a lovely wife and family, and that old buzzard wouldn't hesitate to destroy them along with you."

"I'll be careful. Can you give me anything else to go on?"

"Yes. There is one piece of information I have for you. Last June, they asked me to authorize expenditures from the presidential funds for something called Strike Force Alpha. It's got something to do with the illegal detention of Americans. I'm sure it's related to Operation Migrant."

The President glanced at his watch and grimaced. "Nine AM, Senator. I have a photo session with Miss Wisconsin, followed by a meeting with a congressional delegation."

Porter rose to leave. "Thank you for your direction, Mr. President."

"It's the least I could do. But remember this:

When you walk out that door, I dissociate myself from your activities. I want a quiet, dignified retirement."

"I understand."

The President and Porter shook hands warmly.

"Good day, Mr. President."

"Good day, Senator. Be careful."

Porter nodded slightly, then left the Oval Office.

Chapter Two

llll llll llll llll llll

At Langley, Stanton and the senior analyst, John McKarren, were still discussing their meeting at the White House with the President and President-elect.

"Porter seems like a headstrong man," Stanton said.

"They all are at the start," McKarren replied.

"I wonder what they discussed after we left," Stanton said.

"I don't know, but I don't like it," McKarren said. "Everything is reaching the critical stage. Things are falling into place nicely, and I don't want anyone making waves.

"Strike Force Alpha goes down tonight, and I

don't want any hitches. While I'm handling Alpha, you keep tabs on the President. I don't want him getting any last-minute ideas about baring his soul to the public."

Stanton said nothing, but yielded a reluctant nod of assent. McKarren glanced repeatedly at his companion as they walked down the halls toward their respective offices.

"And don't you get any clever ideas, either."

"Just a minute..."

"Shut up."

The director said nothing more. McKarren smiled. "You brought this on yourself, Stanton. If you didn't have a taste for women other than your wife, I never could have entrapped you, could I?"

Stanton grimaced but did not answer.

"Not to mention your bad timing. Not many men in our business would be brainless enough to start an affair during the Senate confirmation hearings," McKarren said sarcastically. "That was a true stroke of genius."

He began to laugh uncontrollably. They were near the executive office complex, and Stanton scurried for the safety of his office while McKarren continued to laugh.

Still smiling, McKarren stepped inside a waiting elevator and pushed the single button on the control panel. The elevator moved downward, past the lower level of Langley, to the last subbasement.

Only McKarren was allowed on this level. The elevator stopped, and the doors opened. He stepped out into a short, dimly-lit corridor that ended at a brick wall. The apparent dead end was part of the security system he had devised to protect his private underground complex.

As he moved forward, the lights became brighter. "Identify yourself," a serene female voice said. The voice was that of an elaborate security computer McKarren had designed himself.

"I am John McKarren."

"Please stand where you are while I verify your identity."

McKarren's wait was not long. "My preliminary identification indicates that you are John McKarren. Please step forward."

As McKarren complied, a section of the wall slid away to reveal a glass panel.

"Place your palms against the glass."

The machine analyzed his palm and finger prints and compared them to those on file. Finally, the computer spoke, almost reverently, "You are the senior analyst. Only you may enter here."

As soon as the computer was done speaking, the brick wall slid away, revealing rooms on the other side. McKarren stepped forward into the nerve center of his personal empire. As he entered the complex, more lights went on, and a second door opened, revealing McKarren's inner office.

The room was semicircular—dominated by a huge display screen on one wall. Six smaller monitoring screens flanked the main one, and a comfortable armchair sat before them. McKarren sat down and leaned heavily on the armrests. He clasped his hands together and rested his chin on them.

He stared blankly at the screen, driving the events of the day from his mind, savoring the fact that he was sitting in the most powerful chair in the world.

He loosened his tie, then leaned forward and pushed the buttons that activated his console. The main screen before him came on, showing one word in the center of the screen:

WAITING...

"Computer, acknowledge my voice."

There was a pause, then the familiar female voice said, "You are John McKarren. Only you can command me."

"Give me a security analysis for the last twenty-four hours."

"No security incidents."

"Good. Now give me the disposition of our forces for Operation Migrant."

"Yes, sir." An electronic map of the Western Hemisphere appeared on the screen. A graphic of a tank appeared within the U.S. at Fort Hood.

"All armored units of the Northern Attack Force are TOE and ready to go. They're being moved from Fort Hood to Fort Bliss as part of the preparations for the maneuvers we're staging to cover Operation Migrant."

The tank symbol moved from Fort Hood to Fort Bliss.

"Infantry is being massed at Fort Hood, Fort Polk, and Fort Sam Houston." Crossed rifles appeared at the three bases on the map.

"Artillery support at Fort Sill is almost ready, including all available self-propelled howitzers." The crossed cannons of the artillery insignia appeared at Fort Sill.

"Fort Bragg's 82nd Airborne and 101st Airmobile divisions are not quite ready, but will be soon." The parachute insignia of the 82nd and the helicopter insignia of the 101st appeared at Fort Bragg.

"Ten infantry divisions will form two invading armies—one to cross at Laredo and the other at El Paso. They will form the eastern pincer of our Northern Attack Force."

"What about the marines?"

"The marines are ready to go." The marine insignia appeared at Camp Pendleton. "They will form the western pincer of our Northern Attack Force, seizing Baja with a few companies, but sending the main force into Mexico along Highway 2."

"And the air force?" McKarren asked.

"The picture is not as bright with the air force. As you know, General Caldwell on the Joint Chiefs is opposed to the May maneuvers. He was quoted yesterday in several newspapers as calling them a 'boondoggle' and a waste of taxpayers' money."

McKarren thought about the report on Caldwell. "We may get even more flak from Caldwell with a new President coming into office. Review

the files of general officers who could replace
Caldwell. I think we'd better retire the old fool
at the end of the year."

"Yes, sir."

"How about the navy?" McKarren asked.

"The navy is in fair shape." An electronic ship
appeared at the Norfolk Naval Base. "Norfolk is
up to strength."

"What about the Canal Zone Attack Force?"

"There are fourteen army divisions and an
elite marine brigade now training in the national forest on St. John." Crossed rifles appeared on the schematic in the U.S. Virgin
Islands. "The island has been declared off limits
to tourists."

"How will those troops be used?" McKarren
asked.

"The marines will attack Veracruz from the
sea and move inland to Mexico City, where
they'll link up with the three armies of the
Northern Attack Force.

"The fourteen army divisions will be moved to
our secret bases in the Panama Canal Zone a
week before the operation begins. We plan to
start anti-American riots in Panama and use
them as a pretext to land the troops."

"What's the battle plan for those troops once
in Panama?"

"One division will move north into Central
America. The rest of the Canal Zone force will
strike south into Colombia, where it will split
into two armies. One army will roll down the

western coast of South America—the other will seize Venezuela and its oil."

"What about the support fleet for the Canal Zone force? Have those ships reached St. Thomas yet?"

"Yes, sir." An electronic ship appeared in the harbor at Charlotte Amalie. "The fleet has been split up into three squadrons. One will land and support the Canal-Zone army. The second squadron will land and support the marines at Veracruz. The third squadron is nearing the edge of the British quarantine area. When Operation Migrant is launched, that third squadron will help support the Falklands Attack Force."

"Do we have adequate tactical air support for the Northern and Canal Zone Attack Forces?" McKarren asked.

"Yes. In addition to U.S.–based aircraft, we have begun moving planes to our base on the Corn Islands off Nicaragua." An electronic plane appeared next to the two small islands off Bluefields, Nicaragua.

"Very good. Now, what about my Southern Attack Force? I'm most concerned about Brazil and Argentina—they're the two major powers down there."

"Argentina and Brazil will be the targets of strategic bombers based in the U.S. The bombers will neutralize all military targets, concentrating on both military and civilian airports. Airborne rangers will be dropped on the airports at Rio, Brasília, Montevideo, and Buenos Aires."

"That should secure the airports. What's our contingency plan if we are unable to keep control?"

"Strategic and tactical air-force units with low-yield nuclear weapons will be waiting in reserve."

"Very good. Continue."

"As soon as the rangers have the airports, the Norfolk fleet, standing offshore, will land and support the ten infantry divisions at Rio and São Paulo—spearheaded by the 101st Airmobile."

"Sounds like the Southern Attack Force is in good shape."

"Yes, sir. The final crushing blow will be an invasion force of combined British, Canadian, Australian, and New Zealand troops launched from the Falkland Islands. Four, possibly five divisions will attack Bahía Blanca, Buenos Aires, and Montevideo, then move north to hook up with the troops at Rio. This will end phase one of the assault and should secure Central and South America."

"Very good. Are you monitoring military movements in the countries involved?"

"Yes."

"Anything significant to report?"

"Yes, sir."

McKarren was astonished. It was the first time the computer had answered affirmatively.

"Describe the new development."

"A report crossed the Western Hemisphere desk last night about a decision by the Brazilian military to form two new divisions, both to be stationed at Belém on the northwest coast of the country."

"What are the military implications of this move?" McKarren asked.

"There is a first-class railroad between Belém and Brasília," the computer replied. "Brazilian reinforcements from Belém could reach the battle at Brasília before our own troops can move from Rio to the capital. The probability of their reaching Brasília in time is thirty percent."

"That is not an acceptable risk. What stratagem do you recommend to counter this possibility?"

"A fifth attack force is necessary. It should be landed at Belém. This attack will put pressure on the entire northwest portion of the country and neutralize the two divisions at Belém. And our forces could use that same railroad to move on Brasília."

McKarren was impressed with the strategy. "I like the idea, but where will I get the troops for a fifth army, and from what base could I launch them?"

"Two divisions will be necessary. A small carrier force could be detached from the Norfolk fleet for support. Strategic support could come from U.S. bases or from the big British base on Ascension Island."

"Very good. I'll have the President issue the necessary orders."

McKarren stared at the electonic battle map, with its myriad of insignia denoting all of the military units involved in the massive operation.

"Show me a schematic of the world's climate zones as they will be fifty years from now."

"Yes, sir."

Immediately, the screen displayed an equal-area projection map of the world's land masses. A red line bisected the United States.

"The area north of the red line, including all of Canada, Alaska, Iceland, and the upper three-fourths of the U.S. will be covered by glaciers."

The computer filled in the other future climate zones: the areas that would be tundra, and those that would be subarctic.

"That's enough," McKarren interrupted. "Now show me in green the areas that will still be inhabitable." The computer shaded in the designated areas. "These are the areas in the Western Hemisphere that will be inhabitable fifty years from now," the computer said.

"Now show me the areas that will be inhabitable one hundred years from now."

"There will be no inhabitable areas one hundred years from now."

"Accuracy probability?"

"Ninety-nine percent."

"Can human beings survive such conditions?"

"No."

"Very well. Now, give me the latest projection of success for Project Odyssey to survive this ice age."

"Probability of success has increased from sixty-three percent to sixty-eight percent since yesterday."

McKarren grunted. "It's been going up five points a day."

Leaving the schematic of the future climate zones on the main screen, McKarren reached forward and punched a power switch for one of the smaller monitors ringing the big screen.

"Computer, get me Al Howard upstairs on a small screen. He is to see me, but everything behind me is to be blocked out electronically. I want our conversation videotaped, and I want you to analyze what he says and tell me when he's lying. Run your analysis across the bottom of the screen—nothing verbal."

"Yes, sir."

The computer dialed Howard's number on a communications network independent of any other system at Langley. Al Howard's face appeared on the screen.

"Hello, Al," McKarren said.

"Good morning, John."

"Is everything ready for tonight?"

"Strike Force Alpha is ready to roll. All units will be in position early this evening. Operations begin after midnight." The computer's evaluation began to slide across the bottom of the screen like a weather warning.

HE'S TELLING THE TRUTH. HIS CONFIDENCE IS HIGH, AND HE HAS NO REASON TO THINK THE OPERATION WILL NOT SUCCEED.

"Excellent. Have you found someone to replace Driscol as field commander for Alpha?"

"Yeah. Jerry Torrence from my department. He worked with the Counter Terror Program in 'Nam. We're checking him out now."

"Good. As soon as he's cleared, I want to meet him. This afternoon, about three."

"I'll arrange it."

"How's Driscol doing?" McKarren asked.

"He's out of intensive care. Fool waited too long on that appendix of his. But he'll be all right."

"Good. You getting flowers?"

"Yeah. You're already in, John."

"Excellent. Assuming Torrence checks out, proceed as planned with Alpha."

Howard nodded his head slightly. McKarren switched off the small monitor.

"Computer, get me Michael Collins at Project Odyssey."

"Yes, sir."

Collins was the director of Project Odyssey, McKarren's top-secret base in Wisconsin. McKarren hated both his youth and his intelligence. After a short pause, Collins's face appeared on the screen.

"Good morning, Collins."

"Good morning, sir."

"How fares Project Odyssey?" McKarren asked.

"Things are certainly falling into place," Collins replied.

"No more problems with funding?" McKarren asked.

"None at all. NASA is treating us right."

"Why, that's excellent news, Collins."

"But not unexpected?"

"Not to anyone who knows me," McKarren replied.

"Everything's going forward at a much more rapid pace, now. Your intervention last March has really made the difference."

"I'm glad to hear that, Collins, because I'm flying out to see for myself tomorrow."

Collins's face remained expressionless. Finally, he broke into a grin. "We'll be happy to see you, sir."

The computer flashed its message across the bottom of the screen.

HE'S LYING. HIS CONFIDENCE IN THE PROJECT
IS HIGH, BUT HE DEFINITELY WILL NOT BE
HAPPY TO SEE YOU.

"What time shall we expect you?" Collins asked.

"Early," McKarren replied. "0800 hours sharp."

"Very good."

"And when I get there, I don't want to shake hands with your damned staff or read those interminable conference reports on your meetings like the ones you keep sending me."

"No, sir."

"As soon as I walk in, I want to see the revival of your longest living test subjects—"

"That would be the ones placed in suspended animation in 1968."

"Dammit, Collins, I've told you this before,

but apparently you weren't paying attention. I'll tell you one more time. Don't interrupt me. I won't stand for it. Do you read me?"

"Yes, sir. My apologies."

"How many subjects will be revived?"

"Two."

"After they're revived, I want to address the teaching cadre. The first detainees will be arriving tonight and tomorrow. I want to rev up the troops before they start their classes," McKarren said.

"Yes, sir. I'll arrange it."

"Good. Any questions?" McKarren asked.

"No, sir."

"Then I'll see you in the morning."

McKarren abruptly switched him off, then quickly addressed the computer again.

"Get me Marianne on the phone," he said softly.

"Yes, sir."

After three rings, she answered the phone. "Hello."

"Hi."

"Well, birthday boy, I've been sitting here waiting for your call. When are you leaving?"

"In a few minutes."

"All right, but you'd better make it snappy. Don't be late again, or..." She let the threat tail off.

McKarren frowned, then quickly changed the subject. "Where are you?"

"In the bedroom," she said enticingly.

McKarren's lips parted slightly as he envisioned her sitting on the edge of the bed.

"I've got your present waiting for you."

"Oh? What is it?"

"The sooner you get here, the sooner you'll find out," she said.

"See you in a little while, doll."

"All right, John."

By the time McKarren stopped his Mercedes in front of the garage door of the exclusive Georgetown high-rise where he and his wife lived, it was snowing lightly. He waited while the guard inside scanned him and his car. Then the huge door opened upward.

McKarren quickly pulled into the garage. Behind him, the door closed slowly, blocking out the cold, gray November day.

The guard watched McKarren's car pull into parking spot number one. McKarren smiled as he locked his car. He knew the guard was watching him, wondering who he was and how he had gotten the clout and power to park in spot number one. He pocketed his car key and walked quickly to his private elevator. McKarren pressed his palm against a plastic plate identical to the one in his underground complex at Langley.

The door slid open and he stepped in. Quickly, the elevator rose directly to his penthouse. When the door opened, he saw his young wife waiting for him behind the half-open door to their apartment across the hallway.

He smiled and moved toward her, then stopped when she opened the door all the way, revealing what she was wearing. It was a black camisole-style corset, which squeezed her already slim waistline to a mere nothing. The top of the corset supported and uplifted but did not conceal her firm breasts. At the bottom of the corset, a short hem of diaphanous chemise partially concealed her lower belly.

From the bottom of the corset, six delicate red straps trailed downward, supporting midnight-black nylons that hugged her long shapely legs. His eyes moved down her legs to the black stiletto heels.

Shifting his gaze upward, he noticed her long black hair was wrapped into a tight bun. The expression on her face was one of irritation and impatience.

"You're late," she said severely. McKarren stood motionless, powerless before the overwhelming figure. She reached out and grabbed his tie, then pulled him into the room, slamming the door and locking it.

He stumbled into the room and waited for her next move. She reached out and slapped him across the face as hard as she could. "I've warned you over and over about being late. Now you're going to pay. On your knees, Johnny Boy."

Chapter Three

||| ||| ||| ||| ||||

The President-elect entered his Georgetown home still shaken from his meeting with the President. His Secret Service protectors followed him into the house, then walked quickly to the kitchen to report to their commander.

Porter went to his study, where his secretary was typing from a dictating machine. When she saw him, she unplugged the earphones and stood up.

"Hello, Mr. President."

"Good morning, Loretta. Where is everyone?"

"Your wife is with the interior decorator, discussing plans on how to redo the White House. Jeff and Linda are out back playing."

"Are their Secret Service agents with them?" he asked anxiously.

"Why, yes, of course."

"What's my schedule like for the rest of the day?"

"Let's see," she said, reaching for her note pad. "You're due to receive a congressional delegation at two PM. Also, a press conference is scheduled for three, and the president of the auto workers will be here at four. The rest of the afternoon is free."

"Sounds a little too crowded. Keep the rest of my time open today," he said.

"Very well, Mr. President."

"Where's Tom Dean?" he asked, referring to the commander of his Secret Service detail.

"In the kitchen."

"Tell him I'll need the tail car again in about an hour. And I want him in it."

"Yes, sir."

"I'll be in my office."

Porter's office was a small room that could only be reached by passing through the study. He entered the room and locked the door behind him. Everyone understood he was not to be disturbed when he was in his office.

The walls of the office were adorned with numerous publicity shots taken of Porter with various celebrities and politicians during his campaigns for the Senate and for the presidency, and his framed law degree.

Porter walked directly to a print of Van Gogh's *Peach Tree*. The painting opened like a book cover, revealing a wall safe.

He unlocked the safe and removed a thick stack of one-hundred-dollar bills. He counted out twenty thousand dollars into piles on his desk. Then he returned the rest of the cash to the safe and relocked it.

Breathing heavily, he sat down at the desk and slipped the money into a manila envelope. Laying the envelope aside for a moment, he called Ted Amundson. The phone rang seven times before Amundson answered sleepily. "Hello?"

"Ted. It's Adam Porter. You sound like you just woke up."

"I did. Flew back from Europe late last night.

Got a bad case of jet lag...can you hold for a minute?"

"Sure."

There was a long pause before Amundson returned to the phone. "Did you get my cable?" he asked.

"I sure did. I got congratulations from a lot of people, but yours meant more to me than the rest of them combined."

"Well, the system must be working at least half right when we pick a man like you to run the country. Congratulations again."

"Thanks, Ted."

Porter paused before changing the subject. "So, was it business or pleasure in Europe?"

"Both, of course. I was on assignment for your buddy, Senator Marley, on the Intelligence Committee."

"Ah. Business must be good these days."

"Yeah, it is. Thanks for putting in the good word."

"Your assignment for Marley completed?"

"Yeah. I handed him the report this morning. Why, what's up?"

"I've got something for you ..."

"Are we on a secure line?"

"Sure. The Secret Service guys here check everything but my kid's sneakers twenty-four hours a day."

"Oh, yeah. I forgot about the fringe benefits of being President-elect. So what's the problem?"

"We need to talk it over face to face."

"Sure. What's your schedule like?"

"Open until two."

"Hmmm. That gives us two and a half hours. Shall I come over?"

"Yeah. Can you make it by noon?"

"Better give me more time than that," Amundson said. "It'll take me a few minutes to drag myself out of bed."

"All right, twelve-thirty," Porter agreed.

Amundson hung up his phone and turned to face the chaos of his bedroom. His clothes and those of his partner were strewn around the room. The sheets were piled on the floor, and the mattress had slid half off the box spring.

Nude, he walked to the living room. The woman was still on the couch, where he had chased her after answering Porter's call. She had a sheet loosely draped across her body.

As he entered the room, she examined him critically. He was muscular and lean, stood a little over six feet, and weighed about 180 pounds. He was as handsome in the morning light as he had appeared the night before: brown eyes, large, with brows that tapered neatly to the ends of each eye; dark brown hair, thick and a little long; a straight nose that tapered evenly down to the nostrils; high, well-defined cheekbones; and sensuous lips that were formed into a tolerant half-smile.

"Well, Ms. Donahue, do you still like what you see?" he asked.

"Yeah, I do. How'd you get that way?"

"Played middle linebacker in high school and college. Lots of years in the military."

"How do you stay in such good shape?" she said with a lecherous smile.

"I work hard at it," he answered. He plopped down next to her.

"Speaking of work," she said. "Last night on the plane, you told me you're an investigator on Capitol Hill and that you might be able to leak a good story to me from time to time. Is that the truth, or did you just say that to get me into bed?"

Amundson paused, then spoke softly. "And you told me you were a reporter for the *Post*, and that you could publish any hot story I was on to, including the sequel to *The Pentagon Papers*. Is that the truth, or did you just say that to get *me* into bed?"

She grinned. "Touché."

Amundson shrugged. "What else could a liberated lady expect?"

She raised herself to a sitting position, the sheet falling away to expose her breasts. "Got any coffee?"

"Yeah, but that phone call means I don't have time for any."

"Can I wait here until you return?" she asked hopefully.

"Ordinarily I'd say yes, but I'm likely to be gone for days on assignment. Besides, don't you have a deadline to make?"

She pursed her lips at the rebuff, then stood up, letting the sheet fall away completely. She pulled him up off the sofa and enveloped him in a sensual bear hug. "Do we at least have time for a long shower?" she asked.

"Sure," he answered, grinning.

An hour later, Amundson pulled into Porter's driveway, then paused when a Secret Service man popped out from behind a tree, eyeing him suspiciously. The man held his hand up for Amundson to stay where he was while he used a small hand-held radio to report to the house. Finally, he nodded his head and waved Amundson on.

He proceeded up the driveway to where Porter was waiting on the front porch. Porter climbed into Amundson's car.

"Hello, Adam," Amundson said, offering his hand.

"Hi, Ted," Porter greeted.

"Shaking hands with the President of the United States," Amundson said respectfully. "It's hard to believe."

"I know. Sometimes I still have to pinch myself."

"Just goes to show you how long we've been out of touch. How long has it been since I did that last job for you—six months?"

"Hell, I haven't heard from you for over a year—except for the cable."

"Yeah, well, that phone on your desk works both ways, you know," Amundson chided.

Porter's answer was a smile.

At the end of the driveway, they picked up the Secret Service tail car.

"Those guys go with you to the john?" Amundson asked.

"Practically."

Amundson pulled out into traffic, followed closely by the tail car. Porter removed his gloves and placed them on the dashboard. "You got the heat on?"

Amundson nodded. "Car's still cold. Made the mistake of leaving it out last night."

"Damned cold for November," Porter said.

"So what's up?" Amundson asked bluntly.

Porter turned to face his friend. "Think back to 1969."

Amundson winced. "Not a good year."

"I know. You were squeezed out of the CIA. When you told me the story, you described the man who did the squeezing. Do you still remember what he looked like?"

"I'll never forget the sonuvabitch."

"Describe him for me again," Porter said.

"He was in his early fifties, maybe a little older. Good head of hair—brown. His face was thin, and his lips turned down at the corners. I remember his eyes most of all, though. Narrow. They cut right through me the whole time he was reading me the riot act."

"What was his position then?" Porter asked.

"I don't know. But the Saigon station chief brought him in from Washington, so he must have been a heavyweight."

"Have you seen him since then?"

"No. Why? What's with the twenty questions?" Amundson asked.

"I'm pretty sure I saw him this morning."

Amundson bristled. "Where?"

"In the Oval Office. He was introduced to me by the President as a senior CIA analyst—no name given. He and Stanton told me the damnedest story you ever heard."

Porter laid out the entire meeting for Amundson as they drove along Potomac Parkway. When Porter was finished, they were both silent for a few minutes.

"He's older, of course," Porter said, breaking the silence. "His hair is gray, but I recognized him from the way you described his eyes."

"Yeah, it's him. I never knew his name either. And this 'Strike Force Alpha' sounds like it could be a first cousin to the Counter Terror Program in Vietnam."

"What was that all about?" Porter asked.

"That's what started me on my way out of the CIA. The program came down to us for kidnapping, torturing, and assassinating suspected Vietcong. Most of the field officers—including me—objected. We thought the program would alienate our friends and throw the neutrals to the VC.

"The brass said the enemy was doing the same thing. We still balked. That's when they brought in the heavy artillery—the guy you saw this morning. He singled me out as the ringleader. After that, all I ever got was low-grade, high-risk field assignments."

Amundson's words had turned increasingly bitter as he remembered more details. "I think about him a lot."

"The President thinks he may try to use this ice-age problem to seize power."

"I'd say the odds on that are pretty good. The man we're talking about is driven by power. He likes stepping on people. I'm not surprised that he's clawed his way to the top. And believe me, Adam, as senior analyst, he is sitting on the very top."

"The President advised me to find someone who could penetrate Operation Migrant and find out exactly what's going on."

"And you thought of me."

"You're the only person I know who could handle such a mission. Will you help me?"

"Yeah," Amundson said. "I wouldn't miss it for anything. It'll probably be more dangerous than anything I've ever done, but there's no way I'd miss an opportunity to even the score with him."

"Good," Porter said.

"You're the one who ought to think twice about what we're getting into. The man is dangerous."

"I know, Ted. The President already warned me about the possible ramifications."

"Ramifications, my ass. Think of your family, man."

"I am, believe me. I plan to double their Secret Service detail while you're in the field—and maybe restrict their movements."

"Don't do that. If this thing blows up, he'll start to look around for connections. If he sees you and your family surrounded by a wall of Secret Service agents, he'll put you and me together."

"I'll be careful. But I'm willing to take the risk."

Amundson smiled at Porter's reply.

"I'll need a lot of cash to run an operation like this. At least ten thousand dollars to start."

Porter reached into his suit coat pocket. "Here's twenty thousand. If you need more, let me know."

Amundson took the envelope, then stopped the car. They were at the intersection of P Street and Potomac Parkway. The Secret Service car pulled up behind them.

"Just be careful on your end," Amundson said. "Don't tell anyone what's going on. Not even Maureen."

"I'll be careful. But you're the one who'll be in the field. I'd hate to lose you."

"I've never failed in the field against anyone, Adam—except him."

They shook hands. Porter got out of Amundson's car and ran back to the tail car.

Amundson watched his old friend in the rearview mirror until the new President was safely in the tail car with Tom Dean. Then he pulled back out into traffic and continued north on the parkway, while the tail car turned abruptly at the first intersection.

As soon as he spotted a phone booth, he pulled over to make a call.

"One-one-three-zero," Jerry Torrence answered.

Amundson smiled. Nothing had changed. CIA officers still answered with the four digits of their telephone extensions instead of with their names.

"Jer, this line still scrambled?"

"Ted!" Torrence exclaimed happily. "How are you, old friend? Yes, of course it's scrambled. Why, what's up?"

"You had lunch yet?" Amundson asked.

"Nope, and I'm ripe for an offer."

"Good. I need some information."

"Name it," Torrence said.

"I need everything you can find on an expedition to Antarctica around 1952. Also, have you ever heard of 'Contingency Twelve' or 'Operation Migrant'?"

"Nope."

"I need whatever you can find on them— every cross reference."

"Hey, pal, this sounds serious."

"It is," Amundson replied. "How soon can you meet me?"

"I'm going to need about an hour."

"Okay. Where?"

"How about Diamond Jim's?" Torrence asked.

"Okay. See you there."

Chapter Four

‖‖ ‖‖ ‖‖ ‖‖ ‖‖

Amundson arrived first. Diamond Jim's was still crowded with Washington bureaucrats and their secretaries, and there was a long line of people waiting to be seated for lunch.

Amundson looked around the room until he saw what he wanted: a young woman who was eating alone and almost finished.

"Cindy!" Amundson yelled, loud enough for the hostess and the other waiting patrons to hear. Then he quickly walked to her table and sat down.

"Hello," he said to the astonished girl.

"Do I know you?" she said, a little confused and very wary.

"No. But you're almost finished, and I don't feel like waiting in line."

"That's pretty damned nervy."

Amundson flashed a charming smile. "You're right. But I can't risk waiting in that line and being late getting back to the office."

She said nothing more, just frowned at him. She was a cute blonde. Amundson resumed the conversation. "You'll be interested to know that whenever I pull this stunt in a restaurant, I always pick the best-looking unescorted woman in the place. And today, you're it."

"Oh, my, how flattering. Do I win your Queen-for-a-Day award?"

"Hey, I never thought of doing it that way, but that's a hell of an idea!"

"You're too much!"

"Once you get to know me, I'm quite manage-able. Oh, pardon me ... I haven't introduced my-self yet. I'm Phil Crosby." Amundson held out his hand.

"That's nice. I'm not Cindy, but I *am* leaving."

She put on her coat and gloves and then picked up her purse. Then she paused to deliver a parting shot. "Thanks so much for lunch, I'm sure you won't mind handling the check. Good-bye, Phil."

Amundson smiled as she left. He shrugged at his failure, and watched Jerry Torrence make his way to the table.

"Practicing safe harbor?" Torrence asked.

"I think I'm losing my touch. Hey, it's good to see you, Jerry."

"Same here. It's been too damn long."

Torrence sat down and laid a thick manila enve-lope on the table, as their waitress approached.

"Give us a couple of coffees while we look at the menu," Amundson said. She nodded and walked away. "Well, what did you find?" Amun-dson asked.

"Very interesting files you've asked for," Torrence said, spreading the contents of his envelope on the table. "First, the *Norsel* file. There was a combined Norwegian, British, and Swedish expedition to Antarctica in 1952. Actually, it started in 1949 and lasted for three years. How much detail do you want?"

"All of it," Amundson replied.

"The *Norsel* expedition was the brainchild of a Professor Ahlman of Sweden. The Swedes were responsible for glaciology, the British for geology, and the Norwegians for meteorology. They used a refitted icebreaking tug—the *Norsel*—captured from the Germans at the end of the war. She was—"

"How many men involved?" Amundson interrupted.

"Fifteen. Eight scientists and seven technicians. They had dogsleds and a couple of tracked vehicles. One of the technicians was named Kurt Kelly—the only American national on the expedition. Remember the name, because it comes up later."

"Kurt Kelly? What kind of name is that?"

"His father was Irish and his mother Norwegian. His mother got him the job on the *Norsel* expedition."

Amundson nodded.

"They landed on the Eights Coast and worked their way inland to the present site of Byrd Station. There they performed some core drillings through the ice, among other scientific experiments. What they discovered was reported in this," Amundson said, laying a document on the table.

"It's not secret and it made its way into some of the scientific journals. Briefly, the report says the area under the West Antarctic ice sheet is slowly being liquefied and changed to slush. As a result, under the right conditions, the entire ice sheet may someday surge off the continent, precipitating a new ice age.

"Immediately, the Company devised a contingency plan, coded Contingency Twelve."

Torrence stopped talking when the waitress brought their coffees. "I'll have the club sandwich," Torrence said to her.

"Same here," Amundson said.

When she left for the kitchen, Torrence continued, "From 1955 to 1957, the U.S. conducted Operation Deep Freeze in Antarctica. It was supposedly a combined-force military maneuver to test combat readiness under conditions of severe cold. Actually, its real purpose was to verify the *Norsel* discovery."

"And they confirmed the report," Amundson guessed.

"Yeah. Contingency Twelve and its cross references are marked for deputy directors or higher. The computer identified the titles of the operations but would provide no details unless I could supply the identification key."

"Sounds like they're keeping everything in a close little circle," Amundson said.

"The only other piece of information I found was on Kurt Kelly, the mechanic from the *Norsel* expedition. He eventually took a job with the Scott Polar Research Institute in Cambridge, England."

"Sounds like he developed quite an interest in Antarctica," Amundson said.

"Yeah."

"It's not much of a lead. Do you have an address for him?"

"Unfortunately, Mr. Kelly died in February of this year—car accident. Some meticulous Company officer found the newspaper clipping—four lines—and put it into the *Norsel* file.

"I also found a Chicago police report in the file. Apparently, his daughter doesn't believe it was an accident. She claimed foul play, so the Chicago police did a routine inquiry through the FBI."

"Hmmm," Amundson murmured, remembering Porter's story. February was also when the Antarctic ice sheet had begun to surge.

"Sounds like Mr. Kelly was a loose end that needed tying."

"The neatness of it all certainly suggests Company business," Torrence agreed.

"I'd like to follow the Chicago lead," Amundson said. "What's the daughter's name?"

"Ellen Kelly," Torrence said, producing another envelope. "Her address and phone number are in here. And a copy of the police report."

"You're a step ahead of me, old friend," Amundson said. "I really appreciate this information. I have one more lead I'd like to ask you about ..."

"Shoot."

Amundson paused while their waitress delivered their sandwiches.

"Jer, do you know anything about an operation called Strike Force Alpha?"

Torrence was dumbfounded, pausing with his sandwich halfway to his mouth. "Jesus Christ, Ted, how the hell do you know about Alpha? I just learned about it myself this morning. In fact, I was in a meeting about Alpha ten minutes before you called. Have you got another contact at the agency—the director maybe?"

Amundson grinned. "No, Jer, you're my main man. What's Alpha all about?"

"Kidnapping and detaining American civilians."

"I thought so," Amundson said. "Are you involved in it?"

"Involved? I'm being promoted to full field commander to run the operation. I got it because of my experience in the Counter Terror Program in 'Nam."

"I knew it would happen sooner or later," Amundson muttered, shaking his head. "It was only a matter of time before we graduated from foreign unfriendlies to American citizens. But someone must have come up with a mighty important end to justify this."

"Damn," Torrence said, savagely biting into his sandwich. "The thing that really bugs me is not knowing the 'why' behind it. Al Howard, my new boss, is Alpha project commander, and all

I've gotten from him so far is, 'You don't have a need to know.' "

"It's got to be big," Amundson said.

"What does Alpha have to do with a 1952 expedition to Antarctica?" Torrence asked.

"That's what I'm trying to find out. My first step will be to talk to Ellen Kelly."

"Then what?"

"Do you know where the kidnap victims are being taken?"

"Nope. I don't have a 'need to know' that, either," Torrence answered. "I just make sure the designated people are taken and trucked off to staging areas. I have no idea where they go from there."

"Hmmm. Do you suppose you could arrange to have me kidnapped?" Amundson asked.

Torrence smiled. "Sure. But procedure calls for each target to be drugged. You'd wind up in the same predicament as the rest of them."

"How about if I were given a smaller dose of the drug? I would come to before anyone expected it, and I could take a look around before anyone knew I was awake."

Torrence considered the idea for a minute. He ate in silence, thinking about what he was getting into. "I'd have to be there to administer the smaller dose," he said finally.

"That's the only way it will work," Amundson agreed. "Jer, you know you'll have to give up the Company and go to ground if you get involved in this."

"I'd do just about anything for you, Ted. You

know that. But I've got to know what's going on. What are you on to? Who are you working for?"

Amundson nodded. "I'm on to a conspiracy of some kind. The opposition is inside the Company—at the very top."

Torrence put his sandwich down and pushed aside his plate. "Who is it?"

"I don't know his name, but he's the guy who rammed through the Counter Terror Program in 'Nam."

"That asshole?"

"Yeah. Seems he's made his way to the top. He's a senior analyst."

Torrence whistled. "One of the 'Wise Men'!"

"Yeah. That means he sits on the Estimates Board and is privy to every piece of intelligence in Washington."

"We're going up against *him?*"

"Yeah. Are you still with me?"

"Wouldn't miss it. But where do we start?" Torrence asked.

"Put a tail on him."

"Okay, but what does he look like? I don't think I met him in 'Nam, and if I saw him at all, it was from a distance."

"He's not hard to pick out. Just look for the oldest sonuvabitch at Langley. And check out his eyes. You'll never forget his eyes once he looks at you. Once you ID him, can you get a tail on him?" Amundson asked.

"Are you kidding? I have a hundred agents assigned to me for Strike Force Alpha."

"But this won't be like following a doctor or a

computer programmer," Amundson said. "And your tail will have to be someone who doesn't know the target's a Company man."

"I'll put together a team we can trust."

"Good. But be careful. This old guy is going to be tough to take down. He's been at this for a long, long time."

"I won't get careless. When do you want to leave for Chicago?"

"This evening. I have a few details I want to take care of before I go," Amundson said.

"Okay. I'll take a military transport tonight. I can use the time to set up the tail and put together a file on you."

"File?"

"Sure," Torrence said. "You'll need a solid identity for the kidnapping."

"Let's use John Harmon."

"Jeez, I haven't thought about that name in years. We had that identity dead and buried in Saigon."

"Let's resurrect him," Amundson said.

"All right. What else do you need?"

"Credentials."

"What would you like?"

"FBI, Company, Chicago police, and Chicago press. Don't put all the credentials in Harmon's name, in case I have to dirty up some of the identities. I'll need a tape recorder, an entry kit, and some artillery."

"A .38 Special to match the police credentials?" Torrence asked.

"Yeah, with a shoulder holster. Plus a sleeve

rig with a Beretta and a .357 magnum with holster."

Torrence whistled. "Who you gonna take down in Chicago, King Kong?"

"If he gets in my way."

Torrence grinned. "Anything else?"

"If you get something on the opposition before I leave, I'd like to have it."

"Okay. If not, I'm sure I'll have something for you by the time I arrive in Chicago tonight," Torrence said.

"Sounds good."

"I have an easy way to get these goods to you. I'll get you on United Flight 121 leaving National at six o'clock. The captain works for us. He can get your goods on board with no hassle and no metal detector.

"He's done it for me many times. He just carries the goods on board, then passes the bag to you during the flight. At the other end, there's no fuss, no scrambling to get your bag, and no worries about someone opening your bag and finding your goods."

"Great," Amundson said.

"And there are fringes to this arrangement. He'll tell the rest of the crew that you're a friend of his, and you'll get the VIP treatment for the entire flight."

Amundson grinned. "I like it."

"I thought you would."

"How will you set up the kidnapping?"

"We'll use one of the Chicago-area safe houses."

"We'll have to make sure no one on the kidnap team knows it's a safe house," Amundson said.

"Good point. Hmmm. Okay, I have one way out in the boonies that will do the trick. I keep it for 'special operations,'" he said with a sly grin. "I'll put a note in your bag with the address and phone number. Call me there tonight after ten. The operation goes down at midnight."

"Everything sounds tight, Jer."

"Damned right! No one ever stopped us before as a team, and they're not gonna start now."

Torrence glanced at his watch. "I've got to get back. See you tonight."

When Torrence arrived back at his office, there was an urgent message from Al Howard waiting for him. Torrence picked up his phone and dialed Howard's number.

"One-one-zero-zero," Howard said.

"Al, what's up?"

"Where the hell have you been?" Howard demanded.

"Took a late lunch."

"Torrence, you better get used to signing out when you leave the office."

"Al, I told my secretary..."

"Never mind. The Old Man wants to meet you. My office at three o'clock."

Torrence glanced at his watch. "Fifteen minutes," he said.

"No, right now. I want to talk to you before he gets here."

"Okay. I'm on my way."

When Torrence entered, Howard was sitting with his back to him, staring at the screen of a PC.

"Sit down," Howard said, not turning.

Torrence sat in one of the leather chairs and surveyed Howard's desk. The only permanent fixtures were a small lamp, a Company pen-and-pencil desk set, and pictures of his wife and kids. He noticed four white envelopes on one end of the long desk. They caught his attention because Howard was meticulously neat and never allowed any paper to sit on his desk longer than five minutes. Torrence stared at the four envelopes, then glanced at Howard's back. He moved closer to the desk until he could see the names and addresses. Middleton, Cox, & Middleton—a prominent Washington law firm. The other envelopes were also addressed to lawyers.

Why is he sending four identical envelopes to four different attorneys? he thought. *Insurance! He's protecting himself from someone.* The contents of the envelopes suddenly assumed a greater significance. He again glanced at Howard's back.

Torrence quickly copied the names and addresses, and was barely finished when Howard suddenly turned around.

He started to speak, then noticed the four envelopes. Howard's face turned red and he became agitated. He glanced at his watch, and without a word to Torrence, walked to the door and yelled for his secretary.

She came running into the room. "What are these envelopes still doing here? I told you specifically to take them to the post office during your lunch break."

"Sorry, sir. But I had to work through lunch to prepare the readiness reports you asked for. I called administrative services for a courier."

"No way, Miss Dotson!" Howard exploded. "I told you before, these are . . . personal. Get them out of here."

His secretary quickly removed the envelopes and left the room.

"She's been with me for twenty years. You'd think she could follow simple instructions by now."

Before Torrence could reply, John McKarren walked into the room unannounced. Howard immediately rose to his feet, and Torrence followed suit. McKarren acknowledged Howard with a curt nod, then offered Torrence his hand.

"I'm John McKarren."

"Jerry Torrence," he replied, accepting McKarren's handshake.

"Good to meet you, son," McKarren said. He pumped Torrence's hand several times.

McKarren moved to the credenza to the right of Howard's desk, leaning against it with his hands spread out on the top. Having taken control of the room, he looked back and forth at the two seated men, his gaze finally resting on Torrence. The eyes Amundson had described earlier bore through Torrence.

"You've been selected for a very important position, based on your experience in 'Nam," McKarren said. "It's a sensitive position, Torrence, and I want you to know that I have a personal interest in this operation. If there's the slightest hint of a snafu, I'll have your ass. Do I make myself clear?"

Torrence nodded.

"Good." McKarren smirked, then abruptly stood up and left.

"Not much on social graces, is he?" Torrence remarked once McKarren was gone.

"Nope. I wanted to prepare you for his... personality, but we didn't have time. I've known John McKarren for thirty-five years. I've seen him destroy people who got in his way or didn't perform to his expectation. Believe me, he doesn't make idle threats."

"I believe you!"

"Well then, you'll have no problems in your new job. Speaking of which...are you ready for tonight?"

"Yes. I'm going in with the first strike team myself to make sure everything's perfect."

Howard smiled. "That's an excellent idea. I'll pass it on to McKarren. Let me know how it goes."

"Yes, sir."

Howard looked at his watch. Torrence took his cue, and left.

Back in his office, Torrence called his field supervisor.

"Corrigan? Listen up. About half an hour ago, a secretary named Dotson left Langley. She's hand-carrying four white envelopes to four different law firms. I'm going to give you the names and addresses. Figure out which address is furthest from Langley.

"I want you to go to that last address, wait for her, and intercept the package without her knowing about it."

Torrence paused and listened while Joe Corrigan spoke.

"I don't give a damn how you do it, just do it! Once you have the envelope, take it directly to Safety One. Do not bring it back to Langley, and do not reveal this mission to anyone. Okay, now here are the addresses."

Chapter Five

▌▌▌ ▌▌▌ ▌▌▌ ▌▌▌ ▌▌▌

Carrying the attaché case the pilot had given him, Amundson deplaned down the ramp between the aircraft and the terminal gate. Entering the first men's room he saw, he locked himself into one of the cubicles and removed his topcoat and suit coat. He unlocked and opened the case. Inside were a tape recorder and a neat row of three pistols.

Taped to the inside of the lid was a sheet of paper with the phone number of the safe house

and a brief message in Torrence's distinctive
handwriting:

> *Call from Barrington after ten tonight.*
> *I've got plenty on the opposition. I'll*
> *give it to you tonight.*

Amundson memorized the phone number and
threw the paper into the toilet.

He withdrew the under-the-armpit holster,
adjusting the straps to make sure it fit comfortably, then examined the .38. Satisfied, he loaded
the pistol and slipped it into the holster.

He put on the sleeve rig next, taking ten minutes to properly install the small Beretta. The
rig was a cumbersome but essential protection.
In two separate incidents, a sudden pistol in his
hand had saved his life.

He left the magnum in the case. It was his
glove-compartment piece—good for stopping
cars, buses, and other hulks.

Amundson re-donned his specially tailored
coats. Everything felt comfortable. He found the
entry kit on the bottom of the case; he opened it
and removed a lockpick and a glass-cutting
blade, which he inserted into specially sewn
pockets on the inside of his suit coat.

Next to the entry kit were four billfolds with
the credentials he had asked for. Each billfold
had credit cards, a driver's license, and pictures
of wife and kids for each different identity.

Amundson examined the documents carefully,
then chose the billfold with the *Chicago Tribune*

credentials in the name of Robert Farrow. There was even a small Press sign for his car.

From his coat pocket, he took an envelope containing $5,000 of the original $20,000 Porter had given him. He counted out $500 and stuffed the bills into Robert Farrow's wallet, then slipped it into his suit coat.

The other wallets contained Chicago police, FBI, and CIA credentials. He put $500 into each one, then returned them to the attaché case, along with the remaining $3,000. He closed and locked the case, flushed the toilet, opened the cubicle door, and left the men's room.

Amundson found a public phone and dialed Ellen Kelly's number. After three rings, she answered.

"Miss Kelly? How are you?" There was a pause while she responded.

"Good. My name is Robert Farrow. I'm a reporter for the *Trib*. I'm interested in doing a follow-up story on your father's death. Would it be possible for me to interview you this evening?" Again, he paused to listen to her.

"Yes, I'll be completely objective. I assure you I have no prior conceptions about this, Miss Kelly. Someone else wrote the original story…"

She interrupted him again.

"Yes, I guarantee I'll listen to your side," Amundson insisted. "How about seven tonight? Good. I'll see you then. Good-bye."

He hung up and walked quickly toward the main terminal and his waiting rental car.

* * *

Amundson turned right off Howard Street onto North Bell, on the far north side of Chicago. The street was a cul-de-sac, lined on both sides with townhouses. He found Kelly's home at the end of the street, helped by the bright yellow porch light that clearly illuminated her address. He parked and walked up to the porch. Before he could ring the bell, the door opened.

The woman who stood before him looked about thirty. The first thing he noticed was the size of her eyes; they were large, and the whites dominated the pupils. Her strawberry-blond hair was thick and straight, falling to just below her shoulders. Her full lips were slightly parted.

"Hi, I'm Bob Farrow," Amundson said, displaying his press credentials.

She nodded slightly and examined his identification carefully before inviting him in. Once inside, she graciously took his overcoat and invited him into the living room.

He sat down in a love seat that faced a long couch, and carefully placed his attaché case on the seat next to him.

"May I get you some coffee or tea?" she asked.

"Not unless you're having some," he replied.

"I have some coffee on the stove. How do you like yours?"

"Black."

"I'll be right back," she said.

Amundson removed the tape recorder from his attaché case and was testing it when she returned with their coffee.

"Is that necessary?" she asked nervously.

"Well, you keep saying that the press isn't covering your father's death accurately. With a tape recorder, there should be no doubt about the accuracy of my reporting."

"Very well," she said, setting his coffee on the cocktail table in front of him. She sat down on the couch across from him, modestly smoothing her skirt over her knees.

"Where should we start?" she asked.

"Let's get the history out of the way," Amundson replied. "The police maintain that their investigation turned up no trace of foul play. The report is quite explicit. As far as they're concerned, it was a routine accident—another case of a drunken driver killing himself."

"But that's not true!" she objected.

"Well, what can you offer to counter their claim? According to the report, he was seen having cocktails at the airport after his flight arrived from London. Apparently, he just had too much to drink, climbed into his rental car, and—"

"Now just a damned minute," she interrupted angrily. "You told me when you asked for this interview that you were going to be impartial. All you're doing is parroting the same bull the medical examiner presented at the inquest.

"My father *never* drank and drove. Period. Not since my mother was killed five years ago, when he lost control of the car because he was drunk. He never forgave himself for that, and he vowed never to drink and drive again. He would sleep over at friends' houses, take cabs, buses, walk—

do anything to avoid driving. Even if he had just one drink."

"And this was presented at the inquest?"

"Yes! Six people, including me, testified that for five years, no one had ever seen him get behind the wheel of a car after even one drink."

"What did they say about that at the inquest?"

"Our testimony was ignored. Everything was twisted around to fit the police version of what happened. Then, when I told them about the phone call, they struck my testimony from the record as irrelevant."

"What phone call?"

"My father called me just before he boarded his flight. He was scared. He told me that the institute where he worked had just been closed down..."

"What institute was that, Miss Kelly?"

"The Scott Polar Research Institute in Cambridge, England." She paused and sighed deeply. "You have to know more about my father. He was one of the few men I know who truly enjoyed his work.

"Dad loved everything about Antarctica. He went there for the first time in 1949. From then on, he built a career around the place, starting with a degree in glaciology and ending with a job at the Scott Institute."

During their entire conversation, her eyes had not left his face. She leaned toward him.

"Anyway, he called and said the institute was being closed and all the employees were being detained."

Amundson's eyebrows arched in surprise.

"Your father said the employees were being *detained?*"

"That's the word he used. And I told them that at the inquest, but they still ruled his death an accident. I know damned well it wasn't, and so do they. It's all some kind of gigantic cover-up," she said angrily. "I don't know why, but some-one had my father murdered, and I'm going to find out who did it."

Amundson said nothing for a moment, then spoke softly. "For the sake of argument, Miss Kelly, I'm going to assume that you are right—that your father was indeed murdered, and I'll begin my research on that basis."

Amundson noticed Kelly shift her weight slightly until her knees were pointing directly at him. She moved her elbow to the arm of the sofa and rested her chin on her hand. Suddenly, she broke into a disarming smile.

"At last I've gotten through to someone in the press," she said.

"Well, let me put it this way," Amundson re-plied. "Since everyone's assuming his death was an accident, there's no point in my tracking over old ground. I'd prefer to try a different ap-proach."

"Whatever your reason, it's nice to have some-one on my side," she said. Again, she flashed that smile at him.

"Let's start with a few questions," he said.

"Okay. Ask away."

"How long had your father been living in England?"

"Ten years. Ever since he got the job in Cambridge. But he spent lots of time here during the summer."

"How did he manage that?"

"My father was involved with radar mapping of Antarctica. American planes would fly over the continent systematically surveying the entire area.

"He and the rest of the scientists would plot radar maps using the data brought back by the planes. But they could only do that during the Antarctic summer—our winter.

"So for three months out of the year, there was nothing for them to do, and Dad would fly home to do research and to be with me."

"Hmmm. Did he have an office here?" Amundson asked.

"Yes, but believe me, I went through it from top to bottom. And so did the police. We found nothing."

"I'd like to take a quick look myself. May I?"

"Certainly." She rose from the couch, paused while Amundson snapped off the tape recorder, then led him upstairs.

Kurt Kelly had converted one of the bedrooms into an office, with a fine oak rolltop desk, file cabinets, and twin wall units lined with books. Amundson went through everything quickly but methodically. On one of the bookshelves, he found a cassette tape player and a stack of tapes. He turned, holding one of the tapes.

"I went through all the tapes," she said, answering his question before he could ask it. "And so did the police. There's just music and some notes from his job."

The books were on a wide range of subjects; Amundson spent thirty minutes checking them for hollow centers. The file cabinets held household papers, bills, receipts, and bank records.

Finally, Amundson gave up his search. "Is there anyplace else your father might have stored something. A safe-deposit box, a household safe—anything?"

"Not to my knowledge. And if he had a safe-deposit box, he'd have given me a key."

"Was there a will?"

"Yes, there was," she answered. "He left me this house, paid for."

"That's all?"

"Well, except for the things that arrived from England."

"What things?"

"His personal belongings," she said. "They arrived about a month after he died—in two large chests."

"Where are the chests now?" Amundson asked.

"In the basement."

"May I see them?"

"Of course."

They went down into the basement. Amundson could see lathes, a radial saw, tool chests, boxes, worktables piled high with hand tools, and shelves crammed with bottles of screws, nuts, and bolts.

"Looks a little disorganized," he said.

"Yes, but Dad knew exactly where everything was."

"Did you or the police search the chests?"

"They closed the case before these things arrived."

"Would it be all right if I go through them now?"

"Yes, I guess so," she said halfheartedly.

"Where are they?"

"Uh—back there." She pointed to the back of the basement.

"Well, let's get to it."

They walked carefully, snaking through the heaps of dusty chests and boxes. Ellen sneezed loudly.

"Gesundheit," Amundson said. "Say, what is all this stuff, anyway?"

"Tools," she said simply.

"Tools? I thought your father was a scientist."

"He was. But before he became a glaciologist, he was a mechanic. He was a technician on the *Norsel* expedition. After he took the job at the research institute, this stuff just started to collect dust."

"So I see," Amundson said.

Finally, they reached two chests. He opened the first one and began to rummage through it. It contained the dead man's clothes and personal gear. Ellen stood by, watching Amundson impassively.

The second chest squeaked loudly when he opened it. Ellen sneezed mightily.

"Gesundheit again," Amundson said, pausing in his search. He turned toward her. "Are you okay?"

"Yes. I have a problem with dust."

"You want to wait upstairs?"

"No!" she said emphatically.

He shrugged, then continued to search through the second chest, which was much larger than the first. He carefully removed layers of books, files, notepads, rolled-up maps, a globe, a checkbook, and some small, framed pictures.

"One of Dad's friends in England packed this up for me," she said solemnly. "He was good enough to sell off the furniture and appliances and the rest of the big things."

Amundson nodded while he continued his search. Suddenly, his hand closed over something wrapped in an old towel.

Gingerly, he pulled the object out of the chest and unwrapped it. It was an elaborate model of a wooden ship. "I completely forgot about that," she said. "That's a model of the *Norsel*. One of the other men on the expedition was a terrific sculptor. He gave that to my dad soon after they came back—God, that means it's been in our family since 1953."

"So that's the *Norsel*," Amundson said.

"Yes. Dad was very proud of that model. We

used to keep it on display here in the living room—until he took it with him to England."

Amundson examined the ship carefully; it was a foot long and four or five inches wide. He shook it carefully. There was no rattle to indicate something hidden inside. But when he rapped on the hull, he realized it was hollow.

"You're examining that ship the way I'd examine an artifact at an excavation site," she said.

Amundson said nothing, but continued to check the hull with his fingertips, until he found what he was looking for: a very well concealed line where the deck and the hull had been joined together.

"Unless you say not to, I'm going to cut it open," he said.

She paused for a moment. "If you think it's important, go ahead," she answered finally.

Amundson looked around the basement and found a hand saw. He placed the ship in a vice and started to saw into it, cutting slowly and carefully right on the parting line.

When it was cut through, they anxiously peered into the two halves. Lodged inside one half, held securely by a bracket, was a tape cassette. The handwriting on the label was the same as on the tapes he had found in Kurt Kelly's office. Using a screwdriver, Amundson carefully pried the tape loose and held it up.

"I think your father has something to tell you."

"Let's take it upstairs." She snatched the tape

out of his hand. "We can play it on your tape recorder."

"Wait a minute," Amundson said, grabbing her arm. "Before you rush up there, a note of caution."

"What?" she asked.

"Well, now we must assume that your father *was* murdered. That tape probably fills in the 'why,' and maybe the 'who' as well."

"All the more reason to play it," she said, trying to pull away from him. He held onto her firmly.

"Miss Kelly, you don't understand. The killers can't be far away. They must still see you as a potential threat, and they've probably taken measures to—uh—keep tabs on you."

"You mean they may be watching us?"

"Watching, listening, I don't know. But I think we should be careful."

"Well, what do we do?" she asked.

"I suggest we leave your house as soon as possible. We can play the tape in my car."

She nodded in agreement.

"And until we're in my car, keep the tape out of sight."

She glanced down to find she had no pockets on her skirt.

"Give it to me," he said. She handed the tape back to him, and he put it into his suit coat pocket.

"We can't leave these here," Amundson said, picking up the two halves of the *Norsel* model. "If they *are* keeping you under surveillance, they're bound to come back here sooner or later to search the basement. I don't want them to find these."

"Okay," she agreed.

"But I don't want them to see us leaving the house with them either. I don't want to do anything to make them suspicious."

"Here, I know just the place," she said. She led him further back into the basement, to an unused fireplace.

"Many years ago, when my mother was still alive, we used this as a family room," she said. She knelt down on the hearth of the dusty fireplace. "We had this fireplace installed to make the downstairs more comfortable. When my dad converted the basement to a workshop, we stopped using it."

She was poking around in several inches of old ash, looking for something.

"What do you want to do, burn the ship?" he asked.

"No. There's an ash pit below the floor of the fireplace," she explained. "Ah, here's the cover. Give me the ship."

He handed her the two halves of the model, and she dropped them into the ash pit.

"That should keep the *Norsel* out of sight," Amundson said. He looked down at their handiwork, and then glanced at the two chests. "Let's use the chests to cover up the marks you made."

They moved two chests into the fireplace opening.

"Okay, I think we're ready to get out of here,"

he said. "When we get upstairs, we're going to need a reason for you to leave the house with me. I'll invite you to dinner. Just go along with whatever I suggest."

Her eyes got big, and she pursed her lips into a bemused O.

"I assume your intentions are honorable, Mr. Farrow."

"They are for now. C'mon, let's go."

They climbed the stairs and returned to the living room. "I'm afraid I've been wasting my time, Miss Kelly."

"Don't tell me you're quitting on me already," she said with disappointment.

"No, but I've had enough of scrounging in your basement. And my stomach's complaining because it hasn't been fed. I'm thinking of treating it to a steak. Would you care to join me? We can continue our interview over a meal. The *Trib* will buy."

"Sounds good to me, Mr. Farrow."

"Please. Call me Bob."

"Okay, Bob."

Amundson packed up his attaché case while Kelly collected their coats.

As they stepped out into the chilly November evening, she shivered. "I can't stand the thought of winter this year," she said. She paused on the porch to raise the collar of her coat to cover her ears. Her teeth started to chatter, and Amundson could see her frosty breath as she spoke.

He led her to his car and held the door open

for her. "I hope your car has a good heater," she said as she got in.

"It does. And the engine should still be warm."

Amundson walked around to the driver's side of the car and got in. She shivered again as he started the car, but then relaxed as warm air immediately poured out through the vents on the dash. "How's that?" he asked.

"Great. Let's go."

At the end of the block, he had to pull over to the left to avoid a double-parked police squad car. One of the two cops was writing a parking ticket and paused to look up at them as they passed.

"I'm glad to see they're finally patrolling our street," Ellen said.

They turned west on Howard. "You did very well back there in the living room," Amundson said.

"Thanks. Let's play the tape," Ellen said. She was barely able to contain her excitement as he opened his attaché case and removed the tape recorder.

He handed her the cassette. Quickly, she inserted the tape and switched it on. After a few seconds of silence, a male voice spoke:

"My dearest Ellen. You must release this tape to the press as soon as you can. I have hidden it to bargain for our safety if I am caught.

"I'm sure you're saying to yourself, 'Who in the world is after my father?' It is all very bizarre, and it still doesn't seem possible that this has happened to me and my colleagues in a free society.

"Our radar mapping has been going on for over two years now, and we've compiled a nice set of maps that clearly show the landforms beneath the ice on Antarctica.

"We've also been monitoring the layer of slush I told you about. Since we first discovered it during the 1952 expedition, it's gotten a lot deeper, and it's spread across the continent.

"The worst scenario we envisioned back then was that the slushy layer might some day become uniform across the continent and cause the West Antarctic ice sheet to slip off, precipitating a new ice age.

"I don't think any of us actually expected this to happen in our lifetimes, but last month, the maps showed a continuous layer of slush across the entire continent. The day after we reported this, the institute was closed down and all of us were placed under house arrest.

"Now we have learned that the ice sheet has begun to surge off the continent. All of this is being kept from the public. We cannot allow this to happen. The consequences for mankind are enormous.

"That's why we've decided to attempt to escape from our house arrest. Somebody has to tell the press what's happened. This tape is my ace in the hole in case my colleagues and I fail in our attempt or if we are rounded up before we get to the press.

"I hope we're successful. If we're not, and if I don't make it...your life may also be in danger. Only full disclosure can protect you. I give you my love and my final wish—that you have a happy life."

The tape continued to play, but the rest of it was blank.

Ellen sobbed while Amundson drove. Finally, he reached down and turned off the tape recorder; he removed the cassette and returned it to his coat pocket.

"Your father sounds like quite a man," Amundson said softly.

"He *was* quite a man," she sobbed. "Until they murdered him!"

"I'm sorry, Ellen. Believe me, I'll do everything I can to help. Do I have your permission to publish the tape?"

"Yes!"

Amundson's thoughts were torn between helping the woman and dovetailing what he had just learned with Porter's story.

There doesn't seem to be much doubt that the ice age is for real, he thought. *And an ice age makes the need for an operation like Migrant obvious.*

Amundson suddenly felt like he wasn't being careful enough. And he had an innocent bystander with him. She had served her purpose, and he wanted her out of danger and out of his way. He checked his watch: an hour and a half before he could call Torrence at the safe house.

When Ellen finally regained her composure, he touched her elbow gently to get her attention. "Ellen, I don't think you should return home until I get this story into the paper. Is there some place you can spend the night—someone you don't see very often?"

"Uhhh, there's my friend Barbara from college. I can call her."

"Good."

He pulled over to a phone booth and waited nervously while she called her friend. When she returned to the car, she was smiling with relief.

"Barb said okay, but I don't think her husband is too excited about the idea."

"Where does she live?"

"In Wheeling."

Amundson looked down at his gas gauge and was relieved to see that the tank was only a quarter full. He had no idea where Wheeling was, but couldn't maintain his cover without revealing his ignorance. He pulled into a full-service gas station.

"I need some gas, and I have to use the john. I'll be right back," he told her. "Tell the guy to fill it up when he comes out."

He got out of the car and walked into the station. As the attendant handed him the key for the men's room, he asked for directions to Wheeling.

When Amundson returned to the car, it was gassed up. "Does the fact that I'm going to Barb's place mean you're not going to buy me dinner?" Ellen asked.

He was annoyed at her perception. He wanted her out of the way, so he could head out to the safe house.

While Amundson was thinking about his answer, he caught sight of a flashing blue light in his rearview mirror. His eyes nervously darted back and forth from the road up to the mirror. The flashing light was closing. The car behind Amundson pulled over to the side of the road, and the squad car moved up behind Amundson.

"Pull over, buddy," a sharp voice commanded over the megaphone.

Something was wrong. Amundson knew he hadn't broken any traffic laws. There was no reason for the cops to stop him.

"Ellen," he said softly, "listen carefully. I want you to reach into the glove compartment. Don't be alarmed when you find a pistol in there."

She hesitated.

"That's not a police car behind us. It's probably the men who killed your father—after us."

She reached into the glove compartment and found the magnum.

"Give it to me," he said.

Trembling, she handed him the huge pistol. He released the safety and cradled the weapon in his lap.

Behind them, the squad car hunched even closer to Amundson's rear bumper. Again the voice commanded him to pull over. Amundson ignored the order.

The squad car accelerated and pulled up next to them on their left. Amundson looked over at the other car and recognized the cop closest to him as the one who had been writing the ticket on Ellen's street. He brought the magnum up from his lap, in his right hand.

The cop rolled down his window and poked a shotgun toward them. Without thinking, without hesitating, Amundson raised the pistol and fired. Two deafening blasts from the magnum blew a huge hole in the door of the police car, and the shotgun disappeared. The squad car lurched drunkenly, swerving away.

Amundson fired again, and the police car flipped sideways, spinning out of control into a ditch along the side of the road. It burst into flames, but Amundson neither looked nor slowed down.

He turned right at the next street. He could hear distant sirens speeding to the scene. The next few minutes would be critical; he had to get out of the area before the police could seal it off.

Amundson realized Ellen was sobbing hysterically. "Don't become a helpless female on me!" he said tersely. "Get a hold of yourself. Our lives depend on staying calm."

She choked back another sob and nodded.

"Take the pistol," he said, flipping the safety back on. She took it gingerly and started to put it back in the glove compartment.

"Keep it on your lap. We're going to switch cars in a moment."

He turned abruptly onto a side street. Away from the streetlights, he found a high-powered Firebird and parked the rental car.

"Stay here," he ordered.

Amundson quickly picked the Firebird's fender and door locks and hot-wired the ignition. He returned to the rental car, took out his attaché case, and searched along the bottom until he found the credentials he wanted: Sergeant Thomas Spencer of the Chicago Police Department.

He closed the case and threw it onto the back seat of the Firebird. He slipped the new credentials into his suit pocket and tossed Robert Farrow's identity into a nearby sewer. He leaned into the rental car.

"Okay," he said to Ellen. "Take the magnum and get into the other car. I've got to get rid of the fingerprints we've left all over this one."

Ellen got out and ran to the idling Firebird. When Amundson was done, he joined her.

"Let's get out of here," he muttered, slipping behind the wheel. He got the Firebird off the side street and onto a thoroughfare.

He turned to check her out; she had placed the magnum in the glove compartment and was turning on the radio. The announcer was just cutting into the music with a special bulletin.

"The Chicago police have asked us to issue a special alert. Ten minutes ago, two Chicago police officers were slain on the city's far north side. Two suspects are being sought. One is Ellen Kelly of 7540 North Bell in Chicago. The other is an unidentified white male. The two were last seen heading west on Howard Street in a late-model Chevrolet, license number ZF–1463. Anyone who sees the car or the suspects should not approach them. They are heavily armed and considered extremely dangerous. If you do see these suspects, call the police at once at 911."

"Your pretty face will be all over the tube tonight," Amundson said wryly.

"How come they don't know your name, too?" she asked suspiciously.

"Because they've checked with the *Tribune* and found no Robert Farrow working there. It's a phony identity—my cover for this operation."

"What operation? Who are you?"

"Right now, I'm Sergeant Thomas Spencer of the Chicago Police Department," he said.

"Another false identity, no doubt," she surmised correctly. "I want to know who you really are."

He said nothing.

"You're obviously not one of the men who killed my father—you would have killed me already," she reasoned. "And those men tried to kill you, too."

"Yeah."

"Why are you running around with phony identities?"

"I told you, it's part of my cover for this operation."

"For what operation?" she asked again.

He hesitated, then said, "I've been hired to investigate why the CIA is covering up the ice-age story," he said calmly. "And I can't tell you who I am."

"Why not? Are you going to dump me somewhere? That's it. You're going to leave me for them, aren't you? And you don't want me to know anything about you. What am I, the sacrificial lamb for this caper?" she asked angrily.

Amundson had to admit she was partially right. His pragmatic sense of self-preservation was telling him to get rid of her, but he was genuinely sorry she'd gotten so involved.

"All of this over the ice age. Men are being killed to keep it secret. Why?"

"Survival," he said. He thought about Porter again, and Operation Migrant. "The survival of governments and civilization."

"But mankind has survived other ice ages," Ellen said. "People simply migrated toward the equator to escape the ice and cold..."

Her voice trailed off as she began to comprehend the implications of a mass migration of twentieth-century man.

"There were no political boundaries then," Ellen said. "But there still must have been conflicts between tribes as peoples of the northern climates fled south."

"And there will be conflicts again—this time on a massive scale. The United States will be too cold to support life, so the government plans to migrate south—to Mexico, Central and South America. And that means war against those nations to the south who get in our way."

"And the CIA is covering it up?"

"One man in the CIA. He's been building his own empire inside the Company for fifty years, and not even the President can stop him."

"And I'm in this up to my forehead," she said.

"Yeah."

"What are we going to do?"

"Get out of town. And since I'm really not from around here I'll need a navigator."

She breathed a long sigh of relief. "Where do you want to go?"

"Barrington. But we have to stay off the main roads."

"What's in Barrington?"

"Help. When we get there, I'll make a phone call that will get me out of this mess."

"What do you mean, 'get *you* out of this mess'? Are we in this together or not?" she asked angrily.

He looked at her. She was half turned on the seat, her right hand clenched into a tiny, ineffective fist.

Amundson smiled in the darkness. "We're in this together," he said softly.

Chapter Six

It was five minutes to ten when they finally reached Barrington.

"Look for a phone booth," Amundson said to Ellen.

"Can we stop at a restaurant to make the call?" Ellen asked. "I'm absolutely starved."

"Yeah, but we'll have to be careful. The ten o'clock news is coming on, and someone might recognize you. Our best bet is a fast-food joint where I can go in, get the food, and make the call while you wait in the car."

"Can't we find a dark bar instead?"

"We'll have to find a place without a TV. Wouldn't do to have your face pop up on the screen while we're sitting there."

They could find nothing in Barrington itself except for a motel restaurant. Northwest of town, on Route 14, they finally found a place called the River's Edge Inn. Amundson pulled the Firebird into the parking lot.

"Wait here until I check it out," he said. "Meanwhile, see what you can do to change your appearance before we go in. More makeup, and put your hair up or something."

"What am I supposed to use for light?"

He shrugged, then got out of the car and went into the restaurant. Ellen flipped down the visor mirror and did the best she could using the light from the car's overhead lamp.

She sighed with relief when she finally spotted him walking back toward the car.

"I thought you decided this would be a good place to dump me," she said.

"I agreed we're in this together. You've got my word on it," he said simply. "This joint is ideal. No TV, and they've got the river all lit up. It's a nice view."

"Is it crowded?"

"The bar is, but there are plenty of open booths in the dining room. C'mon, let's go have a pizza."

Ellen got out on her side. Even in the dark, he noticed the difference her new ponytail made in her appearance. Once they were out of the car, he wiped away their fingerprints.

"Aren't we coming back?" she asked.

"Nope. We'll leave this car here and take a cab to town when we're ready to go. That'll keep our trail cold in case someone tumbles to our car later tonight."

"What about the—item in the glove compartment?"

"Leave it. We don't need it anymore. But we do need the attaché case," he said, grabbing it.

"How many more guys you got in that thing?" she asked.

"Never mind. Just remember that I'm a Chicago police sergeant named Tom Spencer."

"Who am I supposed to be?"

"My wife, of course. Stop asking questions and let's go eat."

Inside, the restaurant was very casual. They seated themselves in one of the empty booths. Out of habit Amundson sat with his right arm on the aisle side in case he had to use the Beretta. The waitress handed them menus.

The waitress left with their order. Amundson picked up the candle on their table and blew out the flame.

"Why'd you do that?"

"The darker the better," he said.

He looked around for the public phone. When he spotted it, he motioned toward it with his head. "There's the phone," he said. "I've got to make that call. Be back in a few minutes."

He dialed the number of the safe house. Torrence answered after only two rings: "Three-eight-eight-one."

"Hello, Jerry."

"Hi, Ted. Been anxious to hear from you. I was afraid the cops would pick you up."

"It's bigger and better organized than we thought. They had the Kelly place bugged. Robert Farrow is in big trouble."

"Don't worry, we'll get you out. You're the first victim on the list tonight."

"So Strike Force Alpha is going down."

"You bet. Where are you?"

"Just northwest of Barrington," Amundson said.

"Good. The safe house is at 910 Waverly, in town. I'm going to wait here for you."

"All right, Jer, but I still have Kelly with me."

"Figured you would. I've already doctored your file to include a Mrs. Harmon. Makes you look more respectable . . . at least on paper."

"Thanks a lot. Now I can invite her to go with me."

"What if she doesn't want to go?"

"She's already figured out the alternative," Amundson said.

"Hmmm."

"But I don't want her to see you. That'll mean she could ID both of us."

"No sweat. I'm in disguise."

Amundson smiled. "What is it this time?"

"Nothing spectacular, just enough to make it impossible for anyone to give the opposition the right description."

"All right. But why wait for me? Why don't you clear out of there before we arrive?"

"I've got some heavy-duty info on the opposition for you."

"What?"

"Al Howard's personal file on the old man from 'Nam."

Amundson whistled softly. "How'd you get it?"

"Tell you all about it when you get here."

"When do you want us there?"

"It'll be set up for you by ten-thirty. Is there anything special you want waiting for you?"

"Scotch."

"Already here. Anything else?"

"No," Amundson said.

"Can you get here all right?"

"Yeah. We'll take a cab, then walk a few blocks just to be sure."

"Good."

"Have you got a line on where the kidnap victims are being taken?" Amundson asked.

"Still zero. You'll have to tell me. Wherever it is, you'll be there in the morning. How you gonna contact me once you find what you're looking for?"

"I'll come back to Chicago and put an ad in the *Sun-Times* personals under the name Harmon."

"Okay, I'll be watching."

"If everything goes right, I should be back within a week. Can you do anything to cool down the murder warrant?"

"Maybe. I'll have one of my men leak a story that the two 'cops' were syndicate hit men. That should get the wheels turning."

"Good. They'll probably turn out to be a couple of free-lancers working for the Company."

There was a pause on both ends. "See you in about twenty minutes," Amundson said finally. "Meanwhile, I've got a pizza getting cold and a beer getting warm."

"What about Kelly? Is she getting hot or cold?"

"So long, Jer."

"So long, friend. Be careful."

"You, too."

Amundson hung up. He opened the Barrington phone book hanging next to him and turned to a map of the village between the yellow and white pages. Using the street index, he found Waverly, then picked out an intersection within walking distance of the safe house.

He turned to the yellow pages, looking for a taxicab company in town. From the size of their ad, Village Taxi looked respectable. He dialed their number.

"Village Taxi."

"Yes. May I have a cab at the River's Edge Inn in fifteen minutes?"

"Certainly, sir. Please be sure you're out in front when he arrives."

"Okay."

Amundson hung up the phone and returned to the booth, where Ellen waited anxiously.

"Again, I was afraid you weren't coming back," she admitted.

"I said you have my word that we're in this together," he said. Then he noticed his pizza was half eaten and his beer completely gone.

"Hey, this is no way to treat me."

"Relax," she soothed. "I ordered a fresh round for you. You were gone so long the beer was going flat and the pizza was getting cold. Besides, I told you I was very hungry," she said, her voice trailing off.

Amundson grumbled, but didn't have a chance to say anything before the waitress arrived with a hot pie and a cold beer. She put them down in front of Amundson and left.

"Now that you've made your call, where do we go from here?"

He bit into the pizza and said nothing. When he looked up, she was flashing that same smile at him that he had seen earlier in the evening. Only this time she was closer to him, and her hazel eyes seemed to be looking right through him.

"Stop smiling at me like that or I'll make a pass at you."

"Make a pass at your own wife, Sergeant Spencer?"

"Hmmm," he mumbled with his mouth full of pizza.

"Where are we going from here?" she repeated.

Amundson glanced at his watch. "In about fifteen minutes, we're going to take a cab to a house in Barrington, where we will assume another false identity. We will retire for the evening, and sometime after one, a special government team will break into our home and kidnap us."

"What!"

"It's part of the next phase of my investigation of this Operation Migrant I told you about. Our kidnapping will be part of a widespread operation, and I need to find out where these people are being taken."

"How are the kidnappings related to the ice age?"

"When the government moves south, it will need skilled specialists to form a vanguard: scientists, technicians, engineers."

"What's your specialty?"

Amundson smiled at the obvious opening, but continued with his explanation. "We'll be Mr. and Mrs. John Harmon. I'm going to be a security analyst and you an ordinary housewife."

"Housewife? That doesn't fit me at all," she complained.

"Why not? What did you do before you got caught up in this mess?"

"I'm a cultural anthropologist. I conduct seminars once a year for teachers, but I spend most of my time at excavation sites. Usually at this time of year, I'm just returning home from a field expedition. This past summer, I was supposed to be with Mendel Arnold and his team in Guatemala. He discovered a classic Mayan city in the Petén district, and I was supposed to be with him when they opened it up." Her voice trailed off as she remembered the opportunity she had missed.

"I had to cancel the trip because of my father's death. I wasn't about to go anywhere until I found out who murdered him. Now that I know the CIA did it, I can't do a damned thing about it."

She paused, then spoke with admiration. "But you're doing something about it, aren't you? You must have some powerful friends to challenge the CIA."

Amundson said nothing. She flashed that smile at him. "Dammit, woman, would you please put away that smile. It's the most disarming thing I've ever seen."

"You make me smile. You're an interesting man: cold and calculating most of the time, but every so often, I get a glimpse of the man you hide inside. When are you going to tell me your name?"

Amundson smiled, then shook his head. "I can't, Ellen."

She smiled wryly. "Well, can you at least tell me if you're married?" she asked softly.

"No."

"'No,' you can't tell me, or 'no,' you're not married?"

"No, I'm not married."

"Good."

Amundson finished drinking his beer. There was an awkward silence until the waitress returned. "Will there be anything else?"

"Two more beers and then the check."

"Tell me more," Ellen said.

"Why?" he asked harshly.

She leaned forward, staring into his eyes and blocking out the restaurant and the other people in it. "Because I'm attracted to you, dammit. I want to know more about you."

"Ellen, I spend most of my life in the field. And when I'm in the field, I spend most of my waking hours trying to hide who I am. I can't afford to develop any long-term relationship. When I meet a woman on assignment, I usually play 'Safe Harbor' with her."

"What is 'Safe Harbor'?"

Amundson looked embarrassed. "It's a—technique for establishing a random safe place once in the field. If I can meet a new woman, a complete stranger, I'll have somewhere to hide in case the operation breaks down."

She shook her head, then covered his hand with her own. "I still trust my judgment about you. I want to know the man inside."

The waitress returned with their beers and the check.

He took her hand in his. "We have to leave

here in a few minutes," he said, breaking her spell. "Let's just try to relax a little."

Ellen drew back. Her hand was still in his, but her eyes moved away from him, and the restaurant came back into focus. Other conversations were suddenly audible again. The smell of pizza was in her nostrils.

Amundson caressed the back of her right hand, running his thumb sensually along the sensitive skin between her fingers.

"Is that an erogenous zone?" she asked suddenly.

"Between your fingers?"

"Uh-huh."

"I don't know if it's an official one, but I have noticed that many women are sensitive there."

"How many subjects have you—examined?" she chided.

"A few."

Amundson sighed, then brought his hand back across the table. "The cab will be here soon. I think I'll hit the john before we leave."

"Where are the rest rooms? I feel the need, too."

"Near the entrance. Here, I'll just pay the tab, and we can stop on our way out."

Amundson helped her on with her coat, then donned his own topcoat and picked up his attaché case. They walked back out through the restaurant toward the entrance. A side corridor led to the rest rooms and the kitchen.

Amundson entered the men's room, checking it carefully, as he always did. He was alone. He stared at himself impassively in the mirror above the sink and checked to make sure there was still no hint of a bulge in his coat under his left armpit.

Satisfied, he rinsed his hands and moved to the towel roll, which had become detached and was dangling to the floor. As he reached for the towel, the washroom door swung open, and two men entered. They were laughing and talking loudly, obviously drunk.

One of them went to the urinals, while the other entered one of the toilet stalls. Amundson watched them in the small mirror above the towel roll. The one in the stall came out again.

Changed his mind, Amundson thought lazily.

Then he glimpsed the man slipping his hand casually into his suit coat, and both of them were coming at him. Amundson whirled to face his attackers, instinctively pulling the long, detached towel as he turned.

One man had a knife and was on him; the other was backup man, guarding the door with a silenced .22 in his hand.

The knife man arched his long blade at Amundson's stomach, but Amundson, waving the streaming towel in front of his body like a matador, caught the blade in the cloth folds. While the knife man was off balance and exposed for a second, Amundson punched his left fist into the man's neck, sending him sprawling. At the same time, Amundson activated his sleeve rig, and the Beretta snapped into his right hand.

He shot the backup man before the silenced
.22 could be fired: three quick rounds that made
a precise triangle in the gunman's heart.

The knife man was on the floor, struggling
to stay conscious and fumbling for another
weapon inside his suit coat. Amundson kicked
him in the head.

Breathing heavily, Amundson wiped the Beretta clean and pressed it firmly into the knife
man's hand to make it look like they had attacked each other. He opened the attaché case,
shoved the wallets and most of the money into
his coat pockets. He scattered the rest of the
money around the room.

Let the police sort it out, he thought, dropping
the case.

Then he remembered Ellen. His attackers had
wanted him dead, and she knew almost as much
as he did.

The narrow corridor outside was empty, so no
one had heard the shots. The women's rest room
was next door to the men's. Amundson paused
before going in. He checked to make sure no one
was looking at him, then removed the .38 from
its holster. With the pistol held loosely in his
right hand, Amundson crouched low.

With one quick movement, he knocked open
the door with his left hand and knelt into the
room, gun leveled.

A woman was standing with a pistol pointed
at one of the stall doors. She whirled and fired
at him as he burst into the room. The bullet
went over Amundson's head into the wall be-

hind him, as he fired three times at the woman. His bullets struck her in the chest and neck, and she keeled over backward, firing into the ceiling as she fell.

"Get your pants on, Ellen!" he yelled from the doorway. While he waited for her, he took control of the corridor, holding the door open.

In a few seconds, Ellen emerged from the stall, her face white with fear. "C'mon!" he screamed at her, holding out his hand, but not leaving the doorway. She rushed to him.

Meanwhile, the shots from the .38 had been heard by everyone in the restaurant, and curious onlooker faces appeared. He was sure more of the opposition was close at hand.

"Fire!" Amundson yelled as loud as he could. "The kitchen's on fire. Everyone get out of here." The crowd grew uneasy and began to mill toward the front door.

"Fire's spreading!" Ellen yelled. "Get out while you can." The milling turned into a sudden stampede.

"That's great, but how are *we* going to get out?" she asked.

"Kitchen is this way," he said calmly. "Every restaurant has a service entrance in the kitchen."

In the kitchen, the two young cooks made way for Amundson when he pointed the .38 at one of them. "Do you guys deliver pizza?" he asked.

"Sure we deliver, mister. Take all the pizza you want, just please don't shoot me," the young man wailed.

"Where's the delivery truck?"

"Right out back. It's right out back. I was loading up for a run just now."

"You the only two back here?"

"Yes, sir."

"Okay, both of you—face down on the floor." They scurried to obey. "If either one of you moves, you both die."

Amundson motioned for Ellen to precede him out the door. He paused on the way out.

"You two stay just like that for fifteen minutes, and you'll be all right," Amundson warned. As he finished speaking, he glanced up at the shelf above their work area. Ellen's face was on the screen of a small TV sitting on the shelf. Amundson grimaced at his carelessness, then hurried out.

Outside, the van was idling. He fired two warning shots high through the kitchen door to keep the two cooks honest, then he and Ellen climbed into the van and drove to Barrington and the waiting safe house.

The safe house was actually a condominium —the top unit of a four-unit building. Amundson knocked softly on the back door, which opened quickly to admit them. They found themselves standing in another kitchen, this one dimly lit by a single light over the sink.

Torrence quickly locked the door. Ellen breathed a sigh of relief. "Are we really safe at last?" she asked.

"If we're not safe here, we might as well turn

ourselves in to the Chicago cops and the rubber-hose squad," Amundson said.

Torrence said nothing, but motioned for Amundson to take Ellen into another room.

"Who's your friend, Marcel Marceau?" she asked.

Torrence choked back a laugh as Amundson grabbed her roughly by the arm and led her out of the kitchen, into the living room. Atop the bar were two unopened bottles of Chivas, glasses, and an ice bucket.

"Hmmm," she murmured, "I can sure use a drink."

Amundson poured two drinks and handed one to her.

"Come with me," he said. He took her hand and led her on an exploration of the small two-bedroom condo. They stopped in the master bedroom, which was exceptionally large and accommodated a table and two chairs.

"I want you to wait in here while I take care of business with my friend."

"And if I don't?"

"He hasn't quite had time to develop the same fondness for you that I have. He might decide you're an unnecessary risk . . ."

"I'll stay here."

"Good idea. If you need another drink, holler. But don't leave this room, please."

"All right, dammit, I get the picture."

Amundson frowned at her, then quickly rejoined Torrence in the kitchen.

His friend was sitting at the kitchen table, still in semidarkness, when Amundson entered.

"She safely tucked away?" Torrence asked.

"In the bedroom. She won't move until I tell her."

"All right. Turn on the light."

Amundson flicked the light switch. Torrence smiled at him, one hand wrapped around a beer and the other draped over a thick manila envelope on the table.

Amundson leaned over the tabletop, peering into Torrence's disguise. "You've done something with your cheekbones," he surmised correctly. "The mustache is good. Different hairline ... I'd say it's a hell of an improvement."

Torrence snickered.

"I'm glad you're with me on this, Jer. It's getting real hairy. The opposition seems to be a step ahead of us. Almost got us again at the restaurant after I talked to you."

"You kidding me?"

"No. I must be losing my touch. Made a stupid mistake."

"Considering who we're up against, it's a wonder you and Ellen are still in one piece."

"What do you have on the old man?"

"Sit down, and I'll show you," Torrence said. Amundson sat, and took a long sip of his drink. Torrence reached into the envelope and pulled out an 8×10 black-and-white photo and placed it in front of Amundson.

"That's him!" Amundson said.

"His name is John McKarren. No files on him, except this one of Howard's."

"How'd you get a hold of it?"

"I was called into Al Howard's office this afternoon, when I got back to Langley after our meeting at Diamond Jim's." Torrence described his meeting with Howard, placing special emphasis on the four envelopes.

"I believe this file is Al Howard's insurance against McKarren—if McKarren should decide he doesn't need good old Al around anymore."

"So what's Howard got on McKarren?" Amundson asked.

"Plenty. It's all here," Torrence said. He removed the first document and passed it to Amundson. It was accompanied by a long handwritten narrative from Al Howard.

"I don't have time to read all of this, Jer."

"I read everything in detail on the plane. I'll give you the highlights. The first one is an army commission for McKarren, dated 1932. No West Point, no ROTC, no OCS. Guts on the battlefield."

"A mustang, eh?"

"Yep."

"How'd he get it?" Amundson asked.

"In China, before World War II. The whole country was up for grabs, one warlord fighting against another. McKarren was a buck sergeant, stationed at a mission near the Yalu River. The word came down to evacuate the mission people.

"By the time his platoon reached the pickup

point on the river, they'd been ambushed twice. The lieutenant and both senior sergeants were killed. He took over and got everyone out."

"So they made him an officer," Amundson said softly.

"Yeah."

Torrence showed him the next item, a picture of a Bronze Star mounted to a plaque. "He got the Bronze Star the next year. China again, only this time, he was wounded."

Next out of the envelope was a marriage license, attached to a faded sepia print of a dour-faced woman.

"Who's that?" Amundson asked.

"His ex-wife, Nancy."

"I can't believe a bastard like him could be married."

"I said 'ex.' It was in 1934, and it lasted six months. Howard's notes include references to the wife complaining about McKarren's 'sexual aberrations.'"

Amundson made a face.

Torrence next removed a picture of three men dressed in heavy winter clothes, with snow all around. "McKarren, Howard, and Wild Bill Donovan," Torrence explained.

"McKarren and Howard were with the OSS?"

"Yeah. That's them together in World War II behind Nazi lines in Norway. They had just finished their drop when one of the team snapped that picture."

The fifth item was a plaque bearing a portion of the text of the National Security Act of 1947.

"What's this?" Amundson asked.

"The National Security Act—the legislation that set up the CIA. According to Howard's notes, McKarren wrote most of it himself."

"Damn!"

"McKarren did very well in the Company. He knew Chinese from his tours there, and he also spoke fluent Ukranian, which he learned from his mother as a child. With that background, he worked the Soviet-bloc countries after the war —until 1948."

"Jerry, this guy *is* the CIA."

"Yeah. There's enough stuff here for a book. Anyway, in '48, he was transferred to the Far East station to help Chiang Kai-shek in his fight with the Communists."

Torrence displayed the next item. "The general was good enough to send a letter of commendation to the chief of the Far East station. Eventually, McKarren got the station chief's job.

"Now, here's where it starts getting interesting," Torrence said. He showed Amundson the next item from the envelope. It was a yellowed news clipping from 1951. Amundson moved closer so he could read it. TWO BRITISH AGENTS DEFECT TO RUSSIA.

"McKarren was the first to know about the defections of Guy Burgess and Donald Maclean from British intelligence to the KGB."

"How'd he find out about it?"

"From his old friend Chiang Kai-shek. It was

Chiang's way of repaying McKarren for all of the help he had given him.

"One of Chiang's agents penetrated the KGB at the very top and came away with the biggest intelligence coup ever. The agent correctly named Burgess, Maclean, and a third man, Kim Philby, as Russian double agents inside British intelligence."

"Christ, this guy's a one-man army," Amundson muttered.

"Chiang turned the incriminating documents over to McKarren. Being an enterprising fellow even then, McKarren didn't bother to pass them on to his superiors. Instead, he used them to go into business for himself. He took the documents directly to the head of MI-6 and worked out a deal with him."

"What kind of a deal?"

"McKarren gave him the three names and copies of the documents in return for continuous information—person to person, direct and unsanitized."

"To McKarren? Not to the Company?" Amundson asked.

"Yep."

Torrence paused to sip his beer. "A great way to start your own empire, eh?"

"Yeah," Amundson said softly.

"Here's McKarren's payoff from MI-6," Torrence said, handing Amundson another document.

"The *Norsel* report!"

"Yeah. McKarren's been following this since

1952. There's a lot more in here. Howard keeps meticulous notes, but here's the most eye-opening," Torrence said, handing Amundson a document with the words *Top Secret* imprinted across it.

"It's a report Howard put together on his own after Kennedy's assassination. It names McKarren as the man behind it."

Amundson's face went blank.

"You don't look surprised, Ted."

Amundson spoke softly, "The man who hired me has the same suspicion."

Torrence shook his head. "When I first read that report on Kennedy, I was ready to go back to Langley and take McKarren out myself."

Torrence scooped everything back into the envelope. "I've got a couple of copies of this stuff stashed away."

Torrence glanced at his watch. "I've got to get the hell out of here. Have to join up with the guys who are coming to take you away."

He closed the envelope and stood up to leave. "Oh, one more thing. Do you have anything that needs safekeeping? If you do, I can take it with me."

Amundson thought of Kurt Kelly's tape. He pulled it out, spilling money he had stuffed into his pockets at the restaurant.

"I completely forgot about this."

"What is it?"

"A tape recording describing what's going on in Antarctica. Add it to your collection."

"All right," Torrence said, stuffing it into the overflowing envelope.

Amundson picked up the money from the floor and slipped some of it into Torrence's coat pocket. "You may need this," he said.

"Thanks."

"There's more where that came from if we need it."

"I'll be knocking down your door sometime after one."

"Good-bye, Jer," Amundson said, shaking his friend's hand. "Be careful."

"I will. But you're the one at risk here. Watch yourself."

Torrence turned to leave, but Amundson grabbed his arm. "Remember, look for my ad in the *Sun-Times* personals, under Harmon."

Torrence nodded, then was out the door.

Nursing his drink, Amundson mulled over everything he had learned about his adversary, then he remembered Ellen still waiting for him in the bedroom.

He went into the living room and poured two fresh drinks before rejoining her. When he entered the bedroom, she was stretched out on the bed, shoeless, an empty glass in her hand.

"I've been a good girl. I haven't left my room. Can I have another drink now?"

He smiled and handed her one of the glasses.

"Has he gone?" she asked.

"Yes."

"What did you talk about?"

"The opposition," he said simply.

She sat up. "The 'opposition.' That's your euphemism for the man who murdered my father."

He nodded. "He didn't do it personally, you understand. But he gave the order."

Amundson quickly glanced at his watch. "It's eleven o'clock," he said, sitting next to her on the bed. "We've got at least two hours before the press gang gets here. Shall we resume our conversation where we left off?"

"What conversation was that?"

"Oh, erogenous zones between the fingers..."

"Hmmm," she murmured. She set her drink down on the nightstand, as he joined her on the bed.

Amundson was still awake. Ellen had fallen asleep within minutes of their final lovemaking. He reached over and caressed her body; she moaned softly. Amundson molded his body to hers and tried to sleep.

Suddenly, the room seemed to explode. The door flew inward, almost knocked off its hinges. Powerful flashlight beams stabbed into the room, enveloping the two figures in the bed. Amundson snapped to a sitting position as a troop of heavily armed men filled the room.

"Get out of that bed," a gruff voice demanded. Amundson used his right hand to shield his eyes from the blinding flashlight beams.

"Who the hell are you?" Amundson asked angrily.

"Never mind. Just get out of that bed."

Ellen awakened from a deep sleep, into a reality filled with grotesque shadows and outlines of men with guns. She started to scream, but Amundson placed his hand over her mouth.

"Easy, honey," he said reassuringly.

Even though they were expecting the kidnap team, her terror was genuine.

"Mr. and Mrs. Harmon," the same voice said calmly, "we are agents of the federal government. We are not here to harm you or to steal anything from you. We're here to take you into protective custody. Do not ask to see a warrant or to call anyone.

"We are placing you in protective custody because your country needs your skills. My men and I will leave you alone for about fifteen minutes. Use that time to get dressed and gather any small valuables you can carry. I will leave a suitcase for you. Pack enough clothing for two weeks. Do not attempt to take any firearms or other weapons.

"You will not return to this home. It will be sold as soon as possible, and the proceeds placed in an account in your name. When we leave the room, please hurry. Your phone service has been cut off, so don't waste any of your fifteen minutes trying to call someone. Do exactly what I have said. Speed is of the essence."

His speech completed, the speaker and his men left the room, closing the door as they went out.

"Geez! Those guys are scary," Ellen said.

She pressed her trembling body against Amundson. "C'mon," he said, "let's make like Mr. and Mrs. Harmon. The closet is full of clothes. Find something that fits you and let's get dressed."

Amundson transferred his remaining money from the nightstand to the suitcase, but left the .38 in the drawer.

In the gloomy darkness, John Bughatti, the commander of the kidnap team, gave a long sigh of relief and plopped into a comfortable armchair. He lit a cigarette, shielding the flare of the match with his hands. Even though the shades were down and the curtains drawn, he didn't want to risk arousing the curiosity of an insomniac neighbor.

Bughatti was nervous. Jerry Torrence, the overall field commander for Strike Force Alpha, had chosen to monitor his team on the first night of the operation.

At that moment, Torrence was standing next to the bar. He had just finished exchanging his own small medical kit for the one Bughatti's men had brought with them.

Torrence watched the glowing tip of Bughatti's cigarette. "That was really fine work," Torrence said.

"Thank you, sir. I'll pass that on to my boys."

"I especially like the way you followed procedure down to the last detail. Very smooth."

Bughatti grunted, and finished his cigarette.

When Amundson and Ellen emerged from the bedroom, Bughatti's men were assembled and

waiting. "Please sit on the couch," Bughatti said
to the couple. "We're going to administer an an-
esthetic drug to you. When you awaken, you'll
find yourselves at a government staging area.
All of your questions will be answered in full by
the authorities there."

Using Torrence's hypos, Bughatti adminis-
tered the shots. In a few seconds, Amundson and
Ellen were unconscious. They and their luggage
were taken to a waiting van in the street below.
Torrence again congratulated Bughatti, shook
his hand, then left in his own car.

The strike team left for another kidnapping
ten miles closer toward the city of Chicago,
while Amundson and Ellen were taken to the
military side of O'Hare Airport and a waiting jet
transport.

Chapter Seven

llll llll llll llll llll

McKarren's sleek, six-passenger jet began its
landing descent through the heavy gray clouds
that hovered over the Wisconsin landscape. The
fields below looked bleak and abandoned, left
fallow for the coming winter snow.

As they broke through the clouds, McKarren
caught sight of the installation below. From the

copilot's seat, he could identify the mall, runway, and buildings.

On the rolls of U.S. government installations, it appeared as a NASA research and development project, code-named Odyssey. Its budget was a mere two million dollars a year, but McKarren had channeled additional Company dollars into the project to make sure it had the equipment and personnel it needed.

The buildings McKarren was looking at were part of the aboveground cover for the base; Odyssey itself was below ground.

The pilot eased the plane toward the end of the runway and nosed down. As they made their approach, McKarren saw a single person waiting at the far end: Michael Collins—standing bareheaded and without a topcoat.

The plane touched down, its tires squealing. McKarren glanced at his watch: 7:58 AM. He turned to the pilot. "Good going. I thought those headwinds were going to make us late."

"Thank you, sir."

The plane braked gently, then taxied to where Collins was waiting. McKarren collected his briefcase and a small overnight bag, then opened the door.

Collins greeted him with a firm handshake. He quickly attached a security badge to McKarren's coat lapel, and they walked briskly toward the hangar. As they walked, Collins blew on his hands to warm them.

"Aren't we paying you enough to buy a topcoat and gloves?" McKarren asked.

"Hmmm? Oh, I just haven't had time to dig them out yet. This cold weather is early."

"Everything going okay with Strike Force Alpha?" McKarren asked.

"Yes, sir. They started arriving last night, right on schedule."

"Good."

Inside the hangar, they were silent as they walked toward the elevator. A guard snapped to attention as they approached. He examined their badges and let them pass. Inside the elevator car, two TV cameras watched them as they began their descent.

"Everything ready?" McKarren asked.

"Yes, sir. My people have been busy all morning getting the experiment ready."

McKarren scowled. "Dammit, Collins, by this time you shouldn't be thinking in terms of an experiment."

"Just a figure of speech," Collins replied hastily.

"Crap," McKarren said. "I hope for your sake this 'experiment' is a success, Collins."

"It will be, sir."

The elevator stopped at the fifth floor. The corridors were filled with white-smocked technicians hurrying back and forth.

McKarren and Collins entered a control room that overlooked a laboratory where the experiment would take place.

"The two subjects are inmates originally sentenced to life imprisonment without parole," Collins explained.

"What did they do?"

"They killed the president of a bank during a robbery."

McKarren was silent for a moment. "So what do they get in return for being our guinea pigs?" he asked.

"A pardon. They've been in suspended animation for ten years."

From the control room, McKarren watched as the two subjects were rolled into the lab in their life-sustaining canisters. The two cylinders were opened slowly, and the gray-skinned nude forms placed on special tables, where they were immediately injected with stimulants. Diathermy was used to raise their pulses, first to eight beats per minute, then to thirty, and then slowly to normal levels.

After thirty minutes of gentle stimulation and massage, the two men were successfully revived. They were immediately taken to a small cubicle to be debriefed and examined by a team of doctors and psychologists.

"I want a copy of the report as soon as it's ready," McKarren said.

"Yes, sir."

"My compliments, Collins. Everything looked perfect."

"Thank you, sir. The hypothermia itself has been perfected. What we're working on now is the refinement of the revival mechanism."

"What do you mean?" McKarren asked.

"Well, as you saw, reviving those two took a whole team of technicians and doctors. We're working on a self-contained mechanism in the cylinders that will do everything those technicians did a few minutes ago."

"How close are you to a solution?"

"We'll have it in a few weeks," Collins replied.

"Excellent. I'm pleased that you've made such progress. But your final system must be foolproof—with backup systems in case of emergencies or power failure."

"Exactly my line of thinking, sir."

"Good. Now I want to address the teaching staff before they start their classes—and I want to look over some of the detainees before they awaken."

"I'll call upstairs to make sure they're ready for us," Collins said.

When they entered the lecture room on Level 3, McKarren saw twelve green-garbed men standing in small groups, talking excitedly. They were all former Company officers whom McKarren trusted. Their loyalty was based partially on dedication to the Company, but mostly on fear of McKarren. He strode to the podium and immediately the room fell quiet.

"Gentlemen," he began softly. "Together we will write one of the most glorious chapters in the history of the United States—indeed, in the history of civilized man. We will initiate a project that will save our country and our people from certain destruction.

"Already it has begun. The West Antarctic ice sheet has slipped into the ocean. The time for us to act has arrived. On behalf of the President, I am now commencing Operation Migrant."

He was interrupted by twelve standing men, clapping and whistling their approval. McKarren smiled at their outburst. When he'd had enough of their applause, he raised his hands for silence.

"In a few hours, your task will begin. Scores of prominent Americans will awaken from their drug-induced sleep. They'll be angry, distrustful men and women. It will be your job to explain to them why they are here, and to show them the way to the Green Belt and national salvation. We've given you the tools you need. The rest is up to you. I know you'll be successful."

McKarren stepped away from the podium. Applause rang in his ears once more, while outstretched hands grabbed at his hand, shaking, congratulating.

Outside the room, McKarren and Collins paused briefly to watch. McKarren smiled broadly as the instructor-officers in the room received their teaching assignments.

"Everything is going well," McKarren said.

"It certainly is," Collins agreed.

"Now I want to see the detainees."

"Yes, sir."

Level 4 had been designed and constructed as a holding area for victims of Strike Force Alpha. Holding cubicles were arranged in clusters of eight. The smaller ones held individuals or couples, while the larger cubicles were reserved for families.

Each small room was equipped with a one-way mirror so the occupants could be kept under observation. The clusters were arranged so one person could monitor all eight cubicles.

The observation posts were not yet manned. Some of the security people were still being briefed. Others were disrobing kidnappees and exchanging their street clothes for light brown uniforms.

Amundson and Ellen were still in their street clothes, covered by sheets, when two security guards, a man and a woman, entered their cubicle. The male guard started to undress Amundson.

As the guard was completing the exchange of clothing, Amundson began to wake up. He forced himself to think, in order to clear his mind faster. He kept himself under control while the guard put on his boots. The drug's aftereffects left him slightly euphoric, with a distinct sense of well-being.

That's a very interesting drug, he thought groggily.

Finally, he was fully conscious. He waited patiently for the guard to finish. As soon as the boots were on, Amundson punched his right fist into the guard's Adam's apple.

The man half choked and half screamed as he collapsed backward, clutching his throat. The female guard, who was still undressing Ellen, reached for her pistol, but Amundson was on her just as she cleared the holster. He twisted her arm behind her back, and the pistol dropped to the floor. Amundson kicked it away and increased the pressure on her arm.

"Owww. Please, you're hurting me," she moaned.

"That's my intention, sweetheart. Do exactly as I say, and that's all the pain you'll feel. If you don't cooperate, I'll break your arm. Understand?" He increased the pressure on her arm again to make his point clear.

"Owww. Okay, okay."

"Okay what? Are you going to cooperate?"

"Yes. What do you want?"

"You can begin by telling me everything you know about this place. And don't leave out anything."

"Okay, but I don't know much."

"I'll be the judge of that," Amundson said. "Just start talking. What's this place called?"

"Operation Migrant."

"What country?"

"America, of course," she said.

"What state?"

"Wisconsin."

"You're doing fine. How's this place laid out?"

"We're underground," she answered. "It's built in the shape of a giant pyramid. There's six levels. Level One is at the top and is for trucks, Jeeps, tanks, artillery—stuff we'll need when we get to the Green Belt."

"What's the Green Belt?" he interrupted.

"The area in South America where the government is moving."

"Maybe you're not being basic enough with me. Why is the government moving to South America?" he asked, feigning ignorance.

She made a face of tolerant disgust. "If you'd just wait until the lectures begin, you wouldn't get a bunch of half-assed answers like you're gettin' from me. How come you're up before the others, anyway?"

"How do I know?" he lied. "All I know for sure is that my wife and I have been kidnapped, and I want to know who, what, why, and where. And unfortunately for you, you're the first person to cross my path who can answer my questions.

"Now, I'll have some answers. Why is the government of the United States moving to South America?"

"Because there's an ice age coming, and the present U.S. of A. will be covered by glaciers."

Amundson paused. *That's additional confirmation of the ice age*, he thought.

"All right, keep talking. So Level One is for vehicles. What about the rest of the place?"

"Level Two is the armory, maintenance equipment, and a lot of electronics stuff. Level Three is the administrative level. It's also where the classrooms are, and the library and listening rooms. Level Four is where we are right now. It's a holding area for detainees like yourself."

"Why was I kidnapped?" Amundson asked, ignoring her euphemism.

"You and the rest of the people here are going

to be in the vanguard of the migration south after our armed forces secure the Green Belt for us. You should feel honored the government thinks you're so important."

Amundson grunted in reply. "What about Levels Five and Six?"

"I can't tell you much about them. Even security people are restricted down there. We're only allowed in the areas right outside the elevators. It's all top secret. Special passes only."

"Any special security?"

"TV cameras everywhere. Intrusion-alert alarms. Guard stations on the surface and on Levels Five and Six. That's the reason I don't mind tellin' you all this," she said smugly. "Sooner or later, they're going to catch you, and besides, it's all stuff they're going to tell you anyway."

Amundson paused. "How long has this base been in operation?"

"As far as I know, it's been here since March. I got here in April." She stopped talking, suddenly realizing she was discussing things the detainees were not supposed to know.

"How much further did you have to go on your rounds, and how long before you're expected somewhere?"

"We had another twenty cubicles to do, and we're due to report back in an hour."

Amundson breathed a sigh of relief. He had time to work.

"That armory you mentioned, what kind of weapons do you have there?" he asked.

"You name it. Rifles, grenades, pistols..."

"Tear gas?"

"Sure. Why? What are you—"

"Never mind. How long before the other kidnap victims wake up?"

"Oh...two hours," she said.

"Good. Is there any other way out of this place besides the main elevator?"

She hesitated.

I'm asking too many questions whose answers are not on the agenda, he thought.

Amundson twisted her arm harder. "I've gone easy on you till now, because you've answered all of my questions. Don't blow it now. My wife and I are getting out of here, and you're going with us to insure our safety. If we don't make it, you don't make it. Do you understand?"

She nodded her head vigorously. "A few months ago, Johnny, the engineer, and me were passing time by ourselves up in the old mill at the other end of the valley. After we drank a few six-packs, he started to brag about how he was probably the only man who knew everything there was to know about this place.

"When I called him out on his braggin', he said he even knew about an escape tunnel on Level Six. But then he clammed up all of a sudden and wouldn't say any more about it. Then he swore me to secrecy."

"Did he say where the entrance was?"

"Nope."

Amundson smiled. He released the guard from his grip, and shoved her hard to the floor.

He picked up her pistol and trained it on her. She glared at him, rubbing her wrist and forearm.

"Stand up," he commanded. She stood, eyeing him nervously.

"Now take off your uniform," he instructed. He watched as she removed her fatigues and stood nervously in her bra and panties.

"Turn around," he said curtly.

Frightened suddenly, she hesitated.

"I'm not going to hurt you," he assured. "Turn around." Shivering, she did as she was told.

Amundson switched the pistol to his left hand and then chopped her on the side of the neck with the flat of his right hand. She crumbled to the floor in a heap.

He lifted her up and dumped her on to one of the two cots in the room. Using her handcuffs, he chained her to one of the cot's metal legs, and then covered her with a sheet.

Finally, he had a chance to examine the room. The cubicle was small—only ten by fifteen feet. It had two cots, the one where the female guard was handcuffed and the one where Ellen lay, still unconscious. There was a toilet and a small washbasin at one end of the room. On the floor in the middle of the room, the male guard lay dead or close to it.

Amundson quickly removed the brown uniform and donned jeans and a shirt from his suitcase. He stripped the green fatigues from the male guard and put them on over his street clothes.

Ellen was still stretched out on the cot, half undressed. The female guard had removed her shoes and blouse and was working on her jeans when Amundson had jumped her.

He pulled Ellen's jeans back on and stood her up, propping her left arm around his neck and supporting her with an arm around her waist. He walked her around the room, stopping at the washbasin on every circuit to splash cold water on her face, neck, and chest. After ten trips around the cubicle, she groaned weakly. Amundson laid her down on the cot and kissed her lips. She revived slowly. Her eyes opened weakly, blinked at the bright light, then fluttered closed.

He continued to kiss her. "Hmmm, this is a nice way to wake up," she murmured, as she finally realized who was kissing her.

"As good as I am, it's not just me making you feel so good. It's mostly the drug they used on us."

"Ummm," she sighed. "Where are we?"

"Inside Project Migrant."

She sat up on the cot. "How do you feel?" he asked.

"Weak, but happy."

"That's the drug," he said, handing her the blouse. "Let's get going."

Then she spotted the man on the floor. "Who's he?"

"Security guard. I think he's dead. There's another one under the sheet there."

"What do we do now?" she asked, struggling into her blouse.

Amundson collected the female guard's boots and green uniform. "Put these on over your clothes. They're our tickets out of this place."

Amundson told her his plan as she dressed. "We need to get to Level Six. That's where the secret of this base is located, and where the way out is." Amundson quickly told her about the guard's description of the escape tunnel.

"So how do we get down there?"

"Create a diversion. We'll need some things from the armory up on Level Two—grenades and tear gas. But we need to move fast. The guards will be missed in about forty-five minutes."

While Ellen finished putting on the guard's boots, Amundson went through their suitcase, removing his lockpick and some of the money.

"Put this where we won't lose it," he said, handing her the wad of bills.

She stuffed the money into her bra. "How's that?"

"Good. Are you ready?"

"As ready as I can be."

"Just let me do the talking and stay close to me. Don't forget this," he said, handing her the guard's holster belt. The pistol was on the cot next to her. He showed her the safety and handed it to her.

"If you have to use it, remember to use both hands, and just point and squeeze," he said. She nodded solemnly.

"Let's go," he said.

They stepped out of the cubicle and walked to the nearby elevators.

They were silent as the elevator rose smoothly to Level Two. The doors opened, and they stepped out. The corridors were filled with other people in green, and no one paid any attention to them.

"You see how well this disguise works? No one in uniform ever pays any attention to anyone else in the same uniform, except to note rank and salute."

"What rank are we?"

"You're a corporal, and I'm a buck sergeant."

"Do we have to salute anyone?" she asked nervously.

"If I salute, you salute. C'mon, the armory's to the left," he said. They followed the signs that pointed the way. "When we get there, I want you to make a pass at the guy behind the counter," he said.

"What if there's more than one?"

"Make a pass at one of them. Get the others jealous—anything to divert their attention so I can get behind them."

She made a sour face. "*You* make the pass at the guy behind the counter. That'll *really* get his attention."

Amundson gritted his teeth. "Just do what I say!"

When they reached the armory, she smiled and went in. A sergeant was sitting at a desk two feet behind a wide counter that stretched the full length of the doorway. The only way to reach the other side was through a narrow opening.

He was alone, and concentrating on a stack of paper on his desk.

"Hi, Sarge," Ellen greeted.

He looked up. "Well, hello, there," he answered, immediately abandoning his paperwork. He leaned against the counter to get a better look at her.

"Where'd you come from?" he asked.

"Oh, I've been hanging around."

"Yeah? Why haven't I seen you before? I'm sure I would remember..."

Out of the corner of her eye, Ellen could see Amundson crawling through the opening. She leaned forward toward the sergeant to distract him even more.

"My name is Ellen," she said.

"Mine's Ritkin—John Ritkin."

"Nice to meet you, John."

"Likewise. Now, aside from your very good taste in men, what brings you here?"

"I thought I'd exchange my pistol."

"Exchange your pistol? What's the matter—"

That was as far as he got. Amundson suddenly straightened up and struck him from behind in the left temple with the butt of his pistol. The sergeant crumbled heavily to the floor. Amundson dragged him to the back of the armory, out of sight.

"Take his place behind the counter, honey, while I get what we need." He glanced at his watch. "If anyone shows up, make out like you're in charge of the armory, and you're getting ready to lock up for lunch."

"Okay," she said, sitting nervously at the desk.

Quickly, Amundson found what he wanted: fragmentary and tear-gas grenades and a submachine gun. He stuffed the grenades into his shirt and slung the submachine gun over his shoulder.

"Okay, we're all set. Let's get of here before someone shows," he said.

He locked the armory and led her back toward the elevators.

"You're doing real well," he said softly.

"I want to faint," she replied.

"We're almost out of here." Amundson pushed the button to summon the elevator. "Just hang together for another fifteen minutes," he said.

The elevator doors opened. There was no one else on board. As soon as they stepped in, he pushed the button for Level Six. When they were between Levels Five and Six, he pushed the Stop button, and they came to an abrupt halt.

"Get down on all fours," he said. With a moan, she did as he asked. Amundson climbed up on her. She sagged from his weight, but he was still able to reach the escape hatch in the ceiling. He pushed it up and out of his way and stuck his head through the opening. Pulling himself higher, he supported his weight by propping his elbows on the roof of the cab.

"I'm okay now," he said. "You can get up."

He heard her groan as she stood. Removing the grenades from his shirt pocket, he placed them on the roof.

"Take your cap off, mess up your hair, and rub some dirt on your face. And do anything else you can think of to make it look like you've been through a riot."

She did what he asked while he arranged the grenades in a circle. "I'm ready," she said.

"Good. When I say go, push the Start button. When we stop on Level Six, I'm going to pull the pins on these grenades. As soon as that door opens, get out and start screaming. Understand?"

"Yes. That won't be hard. I'm ready to scream right now," she said.

"I'll be right behind you."

"You'd better be."

"Okay, go!"

She pushed the Start button, and the elevator continued down to Level Six. As soon as it stopped, Amundson pulled the pins and dropped to the floor of the cab.

The guards at the security station, a captain and two enlisted men, were waiting anxiously, after witnessing the elevator's delay between floors. The moment the elevator stopped, the captain pressed the silent alarm to alert the security command room. With pistols drawn, they waited for the elevator door to open.

As the door opened, a disheveled woman stumbled out, screaming. The three guards froze for a second. Then a wild man emerged from the elevator, shouting at them. "For God's sake, the base has been sabotaged!"

"We're dead if we don't get out of here!" Ellen shrieked convincingly.

The grenades went off, and flames and tear gas belched into the room. Sirens wailed and emergency lights flashed on.

"Damn!" the guard captain cursed. "Let's get the hell out of here."

Without thinking, he headed back toward the interior of Level Six, followed closely by the two enlisted men, Ellen, and Amundson.

A heavy door slid open as they approached it, and the five of them burst into a cavernous well-lit room. The door closed automatically behind them, shutting out the noise and flames. In the room were six white-smocked technicians, who immediately stopped their work and stared wide-eyed at the intruders.

"Quick!" the guard captain shouted as they ran through the room. "There's no time to lose. The base is under attack, and the upper levels are already in flames. Our only hope is the escape tunnel." He headed straight for the concealed entranceway while the six technicians stood petrified.

As soon as the captain opened the escape hatch, Amundson cut him down with a short burst from his submachine gun, then turned his weapon on the other two guards before they could react. The room was alive with the sound of bullets being fired and the clinking of empty shell casings striking the floor. The smell of cordite was heavy in the air.

Slowly, Amundson turned his weapon until it was pointed at the six technicians. They cowered, hands up. "If any of you move, you'll all be laid out next to those three," he said. Still covering them with his submachine gun, Amundson backtracked to the door and locked it.

Ellen stood motionless, staring impassively at the outstretched corpses. Amundson gently touched her elbow, then wrapped his right arm around her waist and pulled her body tight against his.

"It'll be over soon," he whispered. She nodded numbly.

Amundson walked over to the six men. They stood amid dozens of cylindrical machines, each about seven feet long, each lying horizontally on its own cart.

"What are they?" Ellen asked Amundson.

"They look like lung machines," he answered. "The kind they use for polio."

"What are they for?"

"I don't know, but I'm sure our friends here can tell us. Who's in charge?" he asked the small group of cowering men.

No one spoke, but five pairs of eyes shifted toward the eldest man in the group.

"You!" Amundson said, pointing to the man with his submachine gun.

"Me?" the frightened man asked.

"Yeah, you. Step forward."

The man hesitated out of fear, then reluctantly shuffled forward, his eyes fixed on Amundson's weapon.

"What's your name?" Amundson asked.

"Dr. Carlyle," he squeaked.

"Doctor of philosophy, no doubt?"

The man nodded.

"What is your function here?" Amundson asked.

"Ahhh-uhhh—I am the project coordinator."

Amundson smiled. "Good. It sounds like a very important position. I think you may be just the man to answer my questions."

"Well, I'll try."

"Doctor, you'll do more than try. If I get one twitchy feeling that you're lying to me, I'll shoot you in the kneecap. Very painful. And you don't look like a man who can stand much pain. Am I right?"

Carlyle nodded furiously. "Please don't shoot me. I'll tell you anything you want to know—anything."

"Good. That's sound reasoning, Doctor. Now, for starters, what's the name of this project and where are we?"

"This is Project Odyssey, and we're in south-central Wisconsin," Carlyle answered.

Amundson was stunned. He had expected to hear "Project Migrant" again. "And exactly *what* is Project Odyssey?"

Carlyle paused for only a second. "It's a research project to perfect suspended animation. That's what the cylinders are for."

"Suspended animation? Explain."

"The concept?"

"No, Doctor, I'm familiar with the concept. *Why* are you perfecting suspended animation?"

Amundson watched Carlyle closely. The doctor's answer was slow in coming, as though he were getting up the courage to lie.

"Ah, we're part of NASA. We're developing suspended animation for our longer manned space flights."

Amundson fired a round between Carlyle's legs. The doctor screamed and keeled over backward as though he'd actually been struck by the bullets.

"Get up. You're not hurt," Amundson said curtly. The cringing Dr. Carlyle staggered to his feet. "The next bullet's going to shatter your kneecap if you don't tell me the truth."

"It's secret. It's secret. They'll kill me if I tell you."

"It's their secret versus your kneecap..." Amundson raised the submachine gun.

"All right, all right. Do you know about the ice age?" he squealed.

"Yes."

"Do you know about Operation Migrant?"

"Yes."

"All right, that makes it easy," the doctor said, regaining some of his composure. "Operation Migrant is a diversion. The ice age will be much more severe than first thought. The entire planet will be uninhabitable, and there eventually will be no Green Belt. So Project Odyssey has become our only hope for survival. Suspended animation for selected individuals— government leaders, scientists . . ."

"The people being kidnapped," Kelly interrupted.

"Some of them, yes. But most of the detainees are going to the Green Belt as part of the diversion. Only the most important of them will be selected for suspended animation—to wait out the ice age down here, and eventually be awakened by these caretaker machines you see around us. And there are computers to monitor the outside world and store the knowledge we'll need when we resume our civilization."

"Quite a setup," Amundson said. "But why Wisconsin? Why didn't you put the base in southern California or Texas?"

Dr. Carlyle sighed as a person does when explaining elementary facts to people unacquainted with them. "During the four previous ice ages, the glaciers overran the upper Midwest, New England, and New York. This time we expect them to cover the entire country.

"In the past, this area of Wisconsin remained unglaciated. It's called the Driftless Area. Project Odyssey is in the heart of that area.

"We don't know why the glaciers bypassed the Driftless Area, but if we have an emergency or our power breaks down before the end of the ice age, and we have to revive prematurely, at least the surface above us won't be covered with hundreds of feet of ice."

"How long has this base been in existence?"

Amundson asked, anxious to compare Carlyle's answer to what the female guard had told him earlier.

"Since March. We found out about the ice age in February. By March, we had sufficient data to realize the glaciers would make the entire planet uninhabitable. By the end of March, this facility was completed and functioning."

"How close are you to perfecting suspended animation?"

"We've done it," Carlyle said proudly. "We still have a few bugs to work out, and we'll be ready."

"You mean it's taken you only seven months to perfect suspended animation?" Amundson asked.

"Not exactly. You see, Odyssey was an ongoing project before this. Like I said, it was a part of NASA. But we never had much of a priority before."

"Hmmm. Where does the base get its power? Nuclear reactors?"

"We have a reactor, but it's our backup. We don't think it will be reliable enough over such a long period of time. Our main source of power is geothermal. Piping reaches down to a natural fault in the Earth's mantle, where heat from the planet's core rises and accumulates."

Amundson whistled. "How long will the ice age last?"

"We don't know for sure, but based on the last four, we're allowing for fifty-five thousand years of suspended animation. That should give us an ample margin of safety."

"I'm glad to hear that. Doctor, you said we're in south-central Wisconsin—exactly which county?"

"Sauk."

"Good. Just keep the answers coming, Doc, and I think your right kneecap might make it in one piece. What's above us at ground level?"

"A NASA tracking station and a weather station," Carlyle answered.

Amundson nodded his head slowly.

"Who's in charge of all of this?" Ellen asked suddenly.

"The installation director is Michael Collins."

The name meant nothing to Amundson, but he filed it away for future reference.

"Doctor, you've done well," he said. "As much as I'd like to hear more about your work, we must leave you. But we do have a small problem. What to do to make sure you don't interfere with our escape. The only sure remedy I can think of is to kill you all."

The six broke out into a chorus of moans and pleas for mercy.

Ellen didn't want to see six more men die in a hail of bullets from Amundson's submachine gun. "Handcuff and gag them," she suggested. "That should hold them until we can get away."

"Good idea. Get the cuffs from the security guards," he told her.

Amundson cuffed the scientists in pairs with the three sets of handcuffs, and tied everything together with strips of material from one of the smocks. He stuffed cloth balls into their mouths and tied the gags in place with belts. When he was done, Amundson checked the knots, then stood back and surveyed his handiwork.

"Okay," he said to Ellen, motioning toward the escape hatch. "Let's go."

She crawled through the hatch and Amundson followed. When he closed the door behind them, soft green lights blinked on all around them and a reassuring message appeared in green on the door:

> **WHEN THIS HATCH IS LOCKED ON THIS SIDE, IT CANNOT BE OPENED FROM THE OTHER SIDE. TIME TO SURFACE IS TEN MINUTES.**

They turned to see where they were. A tunnel led upward and to their right. Several small rail cars waited for them. Amundson took Ellen's hand and led her toward one of the cars.

As soon as the captain triggered the silent alarm, McKarren and Collins were ushered into the security command room under protective guard.

While McKarren was furious about the incredible breach of security the intruders represented, he was impressed with the professionalism of the security commander on duty and with the security systems.

Even during the first minutes of the alarm, there was no confusion, no hesitation by anyone in the room. The commander quickly sealed the base, then used the sophisticated system of closed-circuit cameras to track the emergency on the main monitoring screen.

Two minutes after the first alert, they were watching the fire in the elevator. One minute later, the scene shifted, and they watched helplessly as the three guards died. Then, McKarren had cursed and gritted his teeth as Dr. Carlyle spilled his guts about Odyssey.

After Ellen and Amundson disappeared through the escape hatch, the command room was silent. McKarren spoke first. "I want Carlyle, his wife, and his children executed," he said vengefully.

"Yes, sir," Collins said softly, looking away.

"Where does the tunnel come out?" McKarren asked the security commander.

"About five miles away from the base."

"Can you show me the exit point on the screen?"

"No, sir. We assumed we would be in the tunnel and the base in hostile hands. We can't stop them or control anything in the escape tunnel."

"No matter," Collins said. "We can have a security team waiting for them when they come out."

"Don't be a fool, Collins," McKarren said. "As much as I want those two, we've got bigger fish to catch. I want whoever's behind them. I want to know who they're working for.

"An enemy has been exposed—one whose existence we didn't even suspect. Commander,

begin a surveillance dragnet. No one is to interfere with their escape, but I want to know where
those two are at all times."

"Yes, sir."

The dragnet procedure had been well thought
out and was precise in every detail. Every public
telephone within five miles of the installation
was tapped. During a security alert, truckers with
CBs would be sent out to cruise the area, ready to
offer a friendly ride to hitchhiking fugitives.
Phony cops in squadrols would patrol nearby
roads, and choppers with fake police markings
would be used for aerial surveillance.

McKarren sat down. Before him, the large
monitor continued to show the room on Level 6,
but he blocked the image out of his mind. It was
time to think. There were questions that needed
quick answers.

"Collins, I want you to personally handle the
investigation of this incident, and I want some
answers before I leave this base. First, how did
they get in—and how the hell did they find out
about the escape tunnel?

"I want to know which floors they were on
and every room they were in. And most important, I want to know who they talked to."

"I'll get started immediately," Collins said.

"Before you go, I need a secure room and a
scrambled line to Langley."

Collins led McKarren to a small cubicle just
off the security command room. "Are you sure
this room and phone are secure?" McKarren
asked.

"Yes, sir. They're checked twice a day."

McKarren grunted, then motioned with his head for Collins to leave the room. Once Collins was gone, McKarren sat down to collect his thoughts.

The girl was Ellen Kelly from the Chicago snafu, he thought. *The man I know from somewhere, too. He's tumbled to the ice age somehow, and he's tracking it through her. But where do I know him from?*

McKarren's mind reached back, unfolding his past.

'Nam, he thought. *He was a Company man in 'Nam.*

McKarren shifted his position in the chair. *And how the hell did they get in here?* he wondered. *They must have gotten themselves kidnapped. Some sonuvabitch in Strike Force Alpha is working with them,* he decided.

He reached for the scrambled phone to call Al Howard at Langley.

Chapter Eight

When Amundson and Ellen sat down in the transport car, soft green lights, identical to the ones on the hatch, blinked on. Ahead of them, they could see the outline of the escape tunnel. A clear plastic roof closed over them, and they began to move. As the car accelerated, the evenly spaced green lights on the tunnel wall flashed past them, until they became a blur.

They hurtled through the tunnel for about five minutes before the car began to slow down enough for them to distinguish the individual lights again. Finally, the car stopped, and the bubble roof popped open.

Before them loomed a brick wall, with a Jacob's ladder clearly visible, illuminated with the omnipresent green.

"End of the line," Amundson said.

"I wonder where we are," Ellen said.

"Wherever we are, the way out is clearly marked. Let's go."

They stepped out of the car and walked to the ladder, which rose up to a trapdoor, also outlined in green. Amundson led the way up the ladder, his submachine gun slung over his shoulder. "Stay close to me," he said. At the top, an illuminated panel said *Press*. He did, and the trapdoor swung upward. Amundson unslung his weapon and poked it through the opening. Immediately, lights went on in the room above.

"Wait here a moment while I check it out," he said.

He climbed up into the room and looked around. The room was circular, with a domed roof, and illuminated with fluorescent white. There were no windows. Ellen poked her head up through the trapdoor. "Is it safe?" she asked.

"Seems to be," he said, reaching down and extending his hand to her. She grasped it and let his strength pull her up through the trapdoor and into the room.

She stood next to him. They turned in a slow circle, examining the room closely. It was made of concrete and was dank.

"It's a mausoleum," she said finally.

"You're right," he said, smiling. "It's perfect. We're in a cemetery, probably miles from Odyssey."

"It's eerie," Ellen said softly.

"Yeah, but it makes sense. Cemeteries are usually granted perpetual charters—it'll always be here."

As soon as he was done speaking, a metallic voice clicked on and filled the room with its message. "Congratulations. You have escaped the emergency at Odyssey. It is impossible to monitor the emergency from here or to tell how many of you have escaped. This mausoleum is your entranceway to the outside.

"Please observe the crypts in the wall. They do not contain bodies, but the supplies you'll need, including arms and clothing. To open the enclosures, simply pull hard on the casket rings, and the crypts will pressurize and open."

The message ended abruptly. Amundson stepped to the wall and grabbed the ring on one of the burial crypts. Ellen grabbed a second ring. They pulled together. Air hissed into the enclosures, and the crypts slid out of the wall like cabinet drawers. The one Amundson had pulled out contained a variety of small arms. Ellen's was full of clothes.

As Amundson started to reach into the crypt full of weapons, the voice came on again. "Take anything you need. To further assist you, view-screens will appear in a few moments. Use them to monitor the area around the mausoleum and check for hostiles. The other controls are self-explanatory. This is the end of my message."

Amundson found a .38 and ammunition in one of the crypts. He laid down his submachine gun and loaded the pistol quickly. Searching deeper, he found a shoulder holster, and was starting to strap it on when Ellen called to him.

"Hey, what's this?" she asked, pulling out what looked like long underwear. Amundson walked over to her and checked it carefully.

"It's bulletproof clothing," he said. "Put it on. We may need it."

They stripped to their underwear and donned the tight-fitting body armor. "What about the uniforms?" she asked.

"Put them into the crypt."

Once her street clothes were back on, Ellen started to try on ski jackets. "Before you put that on, c'mon over here. I want to fit you with a shoulder holster."

He led her to the weapon drawer and found a .38 and shoulder holster for her.

She stood still as Amundson fitted the holster over her upper body. "These things were not designed for women," she said wryly, trying to fit one strap comfortably around her left breast.

Amundson smiled as he alternately caressed her breast and adjusted the strap. He slipped a loaded .38 into her holster, then strapped on his own holster and pistol.

"Okay, now for the ski jackets," he said.

He checked the rest of the supplies, putting a Swiss Army knife into his pocket. A small section of the wall above the crypt opened, and a control panel appeared, complete with a bank of instruments and twin monitoring screens.

The instruments indicated outside temperature, wind direction, and time of day. "The temperature's dropped fifteen degrees from yesterday," Amundson noted.

The two screens showed the areas on either side of the mausoleum. A hundred yards away, a funeral was in progress. There was a thin layer of snow on the ground.

"Here's the button that opens the mausoleum," she said. "Are we ready?"

"Just a minute," he said, peering intently at the screens. "I want to make sure no one is looking this way when we open the door."

She waited with her finger poised above the button. "Okay, go ahead."

A heavy concrete door slid open, and sunlight flooded the room. "God, that sun's bright," Ellen said, shielding her eyes with her hand.

"Yeah, and the snow makes the glare even worse." He grasped her hand and led her out. The concrete door closed behind them. Amundson felt very exposed.

"We need transportation," he said, eyeing the cars in the funeral. The last cars in the procession had just arrived, and the mourners were making their way to the grave site, where the priest and the family of the dead person were waiting.

The undertaker gave a signal, and the hearse driver got out to open the hearse doors and help unload the casket.

"C'mon, now's our chance," Amundson said.

"Chance for what?"

"To get out of here," he growled, grabbing her hand and pulling her toward the crowd of silent mourners. They walked quickly to the rear of the group to the hearse.

He was guessing the hearse would be the first vehicle to leave the cemetery. They got into the back and lay flat. In a few minutes, the driver returned to the hearse and started the engine. He drove slowly down the bumpy road that led out of the cemetery.

Amundson slowly raised himself to all fours, with his pistol drawn. He jabbed the front of the barrel into the back of the driver's skull. The man jumped.

"You know what this is?" Amundson asked.

The man nodded.

"It won't go off if you do what I say."

"Who are you? What do you want?" the driver asked.

"You're in no position to ask questions, friend. Just follow my instructions and don't look back at me. Understand?"

The driver nodded again.

"Good," Amundson said, lifting himself higher so that he could see the road. There were no other cars visible.

"How soon before the rest of the funeral leaves?" Amundson asked.

"Half an hour."

"Does this road have a lot of traffic?"

"Practically zero. Only when there's a funeral."

"Good. Pull over right here."

As soon as the driver had the hearse off the road, Amundson had more questions for him.

"Where are you driving to?"

"Back to Reedsburg."

"Where's that from here?"

"Up this road about half a mile to County V and turn right. Then a mile to State Highway 33 and take a left. Reedsburg is six miles up 33."

"You got a road map?"

"Sure."

"Get it out and mark the route you just described."

The driver did as Amundson said and handed the map back over his shoulder without turning around. Amundson studied it for a moment.

"Good. Now, take off your hat and coat and hand them to me."

The driver removed his gray hat and topcoat and passed them back. "Now, get out of the hearse—slowly. And don't look back at me."

Carefully following Amundson's instructions, the driver climbed out and found himself facing the woods along the side of the road. Amundson got out, still holding the gun.

"Start walking. Straight ahead, until you're in the woods. And don't look back."

Amundson stayed behind the driver; when they were far enough into the woods, Amundson hit him over the head with his pistol, and watched him collapse to the ground.

Amundson hurried back to the hearse, where Ellen waited anxiously. "You didn't kill him, did you?" she asked.

"No," Amundson said. "But he'll have a hell of a headache when he wakes up."

Amundson donned the driver's somber gray hat and coat and took his place behind the wheel. "Why don't you come up front with me for now. When we hit traffic, you'll have to duck out of sight, but for now, I'd rather have you next to me."

Amundson waited until she was in front with him before he started the car. He drove slowly along the dirt road. "God, I'm glad we're finally clear of that place," she said.

"We're not clear yet. We're still on their turf. But at least we're on our way home."

"I'm still waiting for you to tell me where

'home' is and how we're going to get there," she
said.

"You'll know where when we get there. As for
the 'how,' one phone call, and we'll be pulled out
of harm's way."

"Then, let's stop at the first phone booth," she
said.

"No way. We're not stopping for anything
until we're a long way from here."

The hearse bumped along the dirt road, between rock outcroppings on either side. There
was heavy forest right up to the edge of the
road, and no shoulders to pull onto in case of an
emergency.

Finally, they reached an intersection, where
Amundson turned right, onto a paved road.
They passed over a wooden bridge that spanned
a small creek, and they felt the individual
timbers of the bridge vibrating under them.

"This is spooky," she said. "I don't see any
farmhouses or cars or anything."

"I don't much like it either," he said. "Perfect
spot for an ambush, and we don't know if our
pursuers are two miles behind us or around the
next bend. But I sure wouldn't want to be on
foot here. We'd be moving through pretty rough
country. Just look at that underbrush."

"What direction are we going?" she asked,
testing him for her own reassurance.

"Due south. We should be coming to Route 33
pretty soon. We've gone almost a mile."

"There's some buildings on the left," she said
with relief.

Amundson saw farmhouses and outbuildings, then a small road sign that said *Junction 33*. He stopped at the intersection and consulted his map.

"This is Wisconsin 33. Lots of traffic. You'd better get down." She scrunched down onto the floor, her legs drawn up tight to her body and her elbows resting on the seat.

Amundson waited for an opening in traffic and turned left. Once he had the hearse up to sixty, he relaxed a little. "We'll be in Reedsburg in less than ten minutes."

"And then what?"

"We have to find different transportation."

Amundson put his right hand on her shoulder and massaged gently. She placed her hand over his and tilted her head so that his hand was sandwiched between her shoulder and her neck. They drove in silence for a few minutes.

Suddenly, he pulled his hand away. "What's the matter?" she asked, frightened.

"I've got something in my rearview mirror," he said, reaching inside his coat for his pistol. "And it's coming fast."

"What is it?"

"Uh—looks like a van. Wait, there's more than one. I see two or three vans, all coming fast."

He finally counted six of them, traveling in convoy. They bunched up as they were forced to slow down behind the hearse. As soon as they reached an open stretch of highway, the vans all passed, doing about ninety.

When they were out of sight, Amundson relaxed again. There was still no sign of Reedsburg, only the sprawling countryside, dotted with farmhouses. Some were unsuccessful and abandoned, with fallen-down silos and rusting machinery. Others bore obvious signs of success: one or more blue Harvestore silos next to clean, well-kept barns and large herds of dairy cows.

The road curved, and he saw a roadside tavern, then a billboard advertising the Reedsburg Bank. "We must be getting close to town," he said. "The first signs of civilization—taverns and advertising signs."

"Do you see a phone?" she asked.

"Still too early to make our call. I want more distance between us and McKarren."

"I wish we could just stop somewhere and rest," she said longingly.

"I can understand that, honey. We've been on the run since yesterday evening."

"God, it seems a lot longer. I feel like I've known you for ages."

"A lot's happened. But it'll soon be over."

They passed over a bridge, veered right, and suddenly there was a sign welcoming them to Reedsburg. It proclaimed a population of 4,789 persons. Several gas stations and taverns appeared. In front of one of the taverns, Amundson spotted the six vans that had passed them on the road. "There's our new transportation," he said.

"What is it?"

"The vans that passed us before."

He turned onto a side street next to the tavern

and pulled into an alley. "Okay, time to get out," he said, removing the gray coat and hat. He reached his hand down to her and pulled her up onto the seat.

She grimaced in pain when she straightened her legs.

"What's the matter?"

"Leg cramps," she said, rubbing them with her hands.

"Are you okay?"

"Sure. Let's go." They left the hearse and walked leisurely toward the tavern.

The vans were parked where their owners could keep an eye on them from inside the tavern. The backs of the vans faced the alley, making it easy for Amundson and Ellen to approach the vehicles unseen. He selected the largest of the vans, so the two of them could hide comfortably.

He quickly picked the lock on the rear door, and they climbed in. The van interior was completely customized. The back was sectioned off by a partial wall, housing a built-in refrigerator on one side and a closet on the other. In between closet and refrigerator was a narrow passageway connecting the driver's compartment to the rest of the van. A small table faced one of two porthole windows.

The most compelling furnishing was the water bed. It occupied two-thirds of the van's available space and was covered with a red-and-white bedspread that matched the red carpeting on the walls. Above the bed were two music speakers.

"Wow. What a playpen," Ellen whispered.

"I wonder how many young bodies have tossed and turned on this," he said, gently pushing against the water-filled mattress, setting it in motion.

"Quite a few, I would imagine," she said, smiling.

"If we had time, we could give it a try ourselves," he said. "But right now, I'm thinking of something much more basic. Let's see what's in that refrigerator."

They scooted across the water bed to the refrigerator. Ellen opened it, but saw nothing but cans of beer. "Looks like they're ready for a party." She pushed the beer cans aside and peered into the back of the refrigerator. "There has to be something edible in here."

Finally, she found some bread and a package of bologna.

"Smells like it's been here a while," she said suspiciously, her nose turned up slightly.

"Is it spoiled?" he asked.

"Not quite."

"Then slap some between two slices of that bread and let's eat. We'll wash it down with beer before our stomachs know what we're doing to them."

She assembled two sandwiches while he popped open two beers. They wolfed down the sandwiches, taking huge gulps of Stroh's to help cover up the taste.

"Gimme another sandwich," he said.

"Glutton for punishment?"

"Who knows when we'll have another chance to eat?"

"I don't call this eating," she said wryly, making another sandwich for him. She stopped. "Hold it, I hear someone coming," she said.

"Quick, into the closet."

Holding the sandwiches and beer, they squeezed into the small closet, displacing hangers and knocking clothes onto the floor. It was dark and very cramped once Amundson closed the door. The voices came closer; the doors of the van opened and then slammed shut again.

"Jesus," a young male voice said, "this is going to be one hell of a party."

"Yeah," a girl answered. "We've just started and already we've been thrown out of two places."

"This last guy was too much. Didja see me moon him when he told us to be quiet?"

The girl giggled. "I'll never forget the look on his face," she said.

The engine started.

"How old would you say they are?" Ellen whispered.

"Teenagers."

"Where do you suppose they're going?"

"I don't know, but this ride should leave our trail stone cold," Amundson said happily.

The van headed east on Route 33. In the closet, Amundson finished his sandwich and beer. When he was done, he wedged the empty can inside a shoe so it wouldn't roll around. He wrapped his arms around Ellen, squeezing her breasts. He kissed her as best he could in their tight quarters.

"I think that's as far as I can go," he whispered, fondling her. Ellen smiled in the dark and nestled as close as she could.

Twenty minutes later, Amundson and Ellen were still in the tiny closet. The van slowed, then stopped.

"Where do you think we are?" she asked.

"I don't know. But we're certainly far enough away from Odyssey. Time for us to get out of here and make that phone call."

The van moved forward a little, then stopped again. "Feels like we're at a toll booth," Amundson said.

"God, I hope not. If he gets on a tollway, we may be in this closet for hours."

From outside the van they heard a different female voice. "Are you planning to camp?"

"Yep," the driver said.

"That'll be three-fifty."

"We're in a campground," Ellen whispered. "These kids are going camping."

"Perfect. We couldn't ask for a better cover."

The van moved slowly, bouncing suddenly over railroad tracks. Amundson cursed as they dodged swinging hangers and falling clothes.

Finally, the van stopped, and the driver turned off the engine.

By nightfall, the music was playing loudly, a campfire was blazing, and beer cans were lined up like tin soldiers on the park benches. Amundson and Ellen eased out of the closet, grimacing from the pain of cramped muscles and overfull bladders. Quietly, they slipped out of the van.

"Let's find the rest rooms, and quick," she groaned.

"I can't wait," he said, walking off into the darkness and unzipping his fly. Ellen followed him, cursing the thought of all the clothes she would have to take off.

Once they were back on the road, Amundson took her hand. It was getting colder, and he was concerned about finding shelter for the night in a camping facility without provisions for anyone carless.

"Let's please make that phone call," she said.

"Have to find out where the hell we are, first," he said, turning in a slow circle and peering into a blackness around them. Finally, he spotted a lighted building, partially obscured by trees. "I sure hope that's the office," he said, leading her toward the light.

When they neared the building, they saw it was a narrow, trailerlike structure. Light streamed from a row of windows, which were being systematically closed and shuttered from the inside by a uniformed girl.

"Hi," Amundson greeted.

"Hello," she said. Amundson recognized her voice. She was the girl who had taken the entrance fee as they entered the campground.

"Can you tell me where I can make a phone call?" he asked.

"Sure. At the concession building."

"Where's that?"

"Excuse me, sir, but didn't I give you a copy of the campground newspaper when you came in?"

"I'm sure you gave me one, but I'm afraid I lost it."

"Well, here's another one," she said, handing him a four-page tabloid entitled *Devil's Lake State Park Visitor*. She turned to a map of the park on the back page and pointed to a small circle. "Here's the office—where you're at—and the concession stand is over here. If you walk to the other side of this building, you can see the lights."

"Thank you," Amundson said.

The girl nodded, then resumed her task of shuttering the windows. While she finished, Ellen examined the newspaper, which contained background information, the history of the park, descriptions of the various campsites and hiking trails, and, most important, the map of the park. Amundson checked the map carefully, searching for a solution of their shelter problem.

The girl had shuttered every window except the one where Ellen and Amundson were standing facing her, reading the paper. "I'm sorry, but

I have to close for the night," she said, unhooking the shutter and swinging it down.

Amundson stopped her with a final question. "One more thing," he said. The girl stopped, her frown unconcealed.

"Yes, what is it?" she asked, mustering as much official calm as she could.

"There's a building on here marked 'Nature Center.' What time does it open in the morning?"

"Oh, I'm afraid it's closed permanently from the beginning of November through the end of March. But you can still arrange for a tour. Our resident naturalist lives in Baraboo and comes in twice a week during winter. His name is Bannister, and he'll be in on Thursday. Will you still be here? If so, you can leave your name and campsite number, and Mr. Bannister will contact you."

Amundson shook his head. "No—I'm afraid we're leaving tomorrow. Thank you, anyway."

"That's all right. Have a pleasant evening." Without hesitation, she closed the shutter before Amundson could ask another question. Amundson took Ellen's hand, and they walked to the other side of the office building, where a single yard light illuminated a small parking lot. The concession building, with the public phone they needed, was plainly visible.

As they stood looking, a door to the office opened. Startled, they turned toward the sound, Amundson reaching for his pistol. But it was only the girl leaving. She locked the door, acknowledged them with a quick wave, climbed into a powder-blue Camaro, and sped off.

"She must be late for a hot date," Ellen said.

"C'mon, let's go make that call," he said. He led her toward the concession building.

The building had an old sign in front, illuminated by one determined floodlight: Devil's Lake Concession Corporation. Amundson and Kelly walked through the closed swinging doors, ushering in a draft of cold air. Inside, there were no other customers, only a tired old clerk at the cash register behind the check-out counter. He glanced up briefly, then returned to his magazine.

The room was huge and dimly lit. It was a cross between a quick-stop grocery store and a souvenir shop. Ellen grabbed a shopping cart, scarcely able to contain her hunger. "We need lots of things," she said.

"Is the money still in your bra?"

"My cups runneth over," she answered.

Amundson winced. "Just when I was getting to like you ..."

"What do you need?" she asked.

"Razor, aftershave, deodorant ..."

She nodded her head knowingly.

"While you're shopping, I'm going to make our phone call," he said.

She nodded, and turned her cart in the direction of the sausage and cheese, while Amundson walked to the public phone.

Finally, he hung up the phone and rejoined her. "Did you reach him?" she asked.

"Yes."

"Is he coming for us?"

"Of course. But he won't be able to gear up for a field rescue until tomorrow morning. Meanwhile, we'll have to shift for ourselves tonight."

"How's he going to get here?"

"Helicopter."

"Won't that attract a lot of attention?" she said.

"Not really. The park's almost deserted," he said, pulling the newspaper out of his pocket. "And I arranged for him to pick us up from this bluff overlooking the park." He pointed to a spot on the map. "There won't be anybody up there at this time of year. It should be easy to get a chopper in and out before anyone's the wiser."

Ellen pushed the cart slowly, Amundson escorting her down the aisle toward the check-out counter. She continued to pick items off the shelves as he completed his briefing on how they would be rescued. At the last moment, she added a flashlight and batteries to their supplies.

When they reached the check-out counter, the clerk put down his magazine and smiled at them as they unloaded their cart. He rang up their groceries and bagged them. Ellen paid him, and Amundson picked up the bag. As they left, the clerk returned to his magazine.

"Well, we have food, but no shelter. Where do we spend the night?" Ellen asked.

"At the nature center."

"Oh, so that's what you were up to, asking the girl at the office all those questions."

"Yep."

They started toward the nature center, using Ellen's flashlight to show the way.

In Washington, Porter sat in his office, going over the notes he had taken during his phone conversation with Amundson, who had given him a list of what would be needed for the field rescue, along with the names of people who could supply each item.

There was a soft knock at the door. "Come in," Porter said, and Tom Dean, the commander of his Secret Service detail, entered the room.

"What's up?" Dean asked, a little apprehensive.

"Thanks for getting here so quickly."

Dean shrugged. "You said it was important."

"Sit down, Tom," Porter said, motioning toward one of the armchairs in front of his desk.

"Tom, as chief of my Secret Service detail, how much clout do you carry?"

Dean's eyebrows arched slightly. "What do you mean?"

"I mean I need someone who can get an important job done for me."

"What kind of job?"

"I need to bring an agent in from the field tomorrow morning."

Dean cracked a grin, then shook his head. "Tsk, tsk. Pardon me, sir, but you're not supposed to get involved in this stuff until *after* you're inaugurated."

"I know. But I *am* involved. Deeply involved."

"Where are we pulling him in from?"

"A place called Devil's Lake, Wisconsin."

"Sure. I have some friends in Chicago who can help."

"Good. and I'm going along."

"What? No way. With all due respect, sir, I can't possibly allow that."

"Tom, this man is no ordinary agent. He's a close friend of mine. And I sent him in there myself."

"But..."

"This man pulled *me* out of a burning helicopter in Vietnam. I *owe* him."

"I understand your feelings about him, but be reasonable..."

"I'm going along," Porter insisted.

"I won't do it."

Porter paused before speaking again. "How long will it take you to find another job after I kick you out of the Secret Service?"

"What?" Dean was stunned.

"On the other hand, how quickly do you think you can get to the top if I take you under my wing?"

Dean relaxed a little. "The carrot and the stick, eh?"

Porter did not answer, just sat waiting for Dean's decision. "All right," Dean said finally. "But it's gonna cost you some money."

"How much?"

"Well, we'll need a security team, transportation...How we gonna get him out?"

"By helicopter."

"Couple of helicopters, small arms..."

Porter handed him Amundson's list. Dean read it quickly. "This from your man?"

Porter nodded.

"He knows his stuff—and we'll need these contacts."

"How much will it cost?" Porter asked again.

"Five or six thousand."

"Get the ball rolling...and secrecy is essential. No one is to know where we're going, or what the mission is."

"All right. You'd better get ready, yourself, Mr. President." Dean stood up to leave. "If you'll excuse me, sir, I've got a lot of phone calls to make."

Porter watched Dean leave the room, then breathed a long sigh of relief.

The nature center was perched at the base of one of the trails, away from the campgrounds. Dark and deserted, its outline was dimly visible against the evening sky.

"Looks like we'll have the place to ourselves," Amundson said.

"I hope so," Ellen said.

He picked the lock, then cautioned Ellen to wait outside while he checked the building. After a quick search, he led her into the pitch-black room. "Let's make ourselves comfortable if we can. We need something to make the floor a bit softer."

They searched the room, using Ellen's flashlight sparingly so they wouldn't attract any attention. "Not much here, is there?" she said.

"They must empty out the place at the end of the season."

"Yeah, but the girl at the office said there were guided tours twice a week. The naturalist must keep some kind of equipment here," she said.

"Here we go," Amundson whispered.

"What is it?"

"A locked door. Must be something worth protecting in there." He picked the lock again.

"You're really quite good at that, aren't you?"

"Lots of practice."

They entered a windowless room. Amundson snapped on the flashlight. The beam revealed shelves filled with winter clothing and camping gear, including sleeping bags, tents, blankets, lanterns, boots, stoves, and hand axes.

"The jackpot. You were right," Amundson said. "Why don't you make a nest for us in here while I check out the rest of the place."

There was another door at the far end of the room. He opened it and found himself in a small bathroom, complete with shower. "This is going to be all right," he murmured.

He returned to the storeroom. "I like this setup," he said to her. "No one can see us in here, and there's even a shower back there."

Ellen was laying out a double sleeping bag on

top of a row of air mattresses. He helped her smooth it out and make it more comfortable.

"Now for the hard part," he said.

"What's that?"

"Getting undressed and into the sleeping bag before frostbite sets in."

"Ugghhh. Well, let's do it."

"Just concentrate on the warmth and pleasure to come," he said.

"I think I'll do it in stages," she said. She stripped off her ski jacket, then hesitated as the cold hit her. "Br-r-r," she chattered, quickly removing her pants and flipping off her shoes. Before going any further, she slipped into the sleeping bag, where she struggled to remove the rest of her clothes.

She tossed each item at him: her blouse, then her protective armor, her panties, and finally her bra.

"Hey, watch out for the money!" he said, as the bills fluttered in the air around him.

"We'll find it in the morning. Get in here and warm me up."

Amundson smiled and stripped to the buff, then stood teasingly before her in the cold darkness.

"My eyes are getting used to the dark," she said. "In fact, I can make out every detail of your body."

"Every detail?"

"Yes."

"I trust you still like what you see?"

"Yes. What are you waiting for? Get in here!"

"Be patient. I'm setting my watch alarm. You don't want to miss the pickup, do you?"

Finally, Amundson slipped into the sleeping bag, eagerly pressing his body close to her receptive flesh.

"I need you," she said, grasping him.

"I need you, too," he whispered.

Chapter Nine

▌▌▌ ▌▌▌ ▌▌▌ ▌▌▌ ▌▌▌

Amundson was awake long before his watch alarm went off. He hadn't slept much, and he was afraid his insomnia was back. It had first plagued him during his time in Vietnam, then thankfully disappeared shortly after he'd left the Company.

He slid out of the sleeping bag and stood in the cold darkness of the storage room. A thin band of light from under the door provided the only illumination. He walked to the door and opened it halfway, letting in some of the early morning light so that he could see what he was doing.

He glanced down at Ellen. She lay with her head on a folded blanket, her blond hair spread out in a cascade.

Shivering, Amundson carried the bag full of

groceries and toiletries into the bathroom. When he flipped on the light switch, he was happy to see an overhead radiant heater in the ceiling. He turned it on and luxuriated in the warmth that poured down on him.

There was a small washbasin with a counter and a vanity next to the toilet. Amundson placed the bag on the counter and sorted through the things they had bought, setting aside the items he wanted: razor, shaving cream, towels, and soap. Just as he finished lathering his face and was poised for the first stroke of the razor, another naked body joined his in the small room.

"So you're starting without me, eh?" she teased, pinching his cheek.

"Good morning, darling," he said, bending toward her with a kiss.

"Good morning. You can kiss me after you get that stubble off your face," she complained. She gently pushed him aside and leaned toward the mirror.

"Just look at my face, you brute. It's raw from your beard last night."

"You'd better check the rest of your body," he said, crowding her out of his way so he could finish shaving. She smiled and let him shave, turning her attention to the bag of groceries. She searched through everything, removing the sausage, cheese, bread, and milk.

"We might as well eat in here," she said. "At least we'll be warm enough to enjoy the food." Amundson grunted his assent.

Ellen made two small stacks of sandwiches, using all of the sausage and lunchmeat, and then sliced large chunks of cheese onto two plates. She poured two cups of milk, and placed them on the vanity.

She picked up one of the heavily loaded plates and a cup of milk and sat down on the closed toilet seat. She ate while Amundson shaved.

When he was done, he grabbed one of the sandwiches on his plate.

"One of these days," she said, "you're going to take me to an expensive French restaurant. I'm tired of eating sandwiches everywhere we go."

"Wait a minute," he complained, pausing between bites. "What about the pizza at that classy joint in Barrington?"

She moaned and shook her head. They ate in silence for a minute, until she reached out and touched him lightly on the arm. "I have something to tell you," she whispered.

"Hmmm?"

"I meant to talk to you last night after we made love, but I fell asleep."

"I'll say you did. As soon as we were done, you rolled over and conked out."

She smiled. "I've had that happen to me, and I was very annoyed. I hope you understand. I was dead tired."

"So what was on your mind that you were waiting for just the right moment to talk about it?"

"I—wanted to ask you what's going to happen to us once we're rescued," she said, almost in tears. "When we were in the restaurant, and I spoke about getting to know you better, you drew away from me like I was a leper. Now we're almost out of this mess, and I'm worried you won't want me around once we're rescued. You won't just walk away from me, will you?"

"No, I could never do that," he said. "Two days ago, my answer would have been different, but being with you through all of this...No, I couldn't ever walk away from you. Where I go, you go. If you want to, that is."

"Want to? You—I've always laid down the rules with men before. My work would come first. With you—I'm afraid I'm in love with you."

"What's to be afraid of?"

"I don't even know your name."

"Ted Amundson," he said without hesitating.

Her eyes opened wide. "You're telling me your real name?"

"Uh-huh."

"Are you sure you want to do this?"

"I already did it."

"Ted Amundson?"

"Yeah, that's it."

"Ted," she said softly, letting his name roll around inside her for a while. Then she put her face against his chest, her tears streaming down her cheeks onto his flesh.

He sighed deeply, then reached into the shower and turned it on. He led her under the water with him.

* * *

With a knapsack filled with blankets, the left-over food, a Thermos of water, and their extra ammunition, they left the nature center. There was no one in sight nor any sound that Amundson could identify as coming from a human. A thin layer of fresh snow lay undisturbed on the ground and the sky was filled with threatening gray clouds.

"The trail we want starts right over there," he said, pointing to an opening in the woods about half a mile from where they were standing. "Let's get started. We don't want to be late for our ride home."

When they reached the base of the trail, a small orange sign pointed the way. Hand in hand, they started up the path that would take them to the east bluff, overlooking Devil's Lake. At first, the trail sloped gently upward, a wide, clearly marked lane through the forest. "I don't think we'll have much company this morning," he said.

"Who else would be out here on a day like this?" she replied. She clutched his hand more tightly at the sudden thought that the whole nightmarish episode would soon be over.

The trail gradually became steeper. To make it more easily accessible, the park authorities had constructed stepping-stones along the pathway. Each step was about three feet square.

Fronting the trail on both sides were dense stands of trees and almost impenetrable clusters of thick bushes. Amundson was glad it was November and the trees and plants were stripped of their foliage. In full bloom, they would create a dense forest, capable of concealing a small army. Even so, Amundson was wary; the place reminded him too much of the Vietnamese jungle and its constant threat of ambush or booby trap.

As they climbed higher, the trees became sparser, and the path became narrow and steep. Huge snow-capped boulders dotted the hillside next to the trail.

The path leveled off, and the boulders became even more numerous, finally forming a natural wall to the right of the trail. Kelly paused to rest. In front of them, the path was crisscrossed with animal tracks. To their right was a gap in the rugged wall of boulders. She stepped through the opening and saw Devil's Lake far below.

Carefully, she inched forward to the edge of the sheer cliff, which dropped straight down to the frigid water four hundred feet below them.

"They should import some of those divers from Acapulco," she said.

"We can admire the view from the helicopter," he said. He took her hand and pulled her away from the edge, back onto the trail.

The trail meandered onto rocks, where it was so steep and slippery from the snow, they had to drop to all fours to keep from sliding off. Finally, the trail widened a bit, and the footing improved. They paused for a few minutes so Ellen could catch her breath.

"I didn't realize the trail would be so difficult," he said apologetically. "I'm sure we must be getting close to the top. We've been climbing for almost half an hour."

"I'm glad we're close," she said. "I'm running out of steam. I hope our rescuers have some hot coffee with them."

The trail ended abruptly, and they were at the top, facing a wide clearing. "This is a good spot," Amundson said. "He won't have any trouble getting his chopper in here."

Ellen wondered again who their mysterious rescuer was. She helped Amundson unload his backpack, then spread out a blanket so they could sit while they waited. They sat back-to-back, searching the sky for the helicopter.

As his helicopter began its descent toward the state park, Adam Porter peered intently down at the ground below. Off to his right, their escort, a heavily armed gunship, kept pace.

The lake dominated his vista, stretching north and south, with steep bluffs on the east and west flanks. "They're supposed to be waiting on the east bluff," Porter said to the pilot. "Let's go in and take a look. And tell the gunship to cover us."

"Right," the pilot answered, picking up his mike. "Lifeguard, Lifeguard, this is Rescue One. Do you read me? Over."

"Rescue One, this is Lifeguard. We read you loud and clear. Over."

"Lifeguard, we're dropping down to take a look at the east bluff. Keep us covered. Over."

"Roger, Rescue One. We'll be watching."

The chopper dropped down and banked east, flying above the lake. As they neared the east bluff, Porter saw Amundson and Ellen waving at him.

"There they are! Signal the gunship."

The pilot radioed the gunship that they were going in for the pickup. The copter settled into the clearing. As soon as it touched down, the cargo doors opened, and an eight-man squad of heavily armed men, led by Tom Dean, jumped out to secure the clearing.

Porter waited a moment while Dean and his men took their positions, then jumped out of the helicopter.

Amundson and Ellen, smiling broadly, walked up to greet their rescuer. As soon as Ellen recognized the President-elect, she stopped in her tracks. She stood back while Amundson and Porter greeted each other warmly. Finally, Amundson noticed that she was hanging back.

"Don't just stand there, honey. Come over and meet my old friend, Adam Porter."

She approached slowly. Porter smiled and extended his hand to her. "Adam, this is Ellen Kelly, who has shared all of my experiences during the last two days."

"Nice to meet you, Ellen," Porter said. They shook hands warmly.

"Let's get airborne," Amundson said. "We can

all get better acquainted once we're safely out of here."

But just as Amundson finished speaking, a loud explosion shook the clearing. They looked up in time to see the escort gunship erupt into a ball of fire. Simultaneously, automatic-weapons fire from the surrounding woods raked Dean and his men, leaving them all either dead or wounded.

"Goddamn!" Amundson cried. "They've been following us the whole time." He pushed Porter and Ellen toward the second chopper, their only hope of escape.

As the three neared the helicopter door, the President-elect cried out, then stumbled and fell to the ground from the impact of three bullets in his back. He lay face down, his blood staining the snow.

Amundson took one look at Porter and realized his friend was dead. He shoved Ellen into the helicopter and climbed in behind her. With bullets striking all around them, the chopper rose up out of the clearing.

"Don't let them get away," McKarren snarled. His men fired into the chopper as it rose from the bluff and headed out over the lake.

Oily smoke began to trail from the ship, and its ascent slowed. Then it tilted crazily to the left and began to fall.

"That's it!" McKarren yelled. "Pour it on."

The copter fell lazily, the smoke getting heavier, then dropped below the rim of the bluff.

"We got 'em," the commander said.

"Make sure," McKarren said. "And check Porter's troops. If any of them are still alive, kill them."

"Yes, sir."

McKarren stood up and turned to Collins, who was kneeling next to him. "That was like shooting ducks from a blind, Collins. I trust you enjoyed it as much as I did."

Actually, Collins had been screaming inside during the ambush; he didn't like to be directly involved with violence. However, when McKarren had insisted he go along "to get a good dose of hard reality," Collins had been given no choice.

"My compliments, sir," Collins said. "You were right. It was the President-elect. Your strategy was correct, and your execution was perfect."

McKarren smiled at Collins's choice of words. "Indeed. Let it be a lesson for *you* as well— should you ever think about crossing me. Now, let's go see about Mr. Amundson."

McKarren, Collins, and the security commander strode to the cliff edge. Looking down, they saw the helicopter in the water. McKarren's men were firing at the wreckage, and continued shooting until the chopper slid beneath the water. There was no movement on the lake's surface.

"Commander, contact our men down at the base unit and tell them what's happened. And tell them I want to see two more bodies when I get down there. Whether Amundson and the girl are fished out dead or alive, I want to see their bodies when I get there."

"Yes, sir."

"And freeze this whole park. No one gets in or out without a pass signed by you or me. Confiscate all CBs. If the park rangers, or whatever they are, have sidearms, disarm them. If anyone puts up a struggle, cuff 'em and confine them in the office."

"Yes, sir."

"And get the helicopters in here. I want to communicate with Langley, and I want to get to the water's edge down there. Now!"

"Yes, sir, the choppers are already coming in." The helicopters were landing even as the commander spoke. McKarren and Collins climbed aboard.

"Tie up the loose ends here, Commander," McKarren instructed. "And make sure everything is videotaped before you move one item from the scene. Send the tape to me personally via courier."

"Yes, sir."

As soon as they were in the air, McKarren was patched through to the communications rooms at Odyssey and from there to the DCI at Langley. "Stanton, the President-elect has been assassinated by foreign agents. The assassins have apparently been killed by Porter's bodyguards. Contact the other intelligence services. I'll call the President myself."

"I understand," the director said simply.

"Good. I'll see you later. Out."

McKarren clicked the mike switch until he got the com officer at Odyssey. "Put me through to the President on his scrambled line."

"Yes, sir."

McKarren envisioned the Oval Office. The President would be sitting behind his desk, biting down on that ridiculous pipe, as the red phone rang.

"Yes."

"Mr. President, this is John McKarren."

"Yes?"

"I'm at Devil's Lake in Wisconsin. We've just responded to an emergency security call, and I'm afraid we have some bad news."

"What is it?"

"The President-elect has been assassinated, apparently by agents of a foreign government." McKarren smiled at his lie. He heard the President's breathing, but nothing more. *If you had any part in this, I'll have your ass, too,* McKarren thought.

"Are you sure?" the President asked finally.

"Yes, Mr. President. I have seen the body myself."

"I see. Which foreign government?"

"I'd rather not say until I can present the evidence to you myself."

"I hope your evidence is substantial."

"It is, Mr. President. Everything is being videotaped. It'll be flown out to us later today."

"What about the assassins?"

"Apparently killed by the President-elect's Secret Service people. Their helicopter crashed in the lake, so we haven't yet recovered their bodies. When we do, we'll check them out very carefully."

"Very well."

"Meanwhile, I suggest you contact the National Security Council and the Joint Chiefs and place the nation's military on alert."

"Yes, I'll do that."

"I further suggest you conduct a brief press conference after I arrive back in Washington. We've frozen the area to prevent news from getting out until we've had a chance to sanitize it. Mr. President, I believe it will be in the national interest to conceal this conspiracy."

"Why?"

"If we reveal he was assassinated by a foreign power, the nation will demand war."

"What do you suggest?"

"A single assassin, acting alone, Mr. President. We must assure the stability of the country, so that Vice-President-elect Melville can assume power smoothly and without a national crisis."

"I will accept that logic upon your presentation to me of hard evidence about the identity and motivation of the assassins."

"Very good, Mr. President."

As McKarren finished his conversation with the President, the helicopter settled into a clear spot near the edge of the lake, close to the park office. A small group of campers had gathered at the office after McKarren's men had set up roadblocks at the park's exits. They stood milling around like nervous cattle, most of them with their arms folded, speaking in muted tones.

A captain waited for McKarren and Collins to step out of the helicopter. As soon as they stepped down, McKarren spoke sharply to the captain. "Have you found them?"

"No, sir," the captain replied. "But I've got equipment on the way to drag the lake, and men stationed all along the shoreline in case they're still alive and try to make it ashore."

"Good. I like men who anticipate my needs, Captain...uh, Edwards," McKarren said, reading the man's name tag.

"Thank you, sir."

"And you have your orders if you find them alive?"

"Yes, sir. We're to waste them immediately."

"Quite right. And if they swam ashore right here, you'd have this crowd of witnesses to the deed."

"Uh...sorry."

"Don't be sorry. Just never stop thinking. Round up all of the campers in the park and stick them in one building. Make sure none of them are armed."

"Yes, sir."

"Where are the park rangers?"

"Rounded up, disarmed, and interned at the office."

"Good. Keep the rangers separated from each other. I don't want them hatching any two-bit escape plans."

"Yes, sir."

"And if you need any additional manpower, let the commander know."

"I will, sir."

"Collins, let's get back to Odyssey. I've got a few more things to go over with you before I head back to Washington," McKarren said. Then he smiled suddenly as they were getting back into the helicopter. "You know, Collins, not only has our friend Amundson provided a fascinating diversion, you've proven to be a real trooper these past two days. You've really surprised me."

"It hasn't been easy, sir. I'm not used to being in the field."

"Of course it wasn't easy. Surveillance never is. But it's paid off. Amundson led us to Porter. Now Amundson, Porter, and Kelly have been eliminated, and Operation Odyssey is secure."

Amundson fought the controls of the chopper as it fell toward the surface of the lake. The body armor had saved his and Ellen's lives, but the pilot had not been as fortunate. He was dead, slumped over in his seat.

The cockpit was chewed up from scores of bullets passing through, and the chopper itself was on fire. He barely managed to keep the ship level as they neared the water.

"Take off everything but your body armor," he said. As soon as they hit the water, more bullets started to tear through the helicopter. Slugs hit both of them, knocking them over.

"C'mon, we can't wait. Let's get into the water. Can you swim?"

"Yes."

"Fill your lungs with air. We're going to stay under as long as possible."

"Which bank should we swim toward?"

"Over there," he pointed. "I see some debris along the shore. That'll give us some cover."

They reached the shore before Captain Edwards's troops were in position. Shivering, they climbed out of the water.

"We need warm c-c-clothes, qu-qu-quickly," she chattered.

"The nature center," he said.

They made their way back to the nature center and were quickly in dry clothing. Eluding the search parties, the two fugitives slipped out of the park and flagged a semi for a ride to Madison.

Chapter Ten

▌▌▌▌ ▌▌▌▌ ▌▌▌▌ ▌▌▌▌ ▌▌▌▌

Six months later, Amundson and Ellen walked into the Last Chance Saloon in Grayslake, Illinois, north of Chicago. They were there to meet Jerry Torrence, who had read Amundson's contact ad in the *Sun-Times* personals earlier that day.

The first thing that struck them about their meeting place was that the Last Chance wasn't very well lit, and that suited them fine. The shadowy interior was accentuated by black acoustical ceiling tile, black hurricane lamps at the bar and tables, and dim yellow bulbs in the Tiffany-style lamps hanging from the ceiling. The decor was Old West, which suited the frontier atmosphere that had swept through even the urban areas.

They weren't five steps inside the door when the bouncer stopped them. "Check your hardware, friends," he said, placing one hand on Amundson's chest and pointing with the other to the crude gun rack next to the door.

"Rules of the house," he explained. "No gunfights in here."

Amundson surrendered the .38 he kept holstered on his hip, but did not give up the Beretta in his sleeve rig. Satisfied, the bouncer let them pass, and they made their way to an empty booth. They stashed their backpacks under the table, then sat down next to each other, with their backs to the wall.

"This is quite a place your friend has chosen," Ellen said, gazing around the room. Ceiling fans were spaced ten feet apart across the huge room. The walls were hung with crossed sabers, six-shooters, tomahawks, rifles, and bows and arrows. Over the bar were portraits of Indian chiefs, Indian fighters, and famous madames of the frontier.

As they were admiring the furnishings, a waitress appeared to take their order. "Give us two steins of draft," Amundson said.

Their booth faced a TV, where the five-thirty evening news was just coming on. The newscaster's familiar face appeared on the screen. "Good evening, ladies and gentlemen. As has been the case for the last four months, it is the weather that's making news again tonight.

"Prolonged winter weather continues to grip the nation. The contiguous forty-eight states all report temperatures below freezing, a phenomenon without precedent in May. Let's begin our report tonight with Martin Delano in Florida. Martin."

"Good evening from Florida," Delano began. He was standing on a beach, wearing heavy winter clothing. "Florida's tourist trade has suffered a devastating blow. All along the Florida coast, we are witnessing a scene no one could *ever* have imagined: lifeguards wearing parkas.

"The economic damage to Florida's tourist trade is not confined to the coastline. Walt Disney World, Epcot Center, and all the other vacation attractions in the state are closed."

Amundson noted the total silence in the room as the report continued. Even though the evening news had been showing the same story for months, everyone was still intrigued with it, to the point of morbid fascination.

"Also hard hit is Florida's citrus crop," Delano

continued. The camera cut to an orange grove, showing rows of trees laden only with snow. "There will be no citrus crop here this year," Delano continued. "Oranges will be impossible to find in the stores up north."

The anchorman reappeared. "Speaking of cities up north, another blizzard is sweeping across the plains toward the Great Lakes states. Nebraska and Iowa have already felt the fury of this latest storm. Up to twenty-four inches of new snow has fallen there, isolating most rural communities and bringing commerce in urban areas to a standstill. Here is our Chicago correspondent, Aileen Riggins." A woman's face filled the screen.

"Chicago is bracing for this latest blow. There are already forty-two inches of snow on the ground." The screen showed Michigan Avenue, deserted, filled with billowing and drifting snow. "With roads impassable, food is becoming increasingly scarce..."

A bar patron suddenly stood up, holding his stein high. "But we still got plenty of beer!" he shouted, breaking the silence and getting a good laugh from everyone in the bar.

"...and heating oil delivery is spotty and not very dependable," the reporter said, her voice audible again once the laughter in the bar subsided. "O'Hare Field is barely operational, but it's predicted this latest storm will close down the airport once again. We have an emergency situation which appears will get worse very soon."

The anchorman's face reappeared. "The Great Lakes themselves have become completely frozen, and ice is reported in the Mississippi as far south as Arkansas. Snow has penetrated the deep south and southern California, two traditional winter refuges.

"In the nation's capital, snowdrifts are up to the second story of the White House, where President Melville must be wrestling with the problems created by this incredible cold wave, from what seems to be a visitation from our geological past. The White House press secretary has announced that the President will address the nation following this newscast.

"Meanwhile, the prolonged winter weather has had another startling impact. Across the nation, Americans are abandoning their longtime love affair with the automobile. Certainly, the relationship was already strained, first with the oil embargo of 1974 and the long lines it created at the gas pump, then with the meteoric rise in gasoline prices, and finally with the high cost of owning a car—any car.

"The dying love affair, it seems, has been replaced by a budding new romance—with the snowmobile. Once limited to sportsmen, the snowmobile is fast becoming the *only* way to travel. Dealerships have been sold out for months..."

Amundson and Ellen tuned out the rest of the news. Ellen glanced nervously at the clock. Torrence was late for their meeting.

"You don't suppose he's forgotten the time, do you?" she asked nervously.

"Jerry? Not a chance."

"Do you think he sold us out?"

"Not Jerry," Amundson said simply. He took out a copy of the day's *Sun-Times* from his coat pocket and unfolded it on the table. His ad was circled in red:

> Jerry, our need for you increases
> every day. Call home tonight. Harmon.

The first letter of each word in the first sentence was the first digit for the phone number of a public phone booth. Amundson had scrawled the number next to the ad: 663–9433. The second sentence was a code for the time of the phone call: 2:48.

Amundson and Ellen had waited anxiously in the phone booth for Torrence's call. The phone hadn't finished ringing one time before Amundson had the receiver off the hook. During their terse conversation, Torrence had arranged to meet them at five-thirty at the Last Chance.

"He might have gotten caught," she said softly.

"That's the most likely possibility if he doesn't show. If it's true, they'll make him talk. About everything. Including where we are right now."

Meanwhile, the TV anchorman had begun to present the non–weather related news. "There is a confused report tonight from Panama City of an anti-American riot. A battalion of U.S.

troops has been sent in to protect American nationals."

The story of the Panamanian incident triggered Amundson's memory and took him back to the first day he'd heard about the ice age and Operation Migrant, listening to Adam Porter talk about his meeting in the Oval Office.

"That story on Panama!" Amundson blurted, startling Ellen.

"What about it?"

"The riots. That's the cover for sending in troops. They're part of the invasion force. It means Operation Migrant has started, and the whole mess will soon be out in the open. We're running out of time. We've got to find Odyssey again and quick."

As Amundson finished speaking, a bearded Jerry Torrence appeared at the entrance, hesitated a minute to survey the room, then smiled through the beard when he saw Amundson and Ellen sitting at the booth. Amundson acknowledged his friend's arrival by lifting his beer mug in salute. Torrence waved back, then checked his pistol at the gun rack. He walked to their booth and stretched out his hand.

"Hi, Jer," Amundson greeted warmly, taking the offered hand.

"Hi, yourself, old friend," Torrence returned. "You look almost as bad with a beard as I do!"

"Yeah, but it sure makes a different man out of both of us."

"Sure does. It's helped me stay a couple of

steps ahead of the opposition these past six months," Torrence said.

"Ellen and I have had a helluva time," Amundson said.

"I can imagine. For the first two months after Porter was killed, I saw you two on the tube every time I looked at a TV screen. On the evening news, the late news, the newsbrief... of course, you were a blonde back then," he said to Ellen.

"A lot has happened since we were last together at the safe house six months ago," Amundson said.

The waitress arrived to take Torrence's order. "Just bring another mug and a pitcher," he told her.

When she was gone, they resumed their conversation. "How was it for you, Jer?" Amundson asked.

"Well, the moment I left that apartment in Barrington, I went to ground. I contacted some Company men I could trust. I told them to move their families to safety because the plug was about to be pulled. We had prepared for it, but I guess I never thought it would come.

"Since then, we've all been hunted men and women. Fortunately for us, the opposition has been spending most of its time looking for you two. Anyway, we have a place to stay up north from here."

"Why'd you bring them all the way out here from Washington?"

"When Porter was wasted at Devil's Lake, I

figured your objective was close-by. So I set up our base close enough to be within striking distance, but far enough away from Devil's Lake so we wouldn't get caught up in the dragnet McKarren had out for you."

"Hmmm," Amundson murmured, nodding his head. The waitress brought the pitcher and extra mug. Amundson filled Torrence's stein, then lifted his own in a toast. "Here's to us," he said simply, and the three of them clinked their mugs together and drank deeply. Ellen grabbed Amundson's free hand and held it tightly.

"Our base is a dairy farm," Torrence continued. "We've got hay and straw in the barn, oats in the granary, and corn in the silos. We milk twice a day, and the route man picks up the milk three times a week. It's a perfect cover, plus it pays off in cash to finance our operation. We've used the income to buy supplies, weapons, and vehicles."

"Sounds great. How many people are there?" Ellen asked.

"Seven adults, five kids, three dogs, and I lost track of the cats a long time ago."

"Only one farmhouse for twelve people?" Ellen asked.

"There are two separate buildings. The main house was the family homestead—goes back to the 1850s. It has eleven bedrooms. The other building is brand new. The guy we bought the place from had it built two years ago for his older son and his wife as an inducement to stay on the farm. Didn't work.

"And we've just finished a new building of our own—a combination motor pool and hangar."

"Hangar? For what?" Amundson asked.

"We bought a small plane, a Piper. Lands and takes off on the field in back of the house. Another guy is getting ready to join us, and he's going to bring a chopper with him."

"Sounds like you've been busy," Amundson said.

"Yeah, we have, Ted. But what we've done means nothing without you. We've been marking time, hoping you'd stay alive and eventually get back to me.

"You hold the key," Torrence continued, suddenly leaning closer to Amundson. "What did you find on the other end of Strike Force Alpha?"

"We got the answers, all right. Hearing them will make your blood run cold."

"Well, let me get some more antifreeze into my body before you start," he said. He downed what was left in his stein, refilled it, and emptied it halfway. "I'm ready. Shoot."

"I'm sure you've figured it out already, but it was Porter who hired me."

Torrence nodded. "You two knew each other?"

"Yeah. Met him in 'Nam before your time. He was a tenderfoot congressman on one of those damned fact-finding tours, and I was the intelligence officer assigned to give him the fifty-cent tour.

"Only Charlie didn't cooperate. Some Cong penetrated our 'secure' area and knocked down our chopper. I pulled Porter out of the wreck, and we spent the next two weeks making our way back to our base camp. I got to know the guy pretty good. Level-headed. He could think on his feet in any situation. And he had guts and a good instinct for survival. All in all, he was a helluva man.

"When McKarren forced me out of the Company, Porter gave me a job—got me started in investigation and gave good references to other congressmen.

"Anyway, he called me on the Monday after the election and asked for a meeting. He told me about a briefing he was given that morning in the Oval Office by the President, Stanton, and McKarren."

Amundson related the details of the meeting with Porter, including the story of the ice age and Operation Migrant.

"My job was to verify the ice age and to find out what McKarren was up to."

"And Strike Force Alpha was part of it," Torrence said.

"A big part. Those people you kidnapped are to be the first ones resettled in the Green Belt."

"So where did you wind up after you left the safe house?"

"At a government installation in Wisconsin called 'Odyssey.' Funded through NASA. They were researching suspended animation, supposedly for deep-space travel."

"Suspended animation?"

"Yeah, but it's not for space anymore, it's for

Earth. Operation Migrant won't work. The ice age won't make just the northern latitudes un-inhabitable, as Porter was led to believe. It'll make the entire world uninhabitable. End of civilization, end of man. Finis."

"And the only one who knew this was McKarren?"

"And his people. So he plans to deep-freeze himself and his cronies until the ice age is over, when he can start the world over the way he wants it.

"Anyway, Ellen and I were ready to toss the whole story into Porter's lap, but somehow the opposition was with us the whole time—just played us out like bait on a line until Porter showed up—then 'bang,' they closed the trap on us..."

"How'd you two escape?"

"We were wearing bulletproof body armor."

"And you were framed as the assassins."

"Exactly. We've been on the run ever since. It was hard as hell right after Porter was killed. We never stayed in the same place two nights in a row. But as the weather got worse, the police became preoccupied with civil unrest and the big jump in crime. It helped when they stopped broadcasting our pictures on the news every night and substituted reports on which schools were closed and which stores still had food for sale.

"But McKarren is still after us. Of that I'm certain. Ellen and I—and now you—are the only ones who know the truth about Odyssey, and he has the full resources of the Company to find us and eliminate us."

The three of them drank in silence, lost in thought. The rest of the bar patrons had stopped talking and were watching the TV news anchorman.

"The President will address the nation shortly. TV cameras are being set up at the White House, and we'll be going there live momentarily. Our White House correspondent, Paul Jarrard, is standing by."

At the White House, McKarren was giving President Melville last-minute instructions before the telecast. Melville stood before the podium bearing the Presidential seal, while a makeup specialist did a quick once-over on the President's forehead, and a media specialist checked the camera angle against the backdrop Melville would use.

All three slipped off to the side when the program director gave the ten-second signal. Then Melville's image filled every monitor in the room.

"My fellow Americans," he began. "As you know, our nation—along with the other nations of the world—is in the grip of the most bitter, most prolonged winter on record. Our schools, our factories, and our businesses have suffered a terrible blow. Airports, bus terminals, and train stations have been closed more often than they've been open. Citizens in our urban areas are experiencing food and fuel shortages.

"In some northern cities, vital services have broken down because fire trucks, police cars, and garbage trucks can't get through the snow. This has resulted in food riots and outbreaks of lawlessness.

"The stock and commodities markets have been closed and trading halted, while runs on the banks have forced some to close their doors and resulted in the collapse of others. The price of gold and silver has soared.

"In some areas, food and gasoline, along with other basic necessities, are available only on the black market or on a barter basis.

"In some states, governors have responded to these crises by mobilizing the National Guard to keep the peace and provide vital services. These efforts have not been uniformly successful. Only the strength and power of the federal government can restore order to the country."

Melville paused and took a sip of water from a glass at his podium.

"Consequently, I am issuing an executive order, as provided for in our Constitution, taking the following actions:

"One. The call-up of all army, navy, air force, and marine reserve units, including the inactive reserves.

"Two. I am declaring martial law over the entire country. This means the ultimate authority for assuring law and order will rest with the military.

"Three. Stores of food and gasoline, maintained by the federal government for a national emergency, will be distributed through your local National Guard and civil defense authorities.

"These steps are effective immediately. If the national crisis deepens, additional measures may be necessary. I know you share my deep sense of concern over this emergency. But we as a nation have faced perils equal to, and even more threatening than this one. We have always persevered—we have always prevailed. And we will do so again.

"Above all, we must not yield to panic or to the temptation to participate in the lawlessness that has broken out. Under martial law, lawbreakers will face military discipline, which will be sure and swift. These measures may seem harsh to some, but we are determined to hold the nation together.

"I leave you now, but rest assured that I will repeat these conversations with you on a regular basis. For now, good evening."

The President waited for the red light on the camera to go off before he relaxed his smile. He sighed deeply and mopped his forehead with a handkerchief. "How'd I do?" he asked.

"Great!" McKarren said, shaking the President's hand. "Smooth delivery. Very nice."

"Thanks."

The press secretary also congratulated the President. As the technicians began to turn off their lights and disassemble their equipment, the President and McKarren left the Oval Office.

"Is there anyone who can't make our meeting tonight?" McKarren asked.

"No, they'll all be here. After watching my speech, I'm sure they all understand the urgency of tonight's meeting. They should all be leaving their homes right about now."

"Good. I'm going to the Cabinet Room to get set up. Stanton should be here soon. He said he was going to watch your presentation in his limo so he could get here before the others."

"Fine. I'm going to spend some time with my family before the meeting starts. Do you need someone to help you set up?"

"No. I have an officer with me."

"Excellent. I'll see you shortly before seven."

"Yes, Mr. President. Again, congratulations on a fine job."

"Thank you." Melville turned and strode toward the Family Quarters.

McKarren's pleasant smile turned into a tight-lipped grimace of contempt as he watched the President leave the room. Finally, he turned and walked toward the Cabinet Room to prepare for his meeting.

At the Last Chance, all eyes were still on the TV set. The network anchorman had just finished refereeing a spirited instant analysis of the President's speech by three of his fellow network newsmen. He was just bidding his audience good-night.

When the screen cut to a commercial, a dozen

conversations started up throughout the tavern —all of them about the speech.

"The tip of the iceberg is beginning to show," Amundson said.

Ellen winced at Amundson's choice of words.

"So Operation Migrant is unfolding, but it's an elaborate diversion," Torrence said. "We're interested in Odyssey. Where is it?"

"In Sauk County," Amundson replied. "We don't know what it looks like aboveground, because we never saw it. All we know is that it was once a tracking station. However, we do know where the emergency tunnel came out."

Amundson reached inside his shirt, pulled out a much-handled map, and unfolded it on the table. "The escape tunnel comes out in the Hillside Cemetery, at a mausoleum marked 'Kaltmann.' It's a mile and a half northwest of the junction of Route 33 and County V. Here," he said, pointing to a spot on the map he had circled. "The cemetery wasn't on this map originally, so I marked it myself.

"We can find the location of the mausoleum easily enough, but I wouldn't bother. By now, they've probably removed all traces of it and constructed a new escape tunnel. But we can still use its location as the center of our search pattern. They sure as hell can't move Odyssey."

"Shouldn't be hard to find," Torrence said.

"How far is the farm from there?" Ellen asked.

"The farm's in western Dodge County, just southwest of Beaver Dam," Torrence said, pointing to the map. "It looks to be about sixty or seventy miles from Odyssey.

"If you two want to join us, we could be up there in about three hours."

Amundson didn't hesitate. He put out his hand, and they shook on the deal.

"Good. Now, with that out of the way, I want you to meet the rest of the crew." Torrence waved, and one of the men sitting at the bar got up from his stool and joined them.

"Ellen and Ted, I'd like you to meet Joe Corrigan."

Amundson smiled as he shook hands with Corrigan. *Same old Jerry. He had himself covered the whole time,* he thought.

"Joe is our weapons man. He was also one of the best demolition men in the Company.

"Bob Johnson is waiting for us outside, guarding the snowmobiles," Torrence continued. "He's our mechanic and a specialist in electronic warfare systems. You'll see some of his handiwork when we get back to the farm.

"The third man, Roy Romano, and the women are up there holding down the fort until we get back. We'd better get started pretty quick if we want to beat the storm that's heading our way." Torrence laid some money on the table and stood up.

The four of them picked up their gear, collected their sidearms, and headed out the back door to the parking lot. Every parking spot was taken by a snowmobile. As they approached the back of the lot, a lone figure stepped out, weapon at the ready. "It's us, Bob," Torrence said, and the man lowered his pistol.

"Bob Johnson, meet Ellen Kelly and Ted Amundson. They've agreed to join us."

"Great!" was Johnson's enthusiastic reply. He shook Ellen's hand first, then Amundson's.

Johnson produced two snowmobile suits and two pairs of boots.

"These are more than just snowmobile suits," Corrigan said. "I put them together myself. They'll protect you from the cold, all right, but there's also bulletproof material woven into the fabric."

"They're perfect for conditions these days," Torrence said. "The road is full of thieves, murderers, and road agents. Every day, the papers are full of reports of holdups and ambushes. Once we're on the road, we'll be fair game for all of them."

"The suits also give us an edge in case the opposition shows up," Corrigan added.

Amundson and Ellen removed their coats and shoes and donned the snowmobile suits and boots. Amundson carefully wrapped his Beretta and sleeve rig in his coat and stashed them on the snowmobile. The snowmobiles themselves were customized, with storage areas and rifle holsters.

Amundson mounted behind Torrence and Ellen boarded Johnson's vehicle. They headed south to Route 120, where they turned west on the first leg of their long trip into Wisconsin.

Chapter Eleven

President Melville surveyed the eleven people sitting around the ornate table in the Cabinet Room. He had invited every official of importance in the Washington intelligence community, including some from the old National Security Council, which he had disbanded at McKarren's suggestion.

Seated to Melville's left were the Vice-President, whose appointment had finally been confirmed by the Senate; the national security adviser; the secretary of defense; the secretary of state; and the chairman of the Joint Chiefs of Staff.

On Melville's right was McKarren—seated close-by so that those at the meeting would immediately understand just how important the senior analyst was to the President.

Seated to McKarren's right was Henry Turcott, Melville's chief of staff, who handled congressional liaison for intelligence matters; Al Howard, who was at the meeting at McKarren's invitation; and two members of the intelligence liaison group: the deputy secretary of defense; and the undersecretary of state for political affairs.

The deputy secretary of defense was attending on behalf of the Pentagon's intelligence agencies, including the National Security Agency, the Defense Intelligence Agency, and the intelligence agencies of the army, navy, and air force.

The undersecretary of state for political affairs represented the four intelligence agencies of the State Department, including the FBI, the National Regulatory Commission, the Bureau of Intelligence and Research, and the Treasury Department.

At the opposite end of the table was Dr. Stanton, whom Melville had carried over as director of the Central Intelligence Agency on McKarren's advice. On the table in front of Stanton was a slide projector.

Melville rose to his feet. "Gentlemen, I have called you here tonight to outline the steps we will take to deal with a crisis unparalleled in our nation's history." As he spoke, he turned left and right, meeting the poker-faced gazes of those around him.

"First, I know you're all happy about my decision to reconstitute the National Security Council. When we discontinued the regular meetings of the council upon my taking office, many of you expressed extreme dissatisfaction, both privately to me and publicly to the media.

"However, it's obvious to me that my decision did not restrict your intelligence-gathering activities. Over the last four months, each of you has come to me with bits and pieces of data related to the crisis. No one, however, has been able to give me the complete picture.

"As usual, there was an incredible amount of overlapping among your various agencies. A lot of wasted effort. In fact, the events of these past four months have convinced me that the intelligence services must be reorganized."

At the mention of the word "reorganized," there was an immediate outbreak of excited conversation. Melville raised his hands; immediately, the room was quiet again.

"Yes, I have made that decision. Under martial law, I can do anything I deem necessary to preserve the Union—including the reorganization of government agencies."

Melville let his words sink in, then resumed. "The decision's been made, and the subject is not open to debate. I have some slides here that will show the new organization I have in mind."

Melville pulled down a built-in projection screen on the wall behind him. "Dr. Stanton, the lights, please."

As Stanton turned off the lights, Melville picked up the remote control and flipped on the projector. The first slide showed an organization chart, with the President at the top and a row of cabinet positions below. There was a new, unidentified rectangle.

"Gentlemen, previous attempts to reorganize the intelligence community all failed miserably. Why? Because the man put in charge did not have access to the President. I have remedied that. From now on, the man in charge of overall intelligence will be a cabinet officer."

He pushed the projector advance button, and a second slide came into view on the screen. It showed the previously empty rectangle filled in with a title:

SECRETARY OF NATIONAL SECURITY

Again, there was noise in the room. "Gentlemen, I will field all of your questions after my presentation is complete. I will probably answer most of them before I'm through, so if you will just be patient..." The room became quiet again.

"Thank you."

He advanced the next slide, which showed the new secretary at the top of a second organization chart. Directly below the secretary was a box entitled "Deputy Secretary of National Security."

Reporting to the deputy secretary of national security were two additional new titles: director of domestic security and director of international intelligence.

"As you can see," President Melville continued, "I have broken down intelligence into its two natural components: domestic intelligence and foreign intelligence."

He advanced a fourth and final slide. "Reporting to the director of domestic security will be all of the agencies that previously were under the State Department.

"Reporting to the director of international intelligence will be the CIA, and all of the agencies that previously reported to the secretary of defense.

"Please turn the lights back on," Melville said. Stanton complied.

"You are no doubt wondering who will fill these new positions. First, let me introduce you to the man who will be secretary of national security," the President said. He motioned toward the man on his right. "I'd like to introduce John McKarren, senior analyst with the CIA, and the man who has helped me more than any other to hold this government together these past four months. John, the meeting is all yours."

Melville sat down, and McKarren stood up to take his place. He looked around the table, enjoying his ascension to an official, visible seat of power and enjoying even more the frowns of the other intelligence officials seated there.

"Good evening, gentlemen. The question is: Who will fill the new positions within the Department of National Security?

"As deputy secretary, I'd like to have Al Howard. Al, would you stand up?"

Howard stood, his broad smile an obvious betrayal of his delight at being named to the new position.

"Dr. Stanton, I'd like you to be my new director of international intelligence." Stanton accepted with an appreciative nod of his head.

McKarren motioned toward Bill Underwood, the national security adviser. "Bill, would you be our new director of domestic security?" Underwood also nodded his acceptance.

"Good. Naturally, there will not be any physical moving of people to new offices; that would be an awesome task. However, the agencies involved will receive funding through the new channels, and the reporting of intelligence information will follow the new lines of command. Are there any questions?" he asked, looking directly at the secretaries of defense and state, from whom a total of nine agencies had been stripped. They hesitated, then shook their heads.

McKarren looked at the undersecretary of state and the deputy secretary of defense. "With the approval of your superiors, I invite you gentlemen to remain as liaison for State and Defense."

The two deputies glanced at their respective bosses then nodded their acceptance.

"Excellent. At last, we will all be working together, instead of pulling in opposite directions as we did in the past. And believe me, we *must* work together during the coming months. Before we leave this room tonight, we will set in motion the most ambitious plan ever conceived to preserve a nation and its people.

"Exactly what is it we must face?" McKarren asked rhetorically. "The President has already touched briefly on the subject. Let me expand upon what he said."

McKarren paused, and took a sip of water from a glass on the table before him.

"The cold weather we've been experiencing is actually a symptom of a far greater problem. Dr. Stanton, would you get the lights again."

McKarren produced films and slides illustrating the discoveries of the *Norsel* expedition and the events leading up to the slippage of the West Antarctic ice sheet.

"Gentlemen, the facts are now clear, and the conclusions incontrovertible. A new ice age is headed our way.

"What we've seen thus far will seem mild compared to what we'll get next year—and the year after that. Eventually, we'll lose our ability to feed ourselves. And so will the Russians. They'll probably lose the Ukraine and Kazakhstan this year; and there will be no grain-exporting countries to make up their shortages —or those in China, India, or Europe. The political implications are enormous. Such is the magnitude of the problem.

"Is there a solution? Yes!" McKarren paused while Stanton placed a new carousel of slides into the projector. McKarren advanced the first one.

"This slide shows the areas of the Western Hemisphere that will be inhabitable throughout the ice age. Our estimate is based on three-dimensional computer projections from data on previous ice ages, and from the data we have on the cooling that has occurred already."

"Those will be the only inhabitable lands?" a stunned voice asked from the semidarkness. McKarren thought it was the secretary of state.

"Yes. Only these lands will be left. We call it 'The Green Belt.' It's not a very big percentage of the landmasses, but we think we can live with it."

"But none of those areas fall within our own country," the same voice said.

"Only the Canal Zone, Hawaii, some Pacific possessions, and the Caribbean territories—Puerto Rico and the Virgin Islands," McKarren corrected. "Not enough to support the population of the contiguous United States, that's for sure. We'll have to move our people into the countries in the green areas."

"But you're talking about war!" the secretary of state said.

"We're talking about survival," McKarren snapped. "Either we move south, or we cease to exist as a nation."

"Do we have a plan for such an incursion?" the new Vice-President asked.

"We've had a plan for the annexation of Mexico since the Mexican war in 1846. Annexing the other countries involved is a more recent scenario. Overall, the plan is called 'Operation Migrant.' Since it involves the use of our armed forces, General Snowden, our new chairman of the Joint Chiefs, will present the military phase of the operation."

The general stood up and thanked McKarren. He advanced the next slide. "This shows the movement of our troops into Mexico. As you can see, our Northern Attack Force consists of three columns, moving from bases in the U.S. Each front will be two to five miles wide and will consist of armor and mechanized infantry in armored personnel carriers.

"The first column will be composed of marines, who will strike south from Camp Pendleton and seize Guadalajara, before moving on Mexico City. They will be supported by U.S.-based aircraft and by elements of the Pacific fleet at San Diego.

"A second attack group, composed of army troops, is staging now at Fort Bliss. It will cross the border at El Paso, supported by aircraft from Briggs Air Force Base. Special-op troops and rangers will seize the bridge and suppress any resistance to the crossing."

The general was using a pointer to show the flow of troops. "A third attack group, also army, is staging at Fort Sam Houston in San Antonio. They will strike across from Laredo with air cover from Lackland Air Force Base. They'll be spearheaded by the 24th Mechanized Infantry Division and will move south along the first-class highway between Laredo and Mexico City."

General Snowden advanced the next slide. "A second invasion army is standing by aboard ship in the Caribbean, off Veracruz. That army will seize Veracruz, just as Winfield Scott did in 1847, and move inland to take Mexico City. This force is the Marine Amphibious Brigade, supported by a naval squadron from Norfolk. They will also get air support from long-range fighters based in the U.S.

"Once these four armies have consolidated at Mexico City, they will move south to envelop the rest of Mexico and then continue into Central America."

He advanced another slide, showing Central America in greater detail. "We already have fourteen army divisions in bases in the Canal Zone. Four divisions will move north out of Panama and crush Central America in a pincer with the armies of the Northern Attack Force. Our friends in Central America will be invited to help us, our enemies will be punished."

"This is incredible!" the secretary of state interrupted. "Where are all these troops coming from? And why wasn't the State Department told about this long ago?"

"I can answer part of your question," the secretary of defense said. "Preparations have been going on for months for a large-scale military operation in the south. There are at least ten combat-ready divisions in the area."

"Quite right, sir," Snowden said.

"As for why you haven't been told before now," President Melville interjected. "You didn't have a need to know. Until this week, only Mr. McKarren, myself, and Dr. Stanton knew about this operation. General Snowden was filled in after his appointment as chairman of the Joint Chiefs. Sorry we had to keep it from you, Tom," the president said to the secretary of defense.

The secretary of defense shrugged.

"Please continue, General," Melville said.

The general advanced the next slide, which showed the northern end of South America. "The bulk of the Canal Zone force will move south into Colombia, where it will split into two armies, one rolling down the western coast of

South America, capturing Ecuador, Peru, and Chile. The other force will seize Venezuela. The Canal Zone forces will receive air support as needed from our bases on the Corn Islands off Nicaragua."

Snowden advanced his next slide, showing the northeast coast of Brazil. "A carrier squadron is standing offshore from the Brazilian port of Belém, where we will land two army divisions."

Another slide appeared, showing the east coast of South America. "Brazil and Argentina are the two powers of South America. They will be our primary targets. A naval task force of one hundred ships is nearing its rendezvous off Rio de Janeiro. Ten divisions, spearheaded by the 101st Airmobile, will be put ashore at Rio and São Paulo.

"All targets will first be softened by long-range bombers based in the U.S. Airborne rangers will be dropped on all civilian and military airports in Brazil and Argentina.

"Once Rio and São Paulo are taken, the Southern Attack Force will move inland toward Brasília, the capital."

Snowden showed his last slide. "The final blow will come from the Falkland Islands. An invasion force of British, Canadians, Australians, and New Zealanders—five divisions in all—will land at Bahía Blanca, Buenos Aires and Montevideo. As soon as those three cities have fallen, those troops will march north to hook up with our forces at Rio. The Green Belt will then be ours."

The general turned off the projector, and Stanton turned on the lights. "In conclusion, the ships, the planes, the personnel, are in position and ready to go. Once you give us the go-ahead, we estimate it will take two weeks to secure our objectives."

Snowden sat down, and McKarren stood up. "Our special-operations people have been preparing the ground for us for months—fomenting strikes and conducting guerrilla warfare. As a result, many of the target countries are already on the brink of collapse.

"Once the Green Belt areas are secured by the military, we have a vanguard of technicians, scientists, specialists of all kinds, ready to move in. Civilians will follow.

"Starting tomorrow morning, everyone in this room will be evacuated to a place of safety, where we will set up a new seat of government."

McKarren paused, then turned to Melville. "Mr. President, the meeting is yours."

Melville rose to handle the final items of business. "General Snowden, order your forces into action with the first light tomorrow morning."

"Yes, sir."

"I want our military forces worldwide on full alert, starting now. There's no telling what reaction we'll get from friend or foe when we launch our attack."

"Yes, sir. If I may make a suggestion."

"Of course, General."

"Call in your White House military liaison and tell him to convey your order to the Situation Room, where it can be transmitted directly to NORAD, SAC, and the Military Command System. It will be much faster and eliminate the need for verification."

"Very well. Would you ask him to step in?"

"Yes, sir."

"Thank you for your excellent presentation," Melville added, shaking the general's hand.

"It was my distinct pleasure, Mr. President." Then the general turned and left.

"Gentlemen, we all have a big job to do," Melville continued. "I myself am expecting six tired, disgruntled congressmen here in a few minutes. The chairmen of the Armed Services, Intelligence, and Foreign Relations Committees of both houses are on their way here under heavy guard. I need to brief them on what we've decided, and on our plan for tomorrow—before it takes off.

"In the morning, I plan to address the nation again, to tell them about what we've decided here tonight. After that speech, my family and I will depart for the Virgin Islands, where we will remain until after the fighting is over. Dr. Stanton is arranging transportation from Andrews to St. Thomas for you, your families, and your staffs. The next time we meet, we'll be in St. Thomas. Gentlemen, good evening."

The President turned and left the room.

Chapter Twelve

‖‖‖ ‖‖‖ ‖‖‖ ‖‖‖ ‖‖‖

Night had fallen by the time the small convoy of snowmobiles reached the southern edge of Marshall, Wisconsin, nineteen miles from its destination. The road was deserted, as it had been for most of their journey.

As they entered Marshall, Torrence, who was at the head of the column, pulled over to the side of the road. Several blocks ahead, a fire burned in the middle of the highway. The others also stopped their vehicles, and all drew their rifles.

"Looks like pillagers," Torrence said softly.

"Let's take a look," Corrigan said.

"Easy," Amundson said. "Could be a trap. Two advance and two give cover. Ellen, stay here with the snowmobiles. Take a position behind one of those drifts where you can keep an eye on the road without being seen. If anyone but us shows up, empty your pistol at them, and we'll come running."

She walked toward a snowdrift, while the four men advanced into the small town. Ahead of them, gunshots rang out, followed by screams. They heard the high-pitched whine of snowmobile engines. Amundson and Torrence took the point, crouching low, so their white snowmobile suits and boots would blend into the snow.

Corrigan and Johnson stayed fifty yards back, covering their companions. As they neared the fire, Amundson could make out buildings aflame. In the light from the fire, he could see a Jeep, stuck in the snow, and a gang of snowmobilers riding circles around it, firing into the vehicle as they passed close. Return fire from the Jeep was sporadic and ineffective.

Amundson and Torrence lay flat in the snow, cradling their rifles. "Odds look a little uneven," Amundson said. He extended his left hand and positioned the barrel of his rifle. With his right hand, he moved the stock back and forth, trying to pick out a target with his infrared scope.

"I'll take the one with the Nazi helmet," Amundson said, to make sure Torrence wasn't targeting the same man.

"Okay, you got him," Torrence replied, aiming his weapon at one of the other men.

Each man squeezed off a round, and both targets tumbled off their vehicles. The rest of the marauders stopped in confusion, giving Amundson and Torrence a chance for a second shot. "Got the one with the scorpion on his jacket," Amundson said.

"Okay," Torrence said, selecting a different target. Again, they fired, and two more of the gang went down.

"They're awfully stupid," Amundson said, trying to line up another shot. Finally, the remaining four realized they were under attack. They gunned their snowmobiles wildly and took off down the road, their machines zigzagging crazily.

"Too bad. Those last four will probably kill

again before someone stops them," Torrence said. He turned and waved to their backup men to advance.

Corrigan and Johnson hurried to reach the other two men. "Hey, that was pretty good shooting," Corrigan said. "Four shots and four down."

"Bob, go back to Ellen and stay with her until we're ready to bring up the snowmobiles," Amundson said. "Joe, can you cover us from here?"

"Sure."

Amundson and Torrence made their way toward the Jeep. The fire illuminated the entire ambush scene in an unearthly red.

When they were about fifteen feet from the first body, Amundson handed Torrence his rifle. "Keep me covered," he said, drawing his pistol and flicking off the safety.

Amundson walked toward the first marauder, his pistol trained on the man's head. Standing right over the body, he shot the dead man in the heart. Methodically, he did the same to each of the other three bandits.

Then he turned to the Jeep that had been under attack. He couldn't see anyone inside. "What do you think?" Torrence asked nervously.

"I'll move in from this side. You circle around and come at it from the other side."

Amundson waited until Torrence was in position, then cautiously approached the Jeep. He crouched low and moved to the driver's side. He pulled the door open, and a body rolled out at him. Amundson saw at a glance that the man was dead.

On the passenger side, a younger man, still clutching a pistol, was hunched forward with his head against the dashboard. He was gutshot and barely alive.

When Amundson looked into the back seat, he was suddenly staring into the muzzle of a .45 automatic. The pistol was in the hands of a young woman, whose eyes were wide with fear and anger. Amundson saw that the safety was off.

"Put your hands up," she commanded.

Amundson raised his hands, revealing his own pistol.

"Drop your gun on the floor—back here."

He did what she said. "Easy," he whispered. "I'm not part of the gang that attacked you. I drove them off."

"I know that. But I don't know that you're any better than them," she replied.

"I didn't expect a reward for my efforts," Amundson said, backing out of the Jeep, his hands held in plain view. "But I didn't expect to get shot, either."

Amundson was talking to give Torrence time to get closer to the Jeep. "If it's all right with you, I'll be on my way."

"Quiet," she said.

In order to keep her pistol trained on him as he backed away, she rose to a kneeling position. When she did, Torrence reached into the Jeep from her blind side and grabbed her hand, forcing his thumb over the hammer and lifting her hand so that the barrel was pointing straight up instead of at Amundson.

She squeezed the trigger, but no shot could be fired with Torrence's thumb over the hammer. Torrence reached in with his free hand and took the pistol away from her.

"Thanks, old buddy, you're one up on me," Amundson said.

The woman began to cry, while Torrence removed the clip from her automatic and emptied the bullets into the snow.

"Get out," Amundson ordered. She climbed out on the driver's side.

"Lean against the Jeep, feet wide, hands on top of your head."

When she was in the position Amundson wanted, he searched her thoroughly and found another pistol and a knife concealed in hidden pockets.

"Who are the two men in front?" Amundson asked her.

"My father and brother," she sobbed.

"You father's dead, and your brother's barely alive."

Still crying, she went first to her father and then to her brother, who faintly acknowledged her presence. Convinced there was nothing she could do for them, she reemerged from the Jeep, her sobs choked off, her tears brushed away.

Amundson let Torrence handle the woman. He walked toward Corrigan's position and yelled for them to bring up the snowmobiles.

Using the infrared scope on his rifle, Amundson checked the road in both directions. He rejoined Torrence, who was still trying to console the woman. "We'd better get the hell out of here," Amundson said. "The fire and gunshots are sure to bring more yahoos looking for a fight."

Torrence nodded. Johnson, Corrigan, and Ellen rode into the circle of light on their snowmobiles.

"Who taught you to drive that thing?" Amundson asked Ellen.

"It's not hard," she said. "C'mon, I'll give you the same quick course Bob gave me."

While Ellen was showing Amundson how to drive a snowmobile, Johnson and Corrigan checked the machines abandoned by the marauders. They soon had three of them running.

Meanwhile, Torrence had calmed down the woman. "Do you have any family left?" he asked her.

She shook her head.

"You're welcome to join us, if you want. We have a place just north of here."

She nodded.

"What's your name?"

"Alicia Allison."

"I'm Jerry Torrence. I'll introduce you to the others when we're safe. Right now, we want to get out of here. Can you drive a snowmobile?"

"Yes."

"Good. Let's go."

The six of them climbed aboard their vehicles

and sped through Marshall, with Torrence at the point.

Five miles northeast of Columbus, the convoy turned off Route 151, then stopped abruptly at a barbed wire fence with a padlocked gate. Torrence dismounted. "This is the entrance to our private road, Ted. We're only about a mile and a half from the farm."

Illuminated by the snowmobile headlights, a large sign loomed at them from above the snowdrifts:

This is private property.
KEEP OUT!
Trespassers Who Survive This
Electrified Fence Will Be Shot.

Torrence took a walkie-talkie out of his snowmobile. "Hello, Tiger Base, this is Bobcat. Over."

There was no answer. "Hello, Tiger Base, this is Bobcat. Do you read me? Over."

"Hello, Bobcat, this is Tiger Base. We read you loud and clear. What is the password? Over."

"Tiger Base, the password is 'red.' What is the countersign? Over."

"Bobcat, the countersign is 'beard.' Over."

"Roger, Tiger Base. We're at the entrance to the trail. Can you see us on your screen? Over."

"We sure can."

"Good. Would you turn off the juice?"

"Will do, Bobcat. Wait one."

There was a pause, then Tiger Base resumed. "Bobcat, the fence is off. Be sure to test on your end. Over."

"Roger."

Torrence removed his right glove and threw it against the fence. Nothing happened. He retrieved his glove, then spoke into the walkie-talkie again. "Tiger Base, my test shows the juice is off. We're moving through the gate. Stand by. Over."

"Will do, Bobcat."

Torrence unlocked the padlock. As soon as he swung the gate open, the snowmobiles filed past him. He waited while Corrigan hurried back to retrieve the sixth snowmobile, then closed and relocked the gate.

"Tiger Base, we're through. Reactivate the electricity."

"Roger, Bobcat."

"Tiger Base, you'll see six snowmobiles approaching the house in about five minutes. Over."

"Roger, Bobcat. Six instead of three. We'll have hot toddies for everyone when you get here. Over."

"Excellent, Tiger Base, but you'd better be ready with seconds for everyone. Over."

"Will do, Bobcat. Over."

"See you in a few minutes. Out."

Torrence returned his walkie-talkie to the snowmobile and remounted his vehicle. He led the way along the final leg of their journey. The trail turned into a long driveway, and the six machines glided up the approachway and stopped between the clustered buildings. The six of them dismounted from their machines, unloaded their gear, and followed Torrence toward the main house.

Ellen was dead tired. She was grateful when Amundson took her hand and pulled her close to him. Together, they followed the others toward the dark building. When the door opened, bright, welcoming light poured out at them.

Once inside, Johnson and Corrigan rushed into their mates' arms. Smiles flashed as Torrence began the introductions. He started with Allison, to make her feel at ease. When he introduced Amundson and Ellen to the group, the smiles broadened.

They met Roy Romano, the fourth man, and his wife Carol. "Roy is our communications man," Torrence said. "He also taught cold-weather survival to Special Forces and Company personnel. Carol taught four grades, all subjects, at the Company grade school at Langley.

"This poor female, trapped in Bob's clutches, is Betty Johnson. She's a computer-systems analyst and software expert.

"Last, but certainly not least," Torrence said, alluding to the woman's voluptuous figure, "we have Teri Corrigan, Joe's lovely wife."

"It's a pleasure meeting all of you," Amundson said. "Now, how about those hot toddies you promised..."

"As soon as you get your suits off, the drinks

are waiting for you in the family room," Teri Corrigan said.

The weary travelers stripped off their snow-mobile suits and stacked their holsters on the gun racks in the foyer. In couples, they filed through the kitchen toward the back of the house. Ellen noticed that every window was shrouded with heavy blackout curtains to keep the light from showing through to the outside.

In the family room, a huge fireplace with a raised hearth was filled with burning logs. The room itself was warm and comfortable, lit only by the roaring fireplace.

"Now, instead of making a bunch of individual drinks," Teri said, "we've something that's completely maintenance free." She pointed to a huge punch bowl on a table in front of the fireplace.

"The exact ingredients are not known." Roy Romano chuckled. "We kept pouring booze and mix into the punch bowl until it was full."

"It's not hot, but I guarantee it will warm you up," Carol said. "The four of us have been at it for—oh—thirty minutes or so, and it's amazing how warm this room can become." Smiling, she passed out punch glasses.

Ellen dipped her glass into the mixture and tried it. The liquid immediately started a glow in her stomach. She smiled at the pleasant effect.

"Works fast, doesn't it?" Teri asked, noticing Ellen's smile.

"It sure does."

Amundson filled his glass and drank deeply. "That's good," he said. He finished the first round and refilled his glass quickly. "But these small glasses just won't do. Do you have a long straw?"

There was laughter from everyone, and Teri got up and brought in some tumblers.

"Ah, that's more like it," Amundson said.

He filled two glasses, then dragged Ellen into a corner of the room, where they sank into the thick shag carpeting.

The table with the punch bowl was the only piece of furniture in the room. The carpet was covered with cushions, pillows and trays for drinks. There were several wall lamps, but they were turned off.

"What do you think of this room?" she asked.

"I love it. It's comfortable. Makes it easy to be friendly."

He put his drink down on one of the trays and took off his shoes. Then he propped himself against the wall, placing cushions under his head and behind his back. He let out a long sigh.

"Comfortable?" Ellen asked.

"Uh-huh."

"Are you ready for me to snuggle up?"

"Uh-huh."

She rested her head on his shoulder and kissed his neck and the right side of his face. He wrapped his right arm around her and held her tightly.

"Take your shoes off, darling," he said. "I've got this irresistible urge to play footsies with you."

"You're not paying attention, my sweet. I took off my shoes when we came in. They're inside my snowmobile boots. My feet are completely naked and yours for the taking."

Amundson kissed her deeply, then looked around the room to see if anyone was watching. In one corner, Jerry Torrence and Alicia Allison were speaking softly; he had an arm around her waist. On the other side of the room, Bob and Betty Johnson were locked in a passionate embrace. Joe and Teri Corrigan were in another corner, coupled in a deep embrace. Roy and Carol Romano were laid back, watching their friends. Amundson waved at them, and they waved back.

"It's good to be around people we can trust," Ellen said. "I finally feel safe."

"I know what you mean, honey," Amundson said, remembering the abandoned buildings, flophouses, and roadside culverts where they had spent sleepless, desperate nights during their flight from Odyssey and the subsequent manhunt.

He looked into her face, then kissed her deeply. With his right hand, he caressed her back through her clothing. The fire had died down, but he could still make out her face. She was smiling at him—her broad, beautiful smile that came so easily.

"I love your smile, you know," he said.

"You've mentioned that to me several times, but please don't stop saying it."

"I think it's time we find out where our bedroom is."

"Oh? That excited?" she teased.

"Yeah. But I don't even know if we have our own room. We may have to spend the night right here."

"That would suit me just fine—as long as we're the only ones in it," she said.

"I can tell your sexual fires need more fuel," he said, reaching for her empty glass. He crawled to the punch bowl. As he was refilling their glasses, Jerry Torrence joined him.

"Hey, old buddy, you're just the man I'm looking for," Amundson said.

"Oh?"

"Yeah. Ellen and I are getting anxious to be by ourselves. Where do we sleep?"

"Upstairs. When you reach the top of the stairs, turn right. Then go all the way to the end of the hall. The room on the left is yours. But whatever you do, don't stop one room too soon. Two of the kids, Corine and Karen, are doubled up in that room, and you'll have two hysterical teenagers on your hands if you stumble into their room and start taking off your clothes."

Torrence chuckled at the thought.

"My room is across from yours, and the john is right next door t' me," Torrence continued.

"Thanks, Jer."

"Don' menshun it," Torrence said.

"Say, am I hearing things, or are you slurring your words?"

"Beats me. See yuh later." Torrence moved back toward his corner with two full glasses.

Amundson rejoined Ellen. "Anytime you're ready, sweetheart, our room is upstairs."

Chapter Thirteen

IIII IIII IIII IIII IIII

They slept long past daybreak. The fatigue of their long journey, combined with the effects of the welcoming party, had left Amundson and Ellen in a deep sleep that continued after the sun had invaded their room.

Finally, Amundson awoke. Somehow during the night, he and Ellen had gotten turned around, because he was staring at her feet when he woke up. He reached out and gently squeezed the toes of her right foot, until he felt her stir.

"What are you doing down there?" she asked weakly.

"I don't know. You must have forced me to perform some unnatural act for me to wind up like this," he said.

"I hope you're right."

"I wonder how late it is."

"Should we care?" she asked.

"It's our first day here. We don't want anyone to think we're sluffing off."

"Nonsense," she said. "I'm sure they all have hangovers, too. Besides, it feels so good to sleep late—and not have to worry about somebody finding us."

"By the look of the sun, we've already slept too long," he said. He swung his feet out of bed and sat up. "C'mon, get up," he said, tugging on her leg. She groaned.

"Time for a shower and breakfast," he said.

"We're going to need our gear," she said. "Why don't you call down and ask someone to bring it up."

Amundson went to the door and cracked it open, checking the hallway outside their room to make sure no one was there. Their bags were leaning against the wall, just outside the door. "Hey, someone already brought our stuff up for us," he said.

He carried their backpacks into the bedroom. They took out clean clothes and toiletries, then made a naked dash to the bathroom, where they had a long, relaxing shower together.

Refreshed, they finally went downstairs, through the entrance foyer and into the kitchen. Everyone else was already up and sitting around a huge table in the kitchen.

There was an incredible bustle of activity, with Teri Corrigan standing at the stove making pancakes, and Carol Romano scrambling eggs and preparing sausages for the grill. A young girl was serving the food to ten ravenous appetites. Platters passed quickly from one end of the table to the other, sometimes arriving empty at their final destination.

Four teenagers joked and talked with the adults. Under the table, two anxious dogs waited for scraps to hit the floor. A large potbellied stove kept the entire room warm and cheery.

Teri turned to hand a full platter of pancakes to the girl waiting on the table and saw Ellen and Amundson. "Well, good morning," she said. All eyes turned toward them. "Are you two ready to join us for breakfast?"

Amundson hesitated for a moment, but then propelled Ellen toward the table. Torrence was grinning from ear to ear as they approached. He reached out, grabbed his friend's hand, and pumped it furiously.

"Good morning, good morning. Don't stand there salivating, my friend. Sit down, have some breakfast, and meet the kids."

They sat, and he introduced them first to Corine, the dark-haired and attractive twelve-year-old daughter of Joe and Teri Corrigan, and then to Karen, Bob and Betty Johnson's daughter, who was serving the food.

The three boys were introduced in the middle of a fresh batch of pancakes. Their mouths full, each said "hello" as best he could. Tod and Mike were in a hurry to get out to the barn for the morning's milkings. Steve had duty in the garage. The boys finished, then rushed to the foyer to don parkas and boots. As soon as they were out the door, the room became quiet.

"Hey, we thought you two would stay in bed all morning," Torrence said slyly. "And deservedly so," he added hastily.

Before Amundson could respond, Karen brought plates, napkins, and utensils for them, and Teri filled their plates with eggs and sausages, while Carol followed up with pancakes. Finally, the women sat down and had their turn at some of the food they'd been preparing and serving.

"What's on the agenda this morning, Jer?" Amundson asked.

"We want to catch the morning news, so we'll give you a tour of the place beforehand. After the tour, a strategy meeting."

"Sounds good."

After breakfast, Torrence and the newcomers lingered over coffee, while the others hurried off to their assignments.

"How are you today, Alicia?" Ellen asked.

"I'm all right. Jerry's helped a lot. All of you have been great."

"C'mon," Torrence said, standing up abruptly. "It's time for the fifty-cent tour."

They left the kitchen, with Torrence playing the tour guide. Beyond the kitchen was a hallway leading to the rest of the rooms on the lower level. They stopped just past the kitchen. Torrence motioned with his arm to a large, plainly furnished room off to their right. "This is the dining room. We don't use it much, just on holidays or maybe on the weekend when we're having a special meal.

"Across the hall is our meeting room, where we'll be having our strategy meeting later." He ushered them into a big room that would rival the boardroom of an oil company. A massive, rough-hewn oak table and satellite armchairs dominated the room.

Directly across from them, a large bay window looked out onto a snow-covered pasture. Credenzas lined one wall; the other walls held bookcases filled with volumes of political history, philosophy, and reference.

Next was the communications room, equipped with shortwave, CB, and radar. Inside, Roy Romano and Corine Corrigan were on duty.

"Hi, you two," Torrence greeted them.

From his position in front of the radar screen, Romano smiled and said, "I see the tour has started."

"Indeed it has. Could you give our friends a rundown on what we have here?" Torrence said.

"Of course. From this room, we monitor channel nineteen on the citizens' band. Helps keep us on top of local events and calls for help. Our route man uses it to call us when he's ready to enter the main gate. We control our electrified fences from here.

"I learned the electronics trade in 'Nam," he continued. "My section helped develop those listening devices we used to detect Vietcong moving along their supply trails. We have 'em here, all along our perimeters. If someone intrudes into our space, an alarm goes off. These screens give us an electronic picture of the surrounding areas.

"We also have closed-circuit TV," he said, pointing to a bank of monitors. "Here's the entrance road." The screen showed the narrow lane that ran from the gate to the house.

"The barn." They saw Tod attaching milking cups to one of the cows.

"Here's the garage." Bob Johnson's feet were sticking out from under a Jeep. His son Steve was working on a snowmobile.

"Here's the other house. Cameras at either end to warn of intruders.

"But this is my pride and joy. Radar. Primary and secondary units provide early warning against approaching aircraft. It can track aircraft identified as hostile, then tell us when to fire our surface-to-air missiles.

"That's about it. We have enough equipment to require two people on duty during the day."

Amundson nodded. "Thanks, Roy."

They left the communications room. "My Lord, Jer," Amundson said when they were in the hallway outside. "Here I thought I'd find you tucked away in a cave somewhere, scratching for food with nothing to defend yourselves with except a few rifles. I'm impressed as hell. Where'd you get all this hardware?"

"The guys brought it with them. It was all part of our contingency planning. Hardware was stashed away long ago. After I went to ground and assumed my new identity, I began to look for a good cover. This was it. I notified them, and they got the equipment out of mothballs and had it shipped here by truck in boxes marked 'farm equipment.'"

"Fantastic."

"C'mon, we're getting behind schedule," Torrence said. "You're already familiar with our family room from the party last night. There are two johns on this floor, and a sitting room that you can explore at your leisure. Upstairs are nine bedrooms. In the basement we have an armory and an emergency generator.

"We are a complete, self-sustaining unit. As our family grows, we have the second house about twenty yards east from here."

They were walking back toward the kitchen. "Let's get our coats," Torrence said. "We still have time to visit the barn and the motor pool before the news comes on."

They donned parkas and boots and trudged through the snow. Neither Ellen nor Amundson had been in a barn before. The smell of manure was strong as they entered the building. Amundson and Ellen stopped in their tracks at the sight of the twenty-eight dairy cows standing in their stalls. The animals nearest the door turned and stared, chewing mouthfuls of hay grabbed from the bales in front of them.

Tod appeared, carrying two pails of milk. "Hi!" he said, smiling. The pails were heavy, so he continued on past them without stopping.

"Where's he going with the milk?" Ellen asked.

"To the milk house. C'mon, let's follow him," Torrence said.

They backtracked about ten feet, where a door led to a small room that was detached from the barn, but shared a common wall with it. Inside, there was a soft whir of machinery. Tod was standing on a cinder block, pouring one pail of milk into a spotless, stainless steel tank.

"That's the cooler," Torrence explained. "It stores the milk, keeps it cold, and agitates it. Three times a week, the route man comes in, takes a sample of the milk for analysis, then empties the milk into his truck."

Torrence led them back to the barn. "This is a semiautomated operation. Compressed air is piped along both walls. The milking unit is moved from cow to cow and plugged into the compressed-air line. When the can is full, the milking unit is moved to an empty can, and the full one taken immediately to the cooler."

"How long does this all take?" Amundson asked.

"About an hour. Twice a day, every day, 365 days a year. This week, Tod and Mike have barn duty. One milks and the other carries."

"And it takes an hour?" Ellen asked again.

"Yeah, but milking is only part of the job. First, they have to bring down the straw and hay from the loft—straw to bed the stalls and hay for the cows to eat. Then they have to round up the animals and get them into their stalls.

"They give them water and oats, and only then are they ready to start milking. When the milking's done, everything has to be cleaned, and lye spread over the concrete floor."

"Quite a bit of work," Ellen said.

"I think it's how the word 'chore' originated," Torrence said. "But it's a money business. Don't have to worry about how the grain prices are doing, like the grain farmers do. The cost of milk and cheese keeps pace with inflation, and if things really start to get bad, I can't think of a better barter item."

"Except Scotch," Amundson quipped.

"Right!"

"Where do you buy the food for the animals?" Ellen asked.

"We don't buy it. If we did, we'd go broke in a month. C'mon, I'll show you."

They climbed to the upper level of the barn. The loft was immense, stretching up to the curved ceiling some eighty feet above them.

"Everything we need is grown on the farm— at least it was before this year. What you're looking at is left over from last year's harvest— hay on one side and straw up there, above the granary.

"And here I thought cows just ruminated in the pasture all day," Ellen said.

Torrence smiled, then opened a sliding door. "This leads to a dirt rampway. Tractors and other equipment get into the barn through here."

"Hey! You have your own gas pump!" Ellen

said. She pointed to the antique Standard pump just inside the sliding door.

"Sure," Torrence said. "Every farmer has to have a bulk tank for gasoline. We certainly couldn't haul our tractors to the gas station. Besides, we don't use the roads with tractors and farm equipment, so we don't pay any road-use taxes. Of course, we use this gas for other vehicles, too. Bob says he doesn't know where he's going to get the next delivery from. The farmers' co-op has been closed for months, and the local black-market guy's been busted."

"I'm sure the profit motive will encourage someone to fill the void," Amundson said.

"Yeah, well, so much for the barn. Let's take a look at what we have in the motor pool, and then we'd better get back to the house."

The motor pool was a fifty-yard walk from the barn. It was a new prefab building, with an arched roof like the barn's. They kicked the snow off their boots and stepped in.

Immediately, their attention was captured by an awesome military personnel carrier. "Where the hell did you get an APC?" Amundson asked.

"You're looking at an updated cousin of the old APC we knew. This is an M-2 Bradley Infantry Personnel Carrier. One of the first ones they made. It was officially lost while being transported by helicopter during a maneuver. In reality, it made its way into my hot little hands."

Amundson circled the M-2 slowly. He recognized it, the way the inventor of the cavalry pistol would recognize a .38, but it was very different from the APC of the Vietnam era.

"In a pinch, it can get all of us out of here to safety," Torrence said. "And if we're ever attacked by an outfit like that bunch we ran into in Marshall last night, their ass is grass with this baby.

"If we run into a tougher outfit, this thing has an antitank missile launcher—the new ones that you just fire at the target and forget. It's really something. We've all practiced with it, and you will, too. At three thousand yards, it has a ninety-percent first-hit probability."

"Jeez, what else do you have in here? We could take over the State of Wisconsin with this gear."

"Ah, in the armory, I've got enough antitank and antiaircraft missile launchers to arm a detachment of regular troops. Those missiles work the same way these do. In small arms, we have the A-2—latest version of the M-16.

"Back there, you can see the Piper. As soon as the strategy session is over, let's take her up and start looking for Odyssey."

"I'm ready."

"We have more conventional farm equipment," Torrence said, waving at the tractors lined up next to the M-2. "It takes three tractors of different sizes to operate this farm. Plus, a combine to harvest the oats, a chopper for the corn, a baler and a side rake for hay, and, of course, a plow.

"We also have two Jeeps, *nine* snowmobiles,

with the three new ones we brought in last night, and two cars that we haven't used since last October. Somehow, Bob keeps all of this equipment running."

Torrence glanced at his watch. "C'mon, let's get back to the house. Hey, Bob, time for the news," he called.

The only TV in the house was a portable, which had been moved to the meeting room for the newscast. A video recorder was hooked up to record the newscast for the kids who were still on duty or finishing their chores.

The musical introduction for the program came on, followed by the image of one of the show's anchormen. "Good morning," he said curtly. "There's a lot happening today, so let's get right into the news.

"Reaction to the President's speech last night has been both quick and vociferous. Meanwhile, the President has announced yet another major address to the nation this morning. We and the other networks have been told it will last fifteen minutes. We have not, as yet, been informed as to the subject of the address.

"On the weather front, the news is good. The National Weather Service indicates that our long winter may finally be over. With the details, here is our meteorologist, Charles Hackman."

The network's national weather forecaster appeared, standing in front of a map of the country. One fat red arrow stood out from the others, its base in the Gulf of Mexico, and its tip pointed at St. Louis, Missouri.

"A strong warm front is pushing up from the Gulf into the American heartland," he explained. "This mass of warm air will run head-on into the entrenched polar air that has dominated us all these months. The result will be violent weather across the Midwest, including thunderstorms, hail, and the possibility of tornadoes. The warming trend should spread quickly to the east and west as well. It will cause a rapid thawing of snow and ice, resulting in swollen rivers and much flooding. At the bottom of the hour, your local station will have a report on what to expect in your area.

"The Weather Service has released a report prepared by the Central Intelligence Agency explaining our long winter. According to the report, our trouble started last year when a huge section of the Antarctic ice sheet slipped off into the sea. Our science editor, Jim Thornton, will have a report on the possible long-range effects later on in the show. Back to you, Tim."

The anchorman reappeared. "The President's declaration of martial law last night seems to have struck many a raw nerve. An ACLU spokesman has called it, 'completely unwarranted and a flagrant violation of presidential power.'

"Congress has also been quick to criticize President Melville's actions because he failed to consult with them before initiating the action.

"However, the chairman of the key Armed Services, Intelligence, and Foreign Relations

Committees in both houses could not be reached for comment this morning. Reliable sources indicate they are with the President now. Speculation is rampant throughout Washington that the President will have momentous new revelations this morning."

At President Melville's request, the TV cameras had been moved from the Oval Office into the Cabinet Room. Melville was cloistered in the Oval Office with McKarren, who was reviewing the text of the President's speech. In turn, McKarren was briefing the President on the success of the unfolding military action.

"Everything is fine," McKarren assured. "The attacks went off as planned and were a complete surprise. The Mexicans are falling back on all fronts, and so are the South Americans. Not a hint of what's happening has leaked out. Now, let's get to the Cabinet Room. You're on in three minutes."

Under the hot TV lights in the Cabinet Room, six nervous, tired Congressmen were anxious for the broadcast to be over. The arrangement was masterful. The President's podium was center stage. On either side sat three Congressmen—House members on his left, Senators to his right.

The President took his place behind the podium and laid down his prepared text. Behind him were the maps and blowups he would use to explain the Green Belt, the military operation in progress, and the routes Americans would follow in their migration southward. His program director made some last-minute adjustments to the camera angle, then moved off camera.

The red light went on, and a medium shot of the President and the six congressmen appeared on millions of American TV screens. The camera then zoomed in to the President's face and shoulders.

"My fellow Americans. I speak to you today from the Cabinet Room at the White House, where I, and the members of Congress gathered with me, have an announcement that will change the course of history—and help preserve the United States of America."

As Melville spoke, Amundson was mesmerized. The secret operations he and Ellen had discovered were revealed to the TV audience. The President spoke of the ice age as though it had always been a public fact of life, and described Operation Migrant and Strike Force Alpha in precise detail.

Melville was summing up. "We are taking these actions to secure a new homeland for *you*. How will you get there? By whatever means you can arrange.

"We will do our utmost to make your journey safe. Military police will be on duty along the entire route into Mexico. But I must stress again that only the roads I named will be open, and no one will be allowed to cross the border until the fighting has stopped. You have two weeks to gather whatever belongings you can take in your car and prepare for an orderly evacuation.

"At this moment, a helicopter awaits me on the White House lawn. After this address, my family and I will fly to Andrews Air Force Base, and from there, a military transport will take us to the Virgin Islands. Starting this evening, I will broadcast nightly updates on the military action and on the evacuation. I wish you all success in reaching our new homeland."

The camera stayed with the President as he was enveloped by Secret Service officers. Like a victorious team of football players, the President's entourage left the room on its way to the helicopter.

The scene cut back to the anchorman. "Well, ladies and gentlemen, you heard the President. He is now on his way to the Virgin Islands. According to material handed out by the White House press secretary, he will not be taking Air Force One, but one of the specially converted 747s that could serve as the President's airborne command center in the event of a nuclear attack. An ominous fact, in this reporter's view."

Torrence turned off the television and turned to the people gathered in the room with him. "It's all on the table now," he said softly.

"All except the most important part," Amundson said.

"Let's call the strategy meeting to order," Torrence suggested. "The agenda is as follows. First, I want to turn command of this group over to Ted Amundson.

"Second, Ted will give you the scoop on what

he and Ellen found on the other side of Strike Force Alpha.

"Third, we have to devise a plan for returning there in force.

"Fourth, readiness reports."

Torrence stood up to give his next words more weight. "You all know why we came here. I told you a crisis was coming, and we wanted to be in a position to take positive action to save ourselves and our families. Today, we have finally seen the face of that crisis. Now Ted will tell you what even Melville doesn't know about the ice age."

Amundson stood up. "Ellen and I were kidnapped and drugged as part of Strike Force Alpha. When we woke up, we found ourselves in a secret installation called 'Project Odyssey.' What we discovered is that the ice age is going to be much more severe than anyone is telling—resulting in the destruction of civilization and probably of mankind.

"Not even Melville knows this. Only one high-ranking officer in the Company, John McKarren, knows it—along with some of his cronies. The reason he hasn't told the President is that he wants to take power for himself.

"While the glaciers are overrunning the world, McKarren and his chosen few will be sleeping through it all in suspended animation, reviving only when the glaciers have retreated and life can be resumed—in a society molded by them.

"Ellen and I were ready to give the details to

President-elect Porter, but the opposition caught up to us at Devil's Lake. They killed Porter and set us up as the assassins.

"But the important thing is for you all to realize that Migrant is a diversion, a complex operation designed to give credibility to the version of the ice age revealed today. There are only a handful of us who understand that the only way to survive the ice age is at Odyssey, some sixty-five miles west of here."

"When do you think they'll go into suspended animation?" Torrence asked.

"I think McKarren will wait until three or four months from now. He's got to go through with Operation Migrant. That means airlifting all those people down there. He'll wait until the country is pretty well emptied of everyone except outlaws and people who can't travel.

"Then he'll seal the base and destroy anything above it that would reveal their presence below-ground. Especially the tracking station. So, we need to find the installation before he dismantles everything."

"Well, we do have one big advantage," Torrence said. "McKarren can't possibly know how well organized we are, and we know exactly what we're looking for."

"Jer, I underestimated him once. I'm not going to do it again. We must assume he's expecting us to find him, and that he'll have some kind of welcoming committee waiting for us."

"Do you think the ten of us can take the base?"

"Sure. Once they're in suspended animation, we can do it with a small force."

At that moment, Corine popped her head into the room. "I've got radar contact with Mr. Rylander. He's given the right password, and I've cleared him to land."

"Who's Rylander?" Amundson asked.

"He's the guy I told you about who's bringing a chopper," Torrence said.

As everyone else left the room to meet the new arrival, Amundson took Torrence aside. "While they're greeting Rylander, let's get the Piper ready. We have to find Odyssey."

Chapter Fourteen

IIII IIII IIII IIII IIII

Six months later, they were still looking for Odyssey. Amundson and Torrence were sitting in the kitchen having breakfast and going over their flight plan for the morning. The women were having coffee with them.

As usual, their breakfast meeting was subdued. They were the only ones who were still interested in the morning's search plans.

After the first two months, everyone's high hopes had dimmed. Discipline had started to slip as the futility grew. Sometimes maintenance schedules weren't met, and equipment wasn't always ready when it was needed.

The discontent had reached a boiling point one Monday morning, when Corrigan and Torrence got into a heated argument about continuing the search. Amundson had stepped in and reminded everyone that the alternative to finding Odyssey was to join the hordes of people streaming south to Mexico. After that, discipline had returned, but with a distinct lack of enthusiasm.

"Well, today begins our third try," Torrence said dryly.

"I hope three's our lucky number, Jer. Time's running out."

"You ain't shittin'. If the world doesn't blow up, the weather's gonna get us. Report from the west has a big storm crossing the Rockies. We'll get clobbered here in two or three days and get socked in for a week."

Amundson nodded glumly. Ellen, sitting next to him, refilled his coffee cup. He nodded his thanks, then got up. "I'll be back in a few minutes," he said. And left for the meeting room.

Amundson's after-breakfast trip to the meeting room had become a daily ritual. Each day, he entered the events of the previous twenty-four hours in his log.

He set down his coffee and removed a thin notebook from inside his shirt. He opened it to the first empty page, wrote the date at the top and began his entry:

Yesterday, our search was again without success. With TV gone and commercial radio censored, the only hard news we get is on shortwave or CB. Yesterday, there was no news of importance.

It was the shortest entry he had ever made in his log. He turned back to his original entry, a preamble, in which he identified himself and his mission, outlined the events culminating in Porter's assassination, the fact that Operation Migrant was a diversion, and that the only way to survive the ice age was by finding Odyssey.

He turned the page.

May 16—This morning, President Melville announced the ice age and Operation Migrant on national TV. Armed forces of the United States, England, Canada, Australia, and New Zealand invaded Mexico, Central America and South America.

As soon as President Melville announced the invasion, he flew to the Virgin Islands as the first step in moving the entire government south, with the general population to follow. With his announcement, there was worldwide unrest, and most nations placed their militaries on alert.

There are reports of panic, mass evacuation, conflict, and some open warfare. People across the world seem to be moving toward the equator, clogging every north-south highway. Train stations, bus terminals, and airports are also jammed with people. Civil authority is breaking down in many areas.

In Western Europe, the Belgians, Dutch and

French are moving toward Spain. The Spaniards and Portuguese are crossing the Straits of Gibraltar to Morocco. So far, no outright warfare between the armed forces of those countries, but a general panic is driving them, and many have died. Algeria has threatened war if anyone crosses her borders.

So far, the Germans have held fast and are asking for clarification from us. The Scandinavians are moving into Eastern Europe across the Baltic Sea. The Eastern Europeans, in turn, are moving into Italy, while the Italians are moving across the Mediterranean toward Libya, where the Colonel has threatened to greet everyone with a bullet. Italian Air Force elements, acting on their own, are attacking Libyan troops.

China's armies have already crossed over into Vietnam to settle that old score. Their troops facing the Russian border are on full alert.

The South Africans have activated every reserve unit and are massing troops along their borders with Namibia and Botswana for an apparent thrust at Angola.

The Canadian border is calm. The President's speech was seen on Canadian TV. Immediately afterward, their Prime Minister went on and explained how their troops were involved in the operation and assured them all that they'll have a home in the Green Belt when the fighting is over. He's due to join the President in the Virgin Islands later today.

In Great Britain, there have been some isolated attempts to cross the channel into France, but mainly calm. Their Prime Minister was also on TV right after the President, with maps showing how the Falklands attack force was mainly a British operation. He assured them that part of the Green Belt will be for them. He also unveiled a plan for their mass evacuation to South America as soon as the fighting is over. He too will join President Melville on St. Thomas, along with the Royal Family.

The Israelis have asked for clarification and placed their armed forces on alert.

Of greatest concern is the Soviet Union. They've placed their entire military on full alert. The forty-five divisions along the Sino-Soviet border have moved to their southern-most positions. Thirty divisions along Turkey, Iraq and Pakistan have moved south and west and are now facing Iraq.

All Soviet forces in Eastern Europe—some thirty-two divisions—have moved south, to-ward Yugoslavia.

The Soviets are poised and waiting while the Kremlin analyzes our moves. There are unconfirmed reports of a massive power struggle inside the Politburo.

There are also unconfirmed reports that the American government is secretly cooperating with the Russians, to forestall a nuclear shoot-out between the superpowers. Apparently, the Russians have their eye on the Green Belt countries in Africa, and the U.S. is prepared to help them achieve their objectives to prevent a nuclear exchange.

It appears we will have worldwide chaos before the end of the day.

Amundson skipped ahead two weeks:

June 3—We still haven't found Odyssey.
Around the world, old political boundaries
have disappeared; old alliances are gone, and
new ones rising to take their place.

Australia has moved its seat of government
to New Guinea and formed a new federation
with Indonesia, Malaysia, and the Philip-
pines. All of these countries are in the Green
Belt and are feeling the pressure from the
great Asian powers to their north: Russia,
China and India.

China has signed a mutual defense pact
with Korea and Japan, while her armies have
swept into Southeast Asia. Burma, Laos, and
eastern India have been overrun, while bitter
fighting continues in Vietnam, Cambodia,
and Thailand.

China also has her hands full on her northern frontiers, where the Russians are driving
south, using masses of armor and mechanized infantry. Reports are also circulating
that the Russians are using chemical warfare
against the Chinese.

Some of the worst fighting is reported from
the Middle East, where sixteen Russian divisions have attacked Iraq on two fronts and
smashed through to Jordan and Syria. Word
last night was that forward elements of the
Russian Army were nearing the Israeli
border, where new fighting is expected. Other
Russian troops have reportedly turned east
through Saudi Arabia to envelop the Persian
Gulf.

Europeans are pouring through Spain and

Italy toward North Africa. The Russians and Europeans are all trying to reach the same Green Belt countries in Africa: Sierra Leone, Liberia, Ghana, Togo, Benin, Nigeria, Zaire and Zambia.

South Africa wants the same real estate. Her armies have crushed Angola and are pushing north.

June 4—We haven't found Odyssey. Locally, gasoline can't be found. Luckily, our tanks are full. The milk man called on the CB yesterday. Said he was hijacked again the day before and wouldn't be coming any more. Too bad. Not only was he our only source of income, but a good source for local news. Reports are that the cities are mostly deserted, and the people left are having a hard time getting food. Looting and murder are the order of the day, and everyone wears sidearms.

In a TV broadcast last night, Melville announced how he's going to partition the conquered lands. By right of conquest, the U.S. will annex Mexico, Central America, and all of South America except for two-thirds of Brazil.

Melville's decision to leave most of Brazil autonomous is a good one. Those areas left autonomous are already heavily populated. The area of Brazil ceded to the US—the states of Amapa, Amazonas, Rondonia, Roraima, and part of Para are sparsely populated—ideal for settlement by Americans as they arrive from the north.

The new United States of America will be

comprised of Colombia, Ecuador, Peru, Chile, Bolivia, Argentina, Paraguay, Uruguay, and the area of Panama south of the Canal. The new American nation is about 3,800 miles long, from north to south, and 1,500 miles wide.

Resettlement of the people kidnapped during Strike Force Alpha is proceeding around the clock. This means Odyssey will certainly be sealed by the end of summer.

So Melville is all set up down there. Bogata is now renamed New Washington, Colombia is now spelled Columbia, and there's talk of moving our national monuments down to the new capital.

The Canadians are pleased with their new country. For their assistance in the fighting and because they have always been such good neighbors (Melville's description), he has given them all of the Green Belt territory north of Panama, which includes southern Mexico and Central America.

Likewise, the British seem happy with their piece of the spoils. Their new homeland includes Guyana (once their colony), a piece of Venezuela, and a sparsely populated chunk of Brazil. They should feel right at home in their new capital at Georgetown.

Surinam has been handed back to the Dutch, and the French have been allowed to keep French Guiana, which they have renamed New France.

The Swiss also got a very nice new homeland out of the deal. It's south of Surinam and New France, carved out of the former Brazilian states of Amapa and Para, with a nice piece of coastline and control of the Amazon Delta. A shrewd piece of business by Melville, bringing all the secret Swiss accounts closer to home. Melville has announced that he will allow limited migration from selected European countries, notably West Germany.

So the tiresome banana republics are gone forever, replaced by Western democracy.

Again, Amundson skipped ahead in his log:

September 10—Still no sign of Odyssey. Our situation is becoming more desperate each day. We have been running on the emergency generator for a week. Food is getting low.

Locally, a band of army deserters has turned up in our area and joined forces with our local cutthroats. Together, they practically run the county, except for us. We monitor their CB and radio communication at all times.

There is no contact with the Middle East, Africa, or Europe since the Russians used Backfire bombers with nuclear weapons to eliminate the armies standing between them and the Green Belt countries in Africa. China seized upon the moment to launch a nuclear attack against the Russian heartland, and the Soviets retaliated in kind using part of their strategic missile arsenal.

The world has gone mad. We don't know what is going to happen next.

September 20—Still no Odyssey. We are on full alert every other day as the criminals around us get more and more daring.

There is no longer any word on short wave except from New America and from the Far East. We must find Odyssey before the rest of the world blows itself up.

Amundson closed the log, put it back inside his shirt, and rejoined the others in the kitchen. As he headed out the door with Torrence, Ellen handed him a full Thermos of coffee.

Outside, there was a hard frost on everything. They trudged out to the field where the Piper sat under its camouflage net. "We'll have to put her in the motor pool from now on," Torrence said. "Getting too cold to leave her out."

Amundson nodded as they pulled off the camouflage net. They had painted the plane camouflage green and given it U.S. Air Force markings, a nice touch that helped their small plane command more respect during their search for Odyssey.

"We'll have to change the camouflage soon," Amundson said, thinking of the snow headed their way.

"Yeah," Torrence agreed as they climbed into the plane.

Once airborne, Torrence pointed her toward Sauk County. The sky was still a little hazy, but the sun was quickly burning it away.

By the time they reached Sauk County, visibility was almost unlimited. As usual, they were flying low. Amundson scanned the familiar landscape below and to his right with a pair of binoculars, picking out buildings, roads, and natural formations he knew almost by heart.

As they passed over a range of hills into a green, wide valley, Amundson poured some coffee for himself and for Torrence.

"Thanks, old buddy," Torrence said.

Amundson held his own cup in his left hand and the field glasses in his right as they flew over the valley. He saw only trees, roads and farmhouses. No runway.

Damn that old man, Amundson thought. *How the hell can he hide a runway? It has to be there somewhere.*

But there was no clue. Not in this valley nor in any of the others they had flown over. Below, he saw the clear, blue river that cut through the valley. Then the Piper began to climb to rise above the next string of foothills.

Suddenly, a downdraft caught the plane and sucked them violently toward the ground.

"Holy shit, hang on!" Torrence yelled.

Amundson had nothing to hang onto. His coffee cup emptied into his lap, and his binoculars smacked against his forehead.

"Jesus Christ!" Torrence swore, as they neared treetop level. The river loomed near as Torrence finally won his fight to regain control of the plane. They were barely above the trees, and the foothills looked like mountains in front of them.

"Follow the river up," Amundson shouted.

Torrence grunted, and skillfully maneuvered the craft over the river, between the trees on either bank, pulling back hard on the stick to nose the plane upward. Amundson reached over and grabbed Torrence's hands to add his strength to the effort to keep control.

Before them, through the heavy stands of trees, the river headed up into the foothills. They were only about ten feet above the water when the airplane finally began to respond. She lifted her nose up, and they skirted the slopes of the foothills.

The last thing Amundson saw before the plane finally regained altitude was a mill astride the river where it broke over a rock outcrop into a short waterfall. Then they were over the foothills and into the next valley.

"Jesus, that was close," Amundson said softly.

"That would've been a helluva way to go," Torrence muttered, "after dodging the opposition for twelve months."

"Well, we certainly got a good look at that valley. It's the first time I saw that mill," Amundson said.

"I hope you're not suggesting we fly that low over the next one."

"Hell, no. But we did get a good look."

"Crap," Torrence said.

Suddenly, an image came into Amundson's mind. It was the face of the female guard in the cubicle at Odyssey, twelve months before. She was saying something in response to his questions. She was moving her mouth, and he could hear her words, "...a few months ago, Johnny, the engineer, and me were passing time by ourselves up in the old mill at the other end of the valley..."

In the old mill.

"Damn, that's it!" Amundson yelled.

"What's what?"

"That's the valley. That's where Odyssey is buried!"

"My God, how do you know?"

"The old mill. That's it. Odyssey, here we come."

Excitedly, Amundson told Torrence about the guard and her love nest at the mill.

"C'mon, let's go back and have another look," Torrence said. He banked the plane steeply to reverse direction.

They were soon back over the valley. "I still don't see any runway," Amundson said.

"But there must be one. Remember, they were shuttling cargo planes out of here, and you sure can't set those babies down in a field like we do with this thing. You need concrete—and plenty of it."

"It's gotta be staring us in the face," Amundson said. "Hey, wait a minute."

"What?"

"You see that road down there?" Amundson asked.

"Yeah?"

"It dead-ends . . . there by that hill."

"How come we never noticed that before?" Torrence asked.

"It must have been hidden by the foliage of the trees. The leaves are all down, my friend, and it's as plain as day."

"Okay," Torrence conceded. "If that's what

they used, how come we've never seen any of those transports in this area?"

"They must have flown them only at night. This is way out of range of our radar at the farm."

"Wahoo, wait till we get back and hit the rest of them with this news!"

Amundson smiled, but only for a moment. Their radio suddenly crackled with Roy Romano's desperate voice. "Eagle One, emergency, Eagle One, emergency. We are under attack, we are under attack. Do you read? Over."

"Eagle Base, Eagle Base, switch to Frequency E, switch to Frequency E. Over."

There was a pause while they switched to a more discreet frequency. "Eagle Base, do you read me? Over."

"Loud and clear, Eagle One. Over."

"What's the nature of the attack? How many? What equipment? Over."

"About fifty infantry, supported by two tanks."

"Any aircraft?"

"Negative."

"Is the chopper up?" Amundson asked.

"Not yet, but Andy's revving her up now."

"Are you under fire from the tanks?"

"Not yet. They've just broken through the wire."

"They'll be in range in a moment, so watch yourselves," Amundson said. "Is everyone in position?"

"Not yet. The defense teams who were on alert

are ready to engage. The rest of us are just drawing weapons."

Amundson couldn't remember if Ellen was scheduled for security duty.

"Roy?"

"Yes?"

"Tell everyone we've got something to fight for."

"You've found Odyssey?"

"We sure did. Kick the hell out of that bunch. Our ETA is in forty minutes. We expect you to be mopping up by then," Amundson said.

"I hope so," Romano said. "Listen, Karen's taking over communications. I'm heading out with Bob's team in the M-2."

"Tell Karen to patch all communication in on this frequency so we can hear what's going on."

"Roger, Eagle One. Over."

There was a brief pause, then Karen's voice came on. "Eagle Two, this is Eagle Base. Do you read?" she asked, trying to raise Andy Rylander in the helicopter.

Rylander's voice broke in. "Eagle Base, I am fully fueled, fully armed, and airborne. Give me a heading to the target. Over."

"Eagle Two, you are on course to intercept. Maintain your present heading. You should have visual contact in about three minutes. Over."

"Roger, Base. Over."

"Eagle Two, targets are approximately one hundred yards inside our wire and entering minefield. Electronic scanner shows both tanks now inside minefield. Am activating first group of mines."

"Eagle Base, I have visual," Rylander reported. "You got one of the tanks. It's on fire, and the crew is bailing out. But the lead tank is still moving toward the farmhouse."

"Roger, Eagle Two. I am now activating remaining mines. Report effect, Eagle Two."

There was a pause in the radio transmission, then Rylander came back on. "Negative, Eagle Base. The second tank is through the minefield. Infantry has suffered six, seven casualties. Rest of them have fallen in behind the remaining tank. I am descending to engage."

"Roger, Eagle Two. Good luck."

The Apache gunship arched down and loosed a missile. A shattering explosion shook the tank, and it erupted with a geyser of flame.

"Bull's-eye!" Rylander chortled. "Now for the infantry."

There was the sound of cannon fire. "They're retreating!" Rylander reported. "And here come our guys to mop up."

"Tell them to get some prisoners, Eagle Two," Amundson barked into his mike.

As they neared the farmhouse, Amundson and Torrence saw the twin pillars of black smoke to the south where the two tanks were still burning. Everyone had congregated in front of the house to greet them. Torrence landed, and taxied as close as he could to the house. Immediately, the plane was surrounded, and they were mobbed as soon as they stepped out.

Allison threw her arms around Torrence, and Ellen did the same to Amundson.

"C'mon, let's get inside," Amundson said. "We've got a lot to talk about."

He walked Ellen toward the front door, his arm around her waist.

They went straight to the meeting room. "Did you get any prisoners?" Amundson asked Corrigan, once they were all seated around the table.

"Yeah, two. But they were both badly wounded. Neither of them made it, but they both spilled their guts to us before they died."

"How'd you manage that?" Torrence asked.

"Told them we had a doctor back here who could probably save them if we got them here fast enough. Then we gave them the choice of riding in the chopper and telling us about their friends who got away—or taking the long way here in the bumpy M-2. They both chose the chopper, but they both died on the way here."

"So what did they tell you?" Amundson asked.

"They're part of a renegade reserve armor unit from Beaver Dam. They're the ones who teamed up with our local hoodlums. They've all been holed up at a huge farm complex about ten miles from here, just itching to get their hands on our food and our women. They finally decided to give it a try."

"Didn't they know about the helicopter?" Amundson asked.

258   **LAWRENCE DE MARINO**

"Yeah, but they didn't know it was a gunship
—and they weren't counting on the mines."

"Did you get the location of the farm?"

"Sure," Corrigan said.

"Good. We'll have to take it out."

"Already done," Rylander said. "I flew over
there right after Joe pried the location out of
them. There wasn't a soul around. I leveled the
place with a missile and came home."

"Enough war stories," Corrigan said. "Where's
Odyssey?"

"And how did you find it?" Ellen asked.

Amundson and Torrence kept interrupting
each other as they explained how they finally
found the base.

"So let's move in!" Romano said. "We've been
waiting for months, and now we have them."

"But we don't know for sure that the base is
sealed," Johnson said.

"Hell, the airlift to South America has been
over for weeks," Torrence said. "We know that
from Melville's broadcasts."

"I know, but I'd rather wait a few days and be
safe," Johnson answered. "There must be some
way to verify the base is sealed. "Remember, we
only get one shot at them. If we bust in before
they're in suspended animation, we'll get butch-
ered."

"Maybe Bob's right," Corrigan said. "How
about if we put a couple of people into the valley at night. If there's no activity, we can be
pretty sure they're buttoned up."

"Enough discussion," Amundson said. "We

can't wait. We have to go in *now*. We're running out of time. The first big winter storm's on its way. Once that hits, we'll be grounded. Our fuel is getting low, and we've just about hit bottom on food.

"Even worse, it looks like the small piece of the world that's still out there is well on its way to committing nuclear suicide."

"But if it comes to a nuclear exchange, don't you think it's New Washington the Russians'll hit?" Bob asked.

"Sure. But don't forget that at least a third of the U.S. strategic force is land-based—in silos in the *old* United States. We can't afford to wait. I say we go in tomorrow."

The room was silent.

"All right, so how do we get in?" Corrigan asked finally.

"Jerry and I pinpointed the road they used for a runway. I think we can assume it's still functional—that they plan to use it again when they come out of suspended animation," Amundson said.

"But how did they use it? How did they keep their planes hidden underground during the day and get them up on the runway for nighttime operation?" Torrence asked.

"My guess is that part of that road is a hydraulic elevator, like the ones they use on aircraft carriers," Amundson said.

He leaned over the table, spreading out a well-worn map. "We have to find that section of the highway and blow a hole through it."

"Joe, do we have explosives that could handle that kind of job?" Torrence asked.

"No sweat. I'll open it up like a piece of cheese."

"It sounds and looks simple," Amundson said. "But you'd better believe there'll be some surprises waiting for us. We'll be awfully exposed out there in the middle of that valley. We should sandbag our position.

"Boys," Amundson continued, speaking to Tod, Steve, and Mike, "that'll be your job."

"We'd all better wear flak jackets. Even that may not be enough. We may encounter booby traps—gas or chemicals."

"We've got those army CBR suits in the armory," Corrigan said. "We can wear them under the flak jackets. Together, they should protect us from just about anything."

"What's a CBR suit?" Ellen asked.

"Chemical, biological, radiation," Corrigan said. "Protection against anything the enemy can throw at you on the battlefield."

"I'm thinking of what you did with the snowmobile suits, Joe," Amundson continued. "Could you do the same thing with the CBR suits?"

"Sure. But it'll take time, and I'm going to need some help."

"Who do you want?" Amundson asked.

"How about the kids?"

"You got 'em. Get started right now." Corrigan left the room with five eager teenagers in tow.

"Andy, what's the maximum on the chopper?

Can you handle all of us and our gear in one trip?"

"No way," Rylander said. "It'll take two trips."

"All right, we'll have to live with that. I'm still worried about being so exposed," Amundson said. He pointed on his map to the foothills east and west of the valley.

"There are heavy woods here, at the base of the foothills. Let's put a covering squad into those woods on either side. Hey, that works out all right. As long as we have to make two trips with the chopper, we'll put the covering teams in first. Here, and here," he said, pinpointing locations just outside the valley.

"Three-man squads on either side. They can work themselves into position while Andy is making the return trip with the rest of us. The cover teams will go in before dawn—before the rest of us even show ourselves."

"Okay," Torrence said, "but who's going to do what? We're going to be spread pretty thin."

"I don't think that'll be a problem, Jer. The women can handle the covering action—Teri, Betty, and Alicia to the east, and Ellen, Carol, and Corine to the west."

"But that leaves them alone and exposed," Torrence complained.

"Don't be a chauvinist, Jer. They'll be a lot safer in the woods, and they're all good shots."

Torrence grunted, and Allison smiled at him across the table.

"Karen will be Andy's door gunner," Amundson continued. "Andy, the chopper should be up and covering us as much as possible.

"If anyone on the covering teams runs into trouble, use walkie-talkies to call for help. Otherwise, no communication. Roy, draw up an inventory of the communications equipment you'll need.

"Joe is going to be tied up all night with those suits. Bob, would you make sure the weapons, ammunition, and other armaments we need get on the chopper. Check with Joe to see exactly what he wants to take.

"Remember, if we forget anything, we won't have a chance to come back for it. We'll land at first light. We'll need the rest of today to get ready, so let's get to it."

Chapter Fifteen

‖‖ ‖‖ ‖‖ ‖‖ ‖‖

Precisely at dawn, the helicopter cleared the foothills of the valley where Odyssey was buried. Inside the chopper, five men and three boys sat nervously waiting to land. Amundson, Torrence, and Corrigan wore the three protective suits Corrigan and his five helpers had been able to complete. The others had flak jackets buckled over CBR suits.

On the floor were the three bulletproof plastic

hoods Corrigan had fashioned for the protective suits. The headgear had been rigged with short-range radio for easy communication.

As they descended into the valley, Amundson moved up front to direct Rylander. "Andy, you see the short four-lane highway at the end of the valley? Set her down there. Once we're out, get the chopper up and cover us."

Rylander landed on the spot Amundson had picked. The eight passengers jumped out, weapons ready, and Rylander took off immediately.

"Okay, everyone knows the plan," Amundson said. "We need to find where the road ends and elevator begins. Check the seams with your bayonet. There must be a difference between them. The spaces where the elevator joins the road should be wider.

"Joe, while we're looking for the elevator, you'd better double-check your equipment." Corrigan made sure his explosives, wire, and switches were all set to go.

The others spaced themselves about a hundred yards apart and began their search. High above, the helicopter circled, keeping watch. From the woods, the women in the covering squads watched through binoculars.

Suddenly, Torrence let out a yell. "Here it is!" The others rushed to him. His bayonet was sticking in a seam, and only the handle was visible. Amundson tested it. "You've got it. It's not joint compound. It's all one piece, like a rubber seal."

He paced off the distance to the next seam: twenty-five feet. He probed it with his bayonet, and found that it was solid. He tried three more seams before his bayonet sank into the ground. "This is it," Amundson said. "This must be the other end of the elevator. It looks to be about a hundred feet long. Joe, what do you think?"

"The concrete won't give me any trouble, Ted. If it's really thick, I may have to use more than one charge."

"Okay, let's go through right here," Amundson said. He marked a three-foot circle on the concrete. He felt an overpowering sense of anticipation. After all the months of frustration, he was on the verge of success.

Corrigan unrolled a coil of wire to a position about a hundred yards from the road, where the rocks and boulders would shield them from the explosion. Then he selected the plastic explosive he needed from his carrying bags. It took him about twenty minutes to prepare the explosive charge, while the others looked on from a respectful distance.

"Okay, everyone behind those rocks over there," Corrigan yelled. They all scurried for cover. Corrigan attached his detonation wire to the explosives, then calmly picked up his carrying bags and joined the others behind the rocks. He attached the other end of the wire to a detonator, looked around to make sure everyone was there with him, then flipped the switch.

The explosion wasn't as loud as Amundson thought it would be. Most of the force was directed downward, where Corrigan wanted it to go. None of the exploded debris reached them.

When the debris and dust had settled back to the ground, Corrigan stood up. "Let's take a look," he said.

Amundson, Corrigan, and Torrence put on their protective hoods and bellied up to the edge of the crater. Cautiously, they peered over the edge, wary that the opening would give anyone waiting below a clear field of fire.

The crater was five feet deep, but they weren't through to the room below. "Looks like it'll take another healthy charge," Corrigan said.

He placed more of the explosive at the bottom of the crater and detonated it from behind the boulders. Again, they were cautious as they approached.

"Still not through," Amundson said.

"Yeah, and we're ten feet down," Corrigan said. "Wait a minute. We *are* through. Look at the smoke being sucked down. There must be pinholes at the bottom of the crater."

"That last explosion must have broken some kind of vacuum seal," Amundson said.

"But why would the room below be depressurized?" Torrence asked.

Amundson shrugged. "We'll find out when we get down there."

"The very best way to handle what's left of the concrete is with another small charge," Corrigan said.

"You're the boss, Joe."

After the third explosion, the three of them

were even more cautious as they approached the crater's rim. Amundson poked his M-16 into the hole and fired blindly. He emptied five magazines into the room below without a return shot being fired.

Finally, they peered over the edge. "A neat job," Amundson said of the hole.

"Yeah. Through ten feet of reinforced concrete," Torrence added.

Amundson picked up a nearby rock and dropped it through. It took a couple of seconds to hit the floor.

"Sounds like a long drop," Corrigan said.

"Yeah, well, I think we're ready. Let's get the equipment off the chopper," Amundson said.

Torrence stood up and waved for Rylander to land. Amundson motioned for the rest of the group to join them at the opening.

As soon as the helicopter was on the ground, they began unloading gear: a radio, rope, scaling ladders, climbing equipment, tools, a portable generator and lights, weapons, ammunition, and what looked like the entire contents of Torrence's armory at the farm. While the others inspected and organized the equipment, Amundson marked off a ten-foot square on the pavement with his bayonet.

"Okay, let's get going!" he yelled. "Kids, get those bags over here." Mike, Tod, and Steve ran to Amundson with armloads of empty sandbags.

"Use the dirt from the shoulder of the road to fill the bags," he said. "I want a sandbag wall where I marked it on the concrete. Make it six feet tall, and leave an entrance facing the hole. Make sure the entrance is big enough to move our gear through—say, three feet wide. You're building our command post, so make it strong."

The others stood around the hole, waiting for instructions.

"Okay. Joe, Jerry, and I will be the first ones in. The rest of you are going to support us.

"Roy, get your radio set up inside the sandbag perimeter," Amundson instructed. "Stay on the radio as much as possible, because you'll have to monitor us on our suit mikes, Andy in the helicopter, and the women on their walkie-talkies.

"Joe, move your weapons and ammunition inside.

"Bob, get the generator set up as soon as you can, then you'll have to cover us from up here as we descend into the hole. We'll need a steady stream of equipment. We'll call for it over our suit mikes, and you'll have to make sure we get it. Use the boys when they're done sandbagging."

As soon as Amundson was through barking orders, there was a sudden burst of activity. He motioned for Torrence to join him at the hole.

"Let's move the rest of the equipment closer to the opening so it's handy. We'll need the ladders, rope, flashlights . . ."

Torrence nodded, then began to move some of the boxes. Corrigan finished his work with the weapons and ammunition and joined them. The three men in their protective suits peered down into the hole.

"Okay, let's do it," Amundson said. "I'll go first. Jer, you follow me as soon as I reach bottom. Joe, you follow Jerry."

Using pitons, Amundson attached one of the scaling ladders to the concrete next to the opening, then tossed the loose end through the hole.

"How long is the ladder?" Amundson asked.

"One hundred feet," Corrigan answered.

"Should be plenty."

Corrigan handed him a Very pistol and a flashlight.

Amundson slung his M-16 over his shoulder and shoved the flashlight into one of the suit's big pockets. Then he fired a flare into the room below.

Amundson handed the Very pistol back to Corrigan, moved awkwardly onto the ladder, and climbed slowly into the opening.

Inside the underground chamber, the flare was still burning bright, and Amundson could see the room clearly. He first noticed a huge glistening metal cylinder, about ten feet in diameter, that stretched from floor to ceiling in the middle of the room.

The hydraulic shaft for the elevator, Amundson thought. It was thirty feet from where he was dangling.

"Can you see anything?" Corrigan asked over his suit mike.

"Sure. I can see the whole room."

"Anyone down there?"

"Nope. But I see a lot of vehicles. A bulldozer, trucks, tanks, APCs, Jeeps, helicopters, even a couple of fighter planes. Quite an arsenal they've assembled."

"How do they intend to keep all that stuff in good condition?" Torrence asked.

"That's why the room was depressurized," Amundson said. "With no air in the room, the equipment should still be in pretty good shape when suspended animation is over."

Amundson was ready to continue his climb down, but the flare was beginning to fade.

"You want another flare?" Torrence asked, as if reading his friend's mind.

"Yeah, but not from the Very pistol," Amundson said. "They don't last long enough. You got any road flares?"

"Yeah," Corrigan answered. "Coming right up."

Without waiting for the road flares, Amundson continued downward. The protective suit made movement difficult, and he had to be content with moving down a few rungs at a time, then stopping to catch his breath.

About halfway down, he was sweating—from the climb and from the potential danger. The Very flare was fading fast, so he stopped and waited for the new flares. He stared up at the circle of light above him, at the comforting sight of Torrence peering at him, rather than into the gloomy darkness below. Then Corrigan reappeared.

"Heads up," Corrigan said, igniting a flare. He

tossed it past Amundson to the floor below him, then followed up with two more. The three flares gave the room a red glow.

"How soon before the generator lights are working?" Amundson asked.

"Bob said a few minutes."

"Okay, I've got enough light from the flares. Jer, why don't you start down now instead of waiting. I don't think we're going to have any trouble on this floor."

Amundson watched Torrence swing onto the ladder and start down. When he was sure his friend was safely onto the ladder, Amundson resumed his own descent. The flares helped, but there were a lot of dark spots below. Amundson played his flashlight back and forth as he climbed down, cautiously moving only a few rungs at a time.

Finally, he reached the floor and stepped off the ladder. *I wonder how many silent alarms I just triggered*, Amundson thought. He was suddenly aware of how terribly exposed he was in the semidarkness. He unslung his weapon and brought it to the ready position; but there was no target, only the eerie red glow of the flares.

He looked up and saw Torrence's flashlight swinging back and forth, as his friend came down the ladder.

"Ted, you all right down there?" Corrigan asked suddenly over the suit radio. "All I can see is your flashlight."

"Yeah, I'm okay, but I feel like I've descended into Dante's Inferno."

"Jerry, how are you doing?" Corrigan asked.

"This goddamn monkey suit ..."

"Tsk, tsk," Corrigan said. "You'll feel differently about it if someone starts shooting at you."

There was more swearing from Torrence. Then, two powerful floodlights came on.

"Hey, that's just what we need," Amundson said.

"Where do you want them?" Johnson asked.

"When Jerry gets down here, keep one light on the base of the ladder and the other on us."

As he spoke, Torrence climbed off the ladder and unslung his M-16. "Any sign of the opposition?" he asked.

"No. So far, so good," Amundson said. "Hey, Joe, why don't you start down."

"On my way," Corrigan said. He started down the ladder, moving more adroitly than either of the other two. He carried additional lights and power lines, as well as extra ammunition.

"Bob, can you give us cover from the opening?" Amundson asked.

"Sure can."

"Where do we go next?" Torrence asked.

"That way," Amundson said, pointing with his flashlight. "When the Very flare was still lit, I saw some small rooms over there. Could be control rooms or offices. Maybe we can find the light switch for this place."

They moved toward the cubicles, Bob's floodlight following them as they walked. They entered the first cubicle and found a control console. Amundson played his flashlight over the toggle switches.

"Looks like the controls for everything on this level," Amundson said.

"Watch out for booby traps," Torrence warned.

They searched the room carefully, including the control console, the battered desk, the filing cabinet, and the chairs. They found nothing. Finally, Amundson switched on the button marked Power. Nothing happened. In quick succession, he pushed a row of buttons marked Ceiling Lights, and still nothing went on.

"Power must be turned off at a lower level," Amundson said. He examined the other switches on the console. "There's even a control for depressurizing the room."

Suddenly, Corrigan was standing in the doorway. "Find anything?"

"Just a lot of controls that don't work," Amundson said.

"I've got power leads from the generator and more lights. Where do you want them?" Corrigan asked.

"There's an elevator about ten feet to the right of where you're standing. Leads to the lower levels. That's where we're going to be."

"How's everything down there?" Johnson asked over the suit radio. "I can't see any of you."

"We're all right," Amundson said. "Start moving the equipment down into the room. This level is under control..."

Amundson stopped speaking because he heard a faint hissing noise from somewhere. "You guys hear that?"

"What?" Corrigan asked.

"Gas!" Amundson shouted. "Bob, we're under gas attack. Shine one of the lights along the wall so we can see where it's coming from."

"Right."

Using the floodlight, they located and marked the vents where the gas was coming into the room.

"What do you think it is?" Torrence asked.

"If I rigged it, I'd use the deadliest stuff I could get."

"Nerve gas," Corrigan said.

"Yeah. Joe, do you have something that will fuse those vents closed?" Amundson asked.

"Sure. The latest in thermite jelly. Bob, I'll need my bags."

"Okay, coming right down."

"How are you coming with the rest of that equipment?" Amundson asked Johnson.

"I've pulled the boys off the sandbag detail. We're ready to start lowering all of this stuff by rope, but one of you has to release the rope after each load."

"Okay, Joe, that's your job. And get those vents sealed as soon as possible. Jerry and I are going to try the elevator."

"Right. See you later." Corrigan walked off into the gloomy darkness.

"Do you think the gas was triggered automatically, or is someone watching us?" Torrence asked.

"I don't know, but we'd better be ready for anything. Let's try the elevator."

The elevator did not respond when they pushed the button to bring it up. "We'll have to force the door open," Amundson said. They grasped the doors and pulled.

Immediately, there was a tremendous explosion. Amundson and Torrence flew backward and landed heavily. Neither moved for a moment.

Amundson groaned. He was lying on the floor, staring up at the ceiling. He tried to move, but could not. He was afraid the blast had damaged his suit and the nerve gas was attacking his body.

Then a hand touched his foot. "That you, old buddy?"

"Yeah. Are you all right?" Amundson asked.

"I think so. How about you?"

"I don't know. Check my suit."

Torrence played his flashlight over Amundson's form. "Your suit looks okay. See if you can stand up."

With Torrence's help, Amundson was able to get to his feet. "I'm all right, I think."

"God, what a couple of tenderfeet we are," Torrence said. "Letting a booby trap get us."

"It's the gas and the darkness," Amundson said. "Makes you want to hurry."

"Hey, you two all right?" Corrigan asked, appearing suddenly out of the semidarkness.

"Yeah. Just knocked on our asses," Torrence said.

"I can imagine. That blast knocked me down way over by the ladder."

"Thank God for your suits," Torrence said.

"Ahhh...well, I knew your opinion of my work would improve when the going got rough. Some good news...I've got the vents sealed off."

"Good. Let's take a look at that elevator shaft," Amundson said.

The doors were destroyed, and a small fire was burning at the point of the explosion. "Where are those power lines? Let's get some light in here," Amundson said.

"Here they are," Corrigan said. He picked them up from the floor and attached them to the elevator cable. When he switched on the lights, they could see down about seventy-five feet.

"I don't like this at all," Amundson said. "It's a perfect setup for more booby traps."

"Use this," Corrigan said, handing him the Very pistol.

Amundson fired a flare into the elevator shaft. They could see about 150 feet down, to where the elevator car rested on the bottom. The elevator cable was still vibrating from the explosion.

"We're going to need more help to tackle this shaft," Amundson said. "It's time to bring in the rest of our people."

"You think it's safe?" Torrence asked.

"As safe as it's going to get."

"I'd feel better about bringing them down if

we could at least get this damned gas vented out of here," Torrence said.

"We can't do that until we get power to these controls," Amundson replied. "Anyway, our people are all wearing CBR suits." He spoke into his suit radio mike. "Bob, can you hear me?"

"Yeah."

"Get everyone down into Level One and move the equipment to the elevator entrance. Corrigan will help you get started. And Bob, double-check the CBR suits before anyone comes down here."

"Will do, Ted."

"Joe, help them with the equipment until they get a few people down, then get back to us. We need you with us in that shaft."

"All right. I'll be back as soon as I can." He walked off toward the ladder.

Amundson attached another scaling ladder to the floor in front of the elevator shaft. With Torrence covering, he started to descend. When he was down about twelve feet, he stopped.

"Hey, Jer."

"Yeah?"

"I've found an opening here in the side of the shaft. It's as wide as the shaft and about a foot deep."

Amundson illuminated the opposite wall. "Ah, across from the opening is a rectangular groove, same dimensions as the opening. It looks to me like a metal hatch slides out of one wall into the other to seal off the shaft."

"If they're buttoned up, why isn't it sealed?" Torrence asked.

"The elevator car would have to be up and out of the way for this to work. I sure as hell wouldn't want it to slide shut after I'm further down in the shaft. I wonder if Corrigan could seal the opening so that the hatch couldn't slide out."

"Ask and ye shall receive," Corrigan's voice cut in. "Bob and the rest of them are in good shape. I thought you might need me over here."

"Yeah. Come on down."

"Okay, watch your head. I'm going to toss down another ladder."

Amundson clung to his own ladder as Corrigan's dropped past him on the opposite side of the shaft. Corrigan climbed down with his bags and checked the opening. "A little thermite jelly, and this door will never slide out again."

He removed the jelly from his bag and placed a thin bead of it along the groove. Then he and Amundson climbed back up the shaft to where Torrence was kneeling at the entrance.

There was no explosion, just a sudden flare-up of intense white flame. In five minutes, it was done.

Corrigan climbed down and examined his work. "You can proceed with safety," he pronounced.

"Joe, why don't you and your bag of marvels stay with me," Amundson said. "Jer, do you still have a clear field of fire even with both of us down here?"

"Yeah, as long as you both hug the wall."

"Okay, Joe, let's go."

When they were about fifty feet down, Amundson heard a noise below them somewhere and stopped. "What was that?" he asked, pointing his M-16 downward.

"I heard it, too," Corrigan said.

A small light appeared below them. Before either of them could react, someone started shooting. They were both hit many times, dangling like pop-up targets and twisting on their ladders from the impact of the bullets. Torrence returned fire from his covering position above them. Amundson forced himself to look down. The shooting was coming from the elevator doors at one of the lower levels. He could make out the vague outlines of men below, and the flashes from their weapons.

Finally, Torrence's bullets struck home. There were screams, and one of the attackers fell through the open elevator doors to the bottom of the shaft. The shooting stopped, and the elevator doors slammed shut.

"You guys all right?" Torrence asked.

"Yeah. Good shooting," Amundson said.

"Well, Ted, that answers our question. Someone is down there, monitoring our movements and popping little surprises at us," Torrence said.

"The only way to stop it is to reach whoever is directing the show," Amundson said. "Only trouble is, we don't know which level he's on."

"Where would you guess?" Torrence asked.

"If I were running the show, I'd be all the way on bottom—as far away from intruders as possible."

"How many of them do you think there are?" Corrigan asked.

"Hard to say, but I don't think it's a large force, or they wouldn't be playing cat and mouse with us. Some kind of rear guard, left behind by McKarren to protect the place."

"I hear another noise down there," Corrigan said.

"I don't see—"

Amundson's sentence was cut short by the firing of automatic weapons being aimed through the escape hatch in the elevator cab.

Corrigan pulled a thermite grenade from his bag, pulled the pin, and let the grenade fall. When the incendiary grenade struck the elevator cab, there was a brilliant white explosion that set the cab on fire. Immediately, the shooting stopped.

"That's better," Corrigan said. "Gives us some light down there, too."

"God, that's a long way down," Amundson said.

"Hey, guys, the rest of the team is here, along with all of the equipment," Torrence reported.

"Good. We need you down here with us. Bob and Roy can cover from your position."

"Okay, I'm on my way," Torrence said. He climbed out on Amundson's ladder.

Amundson and Corrigan held their positions until Torrence reached them.

"I'm going down first. Jerry, stay about ten feet above me. Joe, ten feet above Jerry."

Amundson descended more quickly. He had the illumination from the burning elevator car to help him. He saw the end of his ladder, a few feet above the spot where the first attack had originated. He suddenly realized that he was down almost a hundred feet into the shaft. There was no movement and no sound from below.

He saw a narrow band of light coming from under the elevator doors on Level 2.

"Joe, I'm about five feet from Level Two. Let's see if the opposition in there is wearing gas masks. You got anything in your bag?"

"Only tear gas."

"That'll do . . ."

Suddenly, the lights in the shaft went on, and Amundson heard the unmistakable sound of the elevator starting. He looked down. The still-flaming car was rising rapidly toward him.

"Jesus Christ, get out of there, Ted!" Torrence screamed.

Amundson didn't hesitate. He started back up the ladder. He never looked back, just kept climbing upward as fast as he could go. Above him, Torrence was also retreating, but Corrigan held his position. He was stretched out from his ladder to the elevator cable.

Amundson could feel the heat from the burning car. Then there was a small explosion above him, and the elevator cable snapped in two, whipping back and forth across the shaft as it fell. The cable caught Torrence and knocked him off the ladder onto Amundson, who desperately clung to both the ladder and his friend.

Below them, the elevator car crashed into the bottom of the shaft, erupting into a billowy fireball of flames and sparks.

Torrence regained his hold on the ladder. "Does that make us even, or are you one up on me again?" he asked. Amundson smiled.

"Joe, that was quick thinking. Thanks," Amundson said.

"Don't mention it. Jerry all right?"

"Yeah, I'm okay, but I sure am tired of being on the receiving end. What do you say we start dishing out some punishment. You got those tear-gas grenades?"

"Sure."

"Then let's get down to Level Two and do it."

The three of them climbed back down, until Amundson was right above the doors, Torrence a few feet higher on the same ladder, and Corrigan across the shaft from them. "Here," Corrigan said, tossing a tear-gas grenade to Amundson. Amundson parted the doors to Level 2, prompting a volley of shots from the other side.

He lobbed in the grenade. When it went off, there were coughs, curses, and shouting as the defenders retreated away from the elevator.

"I wonder how many of them there are?" Torrence said.

"Too many," Corrigan said.

"You're right. And we can't leave them in

there while we go further down," Amundson decided. "We need to bring in some help." He called Bob and told him to start sending everyone down the ladders to Level 2.

While they waited, Amundson and Torrence pried open the doors. Amundson attached another one-hundred-foot scaling ladder for the descent to the remaining levels.

Meanwhile, the others had worked their way down the ladders as far as they could go. "It looks like the gang's all here," Amundson said to Torrence. "Are you ready?"

"Yep."

"Okay, let's go. Joe, cover us."

Amundson swung into Level 2, with Torrence close behind. The corridor lights were on, but their vision was obscured by the billowing tear gas. They took command of the corridors around the elevator while the others filed in behind them.

Amundson waited for Ellen before moving on down the shaft to the next level. When she arrived, he drew her aside and pressed his vision plate against hers.

"Not your typical Mayan excavation, is it?" he said into the suit mike.

She smiled and shook her head inside her helmet. She formed the words "I love you" with her lips. He nodded, then turned her around and inspected her to make sure her CBR suit was tight and her flak jacket buckled on.

"Be careful," he said.

"Where are you going?" she asked.

"We're going on to Level Three, while the rest of you clean up here."

Amundson placed Romano in charge of the mop-up on Level 2. Johnson remained at the elevator shaft to cover Amundson, Torrence, and Corrigan as they continued down to Level 3.

The further down into Odyssey they went, the fiercer was the fighting. Amundson, Torrence, and Corrigan were the cutting edge on each floor. With their protective suits, they would storm through the elevator doors, secure the area around the elevator, and bring in the rest of the group to mop up.

Andy Rylander was killed in the fighting on Level 3, where Tod and Mike were also wounded slightly. Allison was bayoneted in the arm during the cubicle-to-cubicle fighting on Level 4.

While the Level 4 fighting still raged above them, Amundson, Torrence, and Corrigan made their way down to Level 5. They stopped just above the still-smoldering rubble of the burnt-out elevator car. Amundson guessed that they were about 115 feet into the shaft.

"Something's been changed," Amundson said. "The elevator stops at Level Five. It used to go all the way down to Six."

"They must have changed it after you and Ellen escaped," Corrigan said.

"Let's get into Level Five," Amundson said. "There must be some way to reach Level Six from here. Either they put in a stairway or a new elevator that only goes one floor."

Corrigan blew open the elevator doors. Immediately, shots were fired through the open doorway, the bullets ricocheting around them. Again, they lobbed tear-gas grenades into the opening, but this time the shooting didn't stop.

"They finally got some gas masks," Torrence said.

"No matter," Corrigan said. He threw two shrapnel grenades through the opening. There were explosions, followed by cries and moans. The three attackers climbed into Level 5, more bullets striking against their safety suits.

Suddenly, a stream of liquid fire burst in their faces.

"Flamethrower!" Torrence yelled. He was out in front and took the full force of the flames. He crumbled to the ground, firing his M-16 at the source of the flames.

The fire from the flamethrower stopped abruptly. Amundson and Corrigan fired magazine after magazine into the dimly visible enemy soldiers as they tried to restart the flamethrower. Their bodies twisted and fell, one on top of the other, until there were only two left. They threw down the flamethrower and ran.

Corrigan took control of the corridor, while Amundson knelt down over his old friend. Torrence's eyes were barely open. He grabbed Amundson and pulled him down.

"Does that make us even again, or am I one up on you?" he whispered. Amundson's lips tightened into a half-smile, and an unstoppable tear appeared in each eye.

"Take care of Alicia," Torrence whispered. "And Ted, watch yourself with Corrigan."

Amundson tried to ask why he should be wary of Corrigan, but Torrence's eyes closed slowly.

Amundson stared at his dead friend. "Damn!" he swore.

Bob Johnson appeared at the elevator opening. "You ready for us?" he asked. Then he saw Torrence's body.

"Sunuvabitch. How'd that happen?"

"They had a flamethrower waiting for us. Jerry took the full force of it," Amundson said.

"How about you two? Are you okay?"

"I feel like an overcooked tamale," Corrigan answered. "But everything seems to be intact."

"Another couple of seconds, and the two of us would have been roasted along with Jerry," Amundson said.

"Bob, help me move his body off to the side, I don't want Alicia to see him like this."

"She won't be down for a while," Johnson said glumly. "She was wounded on Level Four."

"Serious?"

"No. A cut on her arm."

"Anyone else wounded?" Amundson asked.

"Tod and Mike—just scratches. Karen and Carol are working on them."

"Well, let's finish off this level and get on to Level Six," Amundson said. "And let's be careful."

They secured Level 5 without any more casualties, most of the defenders having been killed in the firefight around the elevator. Once they

were in control, a quick search located a fire
door a few feet from the elevator. Amundson
opened it, revealing a stairway that led downward. With the others staying back about fifteen
feet, he and Corrigan moved cautiously down
the stairs.

On Level 6, an open door led to the security
antechamber that Amundson remembered from
his first visit to Odyssey. A deserted desk and
chair and two TV cameras mounted high were
the only objects in the room. There was only one
door, straight ahead of them.

"Something's changed here, too," Amundson
said to Corrigan. "There was another door over
to the left—the one Ellen and I ran through
with the guard detail. It led to the escape tunnel. They've walled off the door—and probably
changed the escape tunnel."

"So let's see where the door goes," Corrigan
said impatiently.

"Careful," Amundson said.

They flattened themselves against the walls
on either side of the door and motioned for
everyone else to stand clear.

"More flamethrowers?" Corrigan speculated.

"I don't think so. We're too close to the hypothermia chambers and life-support systems for
a big fight down here. My guess is they gave us
their best shot on Level Five..." Amundson's
voice trailed off as he thought of Jerry Torrence.

"So how do you want to handle the door?"
Corrigan asked.

"The door opens toward us. You open it, and I'll go in low."

"All right. I'll be right behind you."

Corrigan jerked open the door, and Amundson knelt into the room, his weapon ready. He saw a man in fatigues to his left, aiming a pistol at the doorway. The man fired at the same time as Amundson. A single shot bounced off Amundson's vision plate, while the rounds from his M-16 almost cut the man in half.

Corrigan stepped into the room and knelt into a firing position next to Amundson. There was no other movement, only the brilliant whiteness of the room and the hum of machinery.

They had control of Project Odyssey.

Chapter Sixteen

▦ ▦ ▦ ▦ ▦

"We've done it!" Corrigan yelled.

"Easy, Joe," Amundson said. "There may be other diehards like the guy with the pistol."

Behind him, the others filed slowly into the room. "Everyone keep your weapons handy and your suits on," Amundson said, reaffirming his authority.

He surveyed the huge chamber. It was not as large as Level 1, but he estimated the ceiling to be 50 feet above them and the room roughly 150 feet long.

Before them, a corridor passed all the way through the room to the opposite wall. "Keep this corridor covered, Joe. I'm going to check the man with the pistol."

Corrigan motioned for Teri, Steve, and Corine to take positions on the floor. Amundson led the others toward the body. The name tag on the bloody fatigues said EDWARDS, and he was wearing captain's insignia.

"Well, Captain Edwards, nice try," Amundson said softly. He knelt down and searched the corpse. Inside the man's shirt, he found a thin book.

"What is it?" Ellen asked, standing beside him.

Amundson opened it. The book was addressed to Captain Edwards. Amundson read the first page:

Captain, you and your brave men and women have volunteered to remain behind because there is still a threat to our security.

Ted Amundson, the same man who escaped us at Devil's Lake, may find us. We've postponed suspended animation several times, waiting for him to show up. Now our food supply is almost exhausted, and we must proceed with suspended animation.

The 6,000 of us in hypothermia are trusting you to deal with Amundson. Your performance at Devil's Lake clearly indicated to me that you're the man for the job. You'll have twenty-five men and women under your command.

Ellen Kelly and Jerry Torrence will most likely be with Amundson. Pictures of all three of them are on the next page.

Amundson turned the page and saw pictures of himself, Ellen, and Torrence. Ellen, who was reading over his shoulder, cursed softly. "So the welcoming committee was tailor-made for us," she said.

Amundson nodded, then turned to the next page:

Make sure your troops study the pictures. You have access to all levels except the locked hypothermia chambers.

Once you have dealt with Amundson and his group, seal the base and get into your cubicles here in this room. Instructions for sealing the base are at the end of these orders.

To begin hypothermia, you need only enter your cubicles without clothes. Once inside, pretaped instructions will tell you what to do. Not only will you be the last of us to sleep, you will be the first to awaken.

Be assured that you will all receive the highest honors in our new society. Your personal reward, Captain, will be substantial, I assure you.

The orders were signed *John McKarren*. Detailed instructions on how to close off the base were on the last page.

"Hey, that's great!" Ellen said. "All we have to do is take their cubicles. Then we'll be up and around before anyone else wakes up."

Amundson nodded as he stood up. He passed

the book to Romano. "Make sure everyone reads it," Amundson said.

Amundson was pensive, his head bowed, as he stared down at the dead soldier. Ellen pressed her vision plate against his. "Are you all right?" she asked. He nodded.

"Thinking about Jerry?"

"Among other things," he said.

Amundson straightened up. "All right, let's take a look at their cubicles," he said. He led them past Edwards's body, to another long corridor that ran parallel to the first one. On their left were the hypothermia capsules reserved for Captain Edwards and his security force.

"There they are," Amundson said. "Our tickets out of this mess."

The cubicles occupied sections of two walls. Each was seven feet high and two and a half feet in diameter. The upper one-fourth was transparent, while the rest was opaque. Above each one was a small storage compartment.

"Hey, look at this," Ellen said, pointing to four of the cubicles. They were punctured with bullet holes.

"Must have been hit with stray rounds from my M-16 during the exchange with Edwards," Amundson said.

"Are there still enough for all of us?" Betty Johnson asked.

"I'm sure there are," Ellen said. She walked along the wall, counting. "Twenty-six. Only four are damaged. More than enough for us."

They continued their tour. Facing the hypothermia cubicles were banks of computers and controls. "Everything in the base must be controlled from here," Amundson said.

There were also rows of TV screens, power consoles, and other equipment Amundson couldn't identify. The computers and equipment occupied sixty feet of space.

"Hey, here's what I'm looking for," Betty Johnson said. She pointed to the only monitor screen that was on. She sat down on the chair facing the screen.

"I wonder why this one is on," Ellen said.

"Captain Edwards must have been using it," Amundson said.

The screen displayed a schematic of the base. For the first time, they had an accurate picture of how big Odyssey was, and how it was laid out.

Odyssey was shaped like a giant pyramid, with the top sliced off. Level 1, at the top of the pyramid, was separated from the five lower levels by a hundred feet of concrete. They could see the elevator shaft, the armory, the vehicles, everything in the base.

"This must be what Edwards used to monitor our moves in the elevator shaft," Amundson said.

"See those red 'L's' scattered throughout Level Six?" Betty asked.

"Yeah?"

"They must represent humans."

"'L' for 'Lifeform'?" Ellen guessed.

"Yeah," Betty said. "There are nine 'L's' and nine of us on this level."

"And look. There are five more on Level Five where Alicia, Tod, Mike, Carol, and Karen are," Ellen added.

"This is the most sophisticated information system I've ever seen," Betty Johnson said.

"Why don't you and Bob stay here and get better acquainted with it while the rest of us continue on," Amundson said.

"Suits me," she said.

Amundson, Ellen, and Romano continued up the corridor. "Where are these six thousand people in suspended animation?" Romano asked.

Amundson pointed to a door in the middle of the wall to their left. It was five feet wide by ten feet high and fused to the wall. There was no doorknob, no handle, and no visible control for opening it. A warning was written across the door:

DANGER! HYPOTHERMIA CHAMBER IS SEALED. ANY ATTEMPT TO OPEN THIS DOOR WILL RESULT IN YOUR DEATH.

"Well, that's pretty straightforward," Ellen said.

Amundson nodded. "We'll deal with that later. Let's see what the rest of this place looks like."

They continued down a side corridor. "I hear running water," Ellen said.

"You're right," said Amundson, pointing straight ahead. In the middle of the corridor was a huge support column that stretched from floor to ceiling. Around the column, a fountain sprayed curtains of water up and out, into a blue-green reflecting pool.

Amundson, Ellen, and Romano entered a small plaza that was created by the intersection of two corridors. Joe and Teri Corrigan were sitting on one of the benches that surrounded the pool, watching the fountain. Their daughter Corine stood next to the edge of the pool.

"The kids spotted the pool in a flash," Teri said. "It was all we could do to keep them from stripping off their clothes and jumping in."

"Where's Steve?" Amundson asked.

"I sent him up to Level Four to help bring down the wounded," Joe said. "I told him not to say a word to Alicia about Jerry."

Amundson nodded his approval. "Have you checked the other side of the room?"

"Yeah. All clear," Corrigan said. "We found a first-aid station, a kitchen, a cafeteria, handball courts, an exercise room, sauna, and a weight-lifting room."

"Sounds like they had enough diversions while they waited for us," Amundson said.

Corrigan nodded. "There's more. There are individual living quarters—small apartments, actually. Apparently, they were also very comfortable while they waited."

"Hey, you guys got everything under control down here?" Carol Romano asked over the suit radio.

Amundson turned to see Carol, Steve, and

Karen leading the three wounded. Alicia's arm was in a makeshift sling.

"Alicia, come over here," Amundson said, holding out his gloved hand. She walked to him and took his hand.

"Are you all right?" he asked her.

"Yes, I am. Where's Jerry?"

"Alicia, Jerry ... didn't make it."

She dropped his hand and stood stunned, looking around at the bowed heads of her friends. Then she suddenly ripped off her CBR hood and collapsed to her knees, sobbing into her right hand. Amundson pulled her to her feet and steadied her. "Put your hood back on, Alicia," he said softly. She shook her head. Amundson motioned for Ellen to help him. Together, they got Alicia's hood back on and fastened tight.

"Say, Ted, the opposition is gone—dead, finished," Corrigan said. "There's no one left to attack us. I think it's time to lighten up a little." To prove his point, he removed his own hood.

"There may still be booby traps, Joe," Amundson insisted.

"Ted, Odyssey is ours."

"Dammit, Joe, we still have a lot of loose ends to take care of. Remember, the base is wide open. That hole we made has to be plugged. And there's all kinds of crap aboveground to show we're down here. And we've got two friends to bury, plus twenty-six of the opposition. Those bodies can't stay down here."

Corrigan held up his hand. "Enough!" he said

acidly. "I get the message. I'll take the clean-up detail. I'll take the boys and Roy—if that's all right with you. But first I'm going to the john." He stalked off.

There was a long silence after Corrigan's abrupt departure. "Please don't mind Joe," Teri said finally. "My husband is very tired, and I think he's becoming unraveled."

"We all are," Amundson said softly. "Roy, do you still have Captain Edwards's book?"

"Yes."

"Good. You'll need it to lock up Level One. And, Roy, when you're done, and you're coming back down the elevator shaft, I want you to cut footholds in the side of the shaft—every two feet."

"What for?"

"We can't count on the rope ladders lasting the whole time we're in suspended animation. And with the elevator gone, we'll have a helluva time getting out of here."

Johnson nodded.

"When Corrigan comes back from the john, ask him what kind of climbing equipment we have. Especially how many pitons are left. Cover the wall with them to make the climb out easier.

"Now," Amundson said, addressing the entire group. "Just so there's no doubt in anyone's mind about how I stand. I'm not convinced that the base is completely safe yet. Until I *am* convinced, I want you to keep your weapons handy and your protective suits on—except to go to the john or eat."

There was an immediate chorus of groans.

"Better to be uncomfortable for a few more hours than to risk everything we've gained so far."

No one said a word, so Amundson continued with his instructions. "Mike and Tod, switch suits with Karen and Corine and get those wounds taken care of. Teri, would you take them to the first-aid station and dress their wounds?"

"Sure."

"Hopefully, Joe can fix the three damaged suits later tonight."

"Did I hear Joe mention a kitchen?" Ellen asked.

"Uh-huh."

"With food?"

Teri nodded.

"Well, I for one am starving," Ellen announced.

Amundson nodded. "Okay. Carol, would you go along and see if you can rustle up some food? Ellen and I are going to see how Betty and Bob are doing with the computer. We'll meet the rest of you there in fifteen minutes. Roy, you and Joe and the kids better eat before you start the repair work."

"Okay."

As the others left for the kitchen, Amundson and Ellen headed back toward the life-support area. Ellen was perplexed about Amundson's inflexibility. "Why are you being such a hard-ass about the CBR suits? Do you think we'll be attacked again?" she asked him.

"I don't know. I guess I'm just uneasy," he replied. They were in the narrow passageway between the life-support area and the spot where Edwards's body still lay. He stopped abruptly and grabbed her arm. Pressing his vision plate against hers, he brought his finger to his lips as a sign for her to be quiet.

Ellen formed the word "why" with her lips. Amundson said nothing, just pulled off his helmet and motioned for her to do the same. He switched off the radio transmitters in the two hoods so they wouldn't be overheard by anyone. Then he grabbed her hand and pulled her down to the floor with him. "What in God's name are you doing?" she whispered.

He rolled over on top of her and kissed her deeply. "I want to make love to you," he said.

"Right now?" she asked incredulously.

"I've lost control of myself," he said.

"No, you haven't. What are you up to?"

"I want it to look like we're getting ready to make love," he said.

"For whose benefit?"

"Shhh. Just listen for a minute. This whole setup makes me nervous. Unless I've misjudged McKarren, there's a final obstacle here, specially prepared for us in case we reached this level."

"No one else is worried about McKarren."

"They don't know him like I do. Everyone else

wants to believe that we've gone as far as we have to go."

She nodded. "You're such a damned realist," she said. "Thank God."

"And we've got another problem to worry about."

"What?"

He told her about Torrence's warning.

"My God. What do you think he meant?"

"I suspect Joe has never been—uh—comfortable with me as the leader of our group. I think Jerry told Corrigan to either play ball with me as captain or go find another team."

"And with Jerry gone, Joe figures it's time to show his stuff," she concluded.

"Right."

"So what are you going to do?"

"My plans are still a little fuzzy, but Joe's antagonism may be helpful."

She looked at him quizzically.

"Just stay close to me, okay?"

"You want me to cover your back," she surmised.

Amundson nodded. "Especially when Joe and I are alone.

"Now let's play our love scene a little further," he said.

"But you said we have to keep our suits on," she quipped. "How far do you want me to go?"

"I'll tell you when to stop."

She smiled, then suddenly rolled him off her. She kept rolling until their positions were reversed. She flattened his body beneath her own, then kissed him deeply on the lips. "Too bad these suits don't have trapdoors in front," she said suggestively. Amundson smiled.

Five minutes later, he stood up and replaced his helmet, then helped Ellen to her feet. "Turn your radio back on," he said. "Let's see if Betty's conquered McKarren's computer yet."

When they reached the computer area, the Johnsons were still hunched over the console.

"Hi," Betty said when she saw them.

"Have you gotten acquainted with the computer?" Amundson asked.

"We sure have," Betty said. "Here, listen to this." She pushed a switch on the console. "Computer, acknowledge my voice."

"Acknowledged," came the reply.

"It's a marvelous system. It can provide a visual of almost anyplace in the base. Captain Edwards was using a heat-sensitive tracking system. There are sensors throughout the base.

"But the system is so flexible," she continued eagerly. "Here, let me show you. Computer, show me all of the lifeforms on Level Six. Top view of the entire floor, please."

Level 6 appeared on the screen. The diagram looked like a blueprint. There were five red "L's" in the kitchen, five more moving through the security antechamber, and four more in the computer area.

"Looks like Joe and his team are done eating and are on their way upstairs," Ellen said.

"Betty, have you seen the warnings on the

doors that lead to the hypothermia chamber?"
Amundson asked.

"No, I haven't."

"They say that anyone attempting to enter the
chamber will die. I wonder if the computer can
enlighten us on exactly what's waiting for us
beyond those doors."

"Let's check. Computer, show me a schematic
of the area between the life-support room where
we are now and the hypothermia chamber."

There was a pause. "I cannot comply with
your request. That information is classified."

"Well, the information is in the system all
right, but it's protected by an access code."

"Hmmm. Let's try a different tack," Amundson said. "Computer, describe the purpose of
the room we're in."

"This is the life-support room. It is self-
sustaining and self-repairing. It monitors, analyzes, and modifies the environment of the
hypothermia cubicles, the overall flow of power,
the life-support for the entire base . . ."

"Thank you, that's enough. Now, describe the
hypothermia procedure."

"The procedure is as follows. First, each individual must be unclothed upon entering the hypothermia cubicle. The individual may have no
object with him, including eyeglasses, jewelry,
money, weapons, or any hand-held objects.

"When the individual enters the cubicle, pretaped instructions are played automatically.
Once the instruction tape is done, the cubicle
door locks, and the hypothermia cycle begins.

The cycle lasts exactly twenty-one minutes. During that time, a complex mixture of gases, including argon, oxygen, and Refrigerant 42, is introduced into the cubicle.

"The individual feels no pain and remains conscious for the first fifteen minutes. The cycle cannot be terminated until it has run its course. Any such interruption will result in death.

"However, hypothermia may be terminated one hour or more after the cycle is complete. Termination takes two hours." Then the computer was silent.

"Okay, I've heard enough. They're preparing food for us in the kitchen," Amundson said to the others. "Betty, you can try to break that access code later. Right now, let's go eat."

It was about quarter to ten when the clean-up crew returned. When they entered the life-support room, the lighting was dim. Amundson and Ellen were waiting at the door.

"What gives with the lights?" Corrigan asked.

"The life-support system automatically regulates 'day' and 'night' by modifying the lighting. Even creates evening noises," Amundson said.

"I *thought* I heard crickets," Corrigan said. He walked toward the living quarters, anxious for a shower. Amundson walked next to him.

"Everything go okay?" Amundson asked.

"Yeah."

"Did you cut the notches in the shaft?"

"Yeah. And we used all but ten of the pitons. My grandmother could climb that wall now."

"Good," Amundson said.

"How'd it go down here?"

"No sign of trouble, but we haven't been able to reach the hypothermia chamber."

"Ah, shit! Who cares if they're in there, Ted. We're going to wake up before any of them."

"But we can't control those six thousand people in there unless McKarren is out of the way."

Corrigan lost his temper. "Your obsession with killing McKarren has destroyed your sense of reason," he said heatedly. "In fact, the five of us talked about it all night. We're tired, hungry, and smell like sewer workers in these suits. We're on our way to wash, eat, and sleep. In the morning, we're going into suspended animation.

"If you want to stay behind and try to blow down Old Man McKarren, that's your business."

Amundson stopped—as a signal for Corrigan to stop and talk some more—but he continued on toward the living quarters. The three boys followed without hesitating. Romano shrugged his shoulders and followed Corrigan.

Amundson turned to Ellen, who had a worried look on her face. He removed his helmet, and she followed suit.

"Everything's working fine," he whispered, wrapping his right arm around her waist.

Above them, the lights blinked off and on several times. "Looks like it's time for bed," Ellen said, looking up at the lights and yawning deeply.

"You go ahead. I want to check the cubicles

one more time to make sure nothing else was damaged during my firefight with Edwards."

"All right. If I'm asleep when you come to bed, wake me up," she said.

He nodded, then watched her as she walked away.

Chapter Seventeen

In the morning, Amundson and Ellen were shunned by the others. The two of them sat conspicuously alone during breakfast in the cafeteria.

Corrigan had systematically taken each adult aside and talked at length about the logic of going into hypothermia without delay. Amundson had made no attempt to dissuade anyone. Even Allison decided to go along with Corrigan.

As a final prelude to their entry into suspended animation, everyone gathered at the pool, where they shed their clothes and entered the water. They formed a circle and held hands.

Amundson gave a long sigh and began to undress. He and Ellen were the only ones still wearing protective suits, so it took them longer to disrobe. They joined the others in the pool.

"I'm glad you're finally coming around, Ted," Corrigan said smugly.

"I'll agree on one condition."

"What's that?"

"Instead of everyone going into suspended animation at once, one of us goes first—just to make sure it's safe."

"Sure. And I'll be happy to be the guinea pig," Corrigan said.

They all climbed out of the pool and walked to the cubicles. "I suggest we avoid the capsules to the left, where the bullets were flying," Amundson said. "Even though only four of them were damaged, some of the rounds may have hit controls or wiring."

"Good idea."

Corrigan led the group to the chosen cubicles. He paused, then kissed Teri, his son Mike, and his daughter Corine. Then he shook hands with everyone else.

"It'll be okay, Ted," Corrigan said, pumping Amundson's hand. Then Corrigan got into a cubicle.

"Ohhh, God, make it be all right," Teri sobbed after Corrigan's door locked shut. Amundson peered into the cubicle and watched Corrigan's face. He waited for five minutes, then slowly formed the words "Are you okay?" so that Corrigan could read his lips.

Corrigan nodded.

After ten minutes, Amundson noticed that Corrigan was getting drowsy. Again, Amundson asked the silent question, and again Corrigan nodded yes.

Above Corrigan were dials that monitored his condition. There was a set of green and red lights for each vital sign: respiration, pulse, and brain-wave function. All of the lights were green.

After twenty minutes, Corrigan was unconscious. The vital signs still showed green, and Corrigan was apparently safely into suspended animation.

The others separated into family groups for their final farewells.

One after the other, they took their places in their cubicles. Amundson and Ellen held back. "Let's make sure they're all safely in before we go," he said to her. Finally, everyone else was in cold sleep, and the lights above each cubicle showed green.

"It's our turn," Amundson said, helping her into a cubicle.

"Ted, are you sure—"

He placed his hand over her mouth. "Don't worry, honey. Everything will be all right." He kissed her passionately, then backed away as the tape started. The door clicked shut, and she waved weakly to him.

Amundson waved back. He waited about ten minutes, then entered a cubicle. Immediately, the prerecorded instruction tape came on and repeated what he'd heard the night before.

"...you will awaken as young as you are now,

healthy and alive, thousands of years from now," the tape concluded.

Amundson waited.

Five minutes after he was locked into the cubicle, he saw a movement out of the corner of his right eye.

And then, suddenly, John McKarren was standing in front of Amundson's cubicle, a tight-lipped sardonic smile of victory on his face. Behind McKarren were twelve green-garbed men and a woman.

McKarren watched Amundson's eyes bulge with terror. He walked up to the cubicle and attached a plastic disk to the front, at eye level with Amundson. McKarren held the other end of the device to his lips.

"The resourceful Mr. Amundson. I have you at last. God, you certainly proved to be a worthy adversary.

"But, you've wasted enough of my time. I've been waiting for you in there for three months—not to mention the man-hours lost hunting for you after Devil's Lake.

"Before you drift off into hypothermia, you should know that I don't plan to kill you—at least, not in the usual sense." McKarren paused to smile malevolently.

"I'm going to keep you and your friends in suspended animation forever, as a kind of eternal trophy—a warning to those who oppose my new society.

"Now, do you have anything to say before I

bid you good-bye?" McKarren released the mike switch so that Amundson could speak.

"I *thought* you'd get tired of waiting in there," Amundson said.

A look of surprise crossed McKarren's face, followed by a frightened look of sudden realization.

It was at that moment that Amundson squeezed the trigger of the .38 in his right hand. The slug blew off the plastic cubicle door and exploded into McKarren's stomach, hurtling him backward. Amundson fired again, and the second bullet struck McKarren's chest as he fell backward.

Then Amundson stepped out of the cubicle, holding a pistol in each hand. He fired at the men in green fatigues. Some of them tried to dig their sidearms out of their handsome buckled-down holsters. Others tried to run back into the hypothermia room. Amundson shot all of them Finally, he turned a pistol on McKarren's woman. She stood still and closed her eyes as he squeezed the trigger.

Amundson surveyed the carnage, then calmly dropped the pistols to the floor. He turned and faced Ellen, who was still locked inside her cubicle. Her eyes were wide with amazement as he unlocked her cubicle door.

As soon as it was open, she flung her arms around him and embraced him. He lifted her nude form into his arms and carried her toward the living quarters.

"You never told me he was in there waiting," she admonished.

"I didn't know for sure, but I suspected."

"You went along with Corrigan just to draw out McKarren," she said.

"Yeah. I figured if McKarren didn't show up, we were all pretty safe in suspended animation. But the chances were better that he *would* show up. I underestimated him before, and I wasn't about to do it again. I realized he wouldn't be satisfied to let Edwards finish the job for him. And that book we found on Edwards. It was *too* helpful. Edwards should have been instructed to destroy it once he read his orders and his troops saw our pictures."

"You're incredible," she said.

"So I was ready for him."

"So I saw. How did you stop the hypothermia in our cubicles?"

"Plugged the gas inlets last night, right after you went to bed. Spent most of the night taking care of the details."

"Like hiding two pistols in your cubicle."

"Yeah. Got that idea from the stray bullets that damaged the four cubicles."

They were entering the living quarters. "Why are we back here? What about the others? Are they safe?"

"They'll be okay. We have to move them into the hypothermia chamber with us. The cubicles they're in now are programmed for indefinite cold sleep. We'll have to terminate their suspended animation later, and then we can take the places of McKarren and his men."

"We're not going to do it right away?" she asked.

"No. We can't interrupt the cycle. It'll be a few hours before they're awake," he said.

"In the meantime, we can say good-night properly."

"Right." He reached out and opened the door to one of the bedrooms.

Reading—
For The
Fun Of It

Ask a teacher to define the most important skill for success and inevitably she will reply, "the ability to read."

But millions of young people never acquire that skill for the simple reason that they've never discovered the pleasures books bring.

That's why there's RIF—Reading is Fundamental. The nation's largest reading motivation program, RIF works with community groups to get youngsters into books and reading. RIF makes it possible for young people to have books that interest them, books they can choose and keep. And RIF involves young people in activities that make them want to read—**for the fun of it.**

The more children read, the more they learn, and the more they **want** to learn.

There are children in your community—maybe in your own home—who need RIF. For more information, write to:

RIF
Dept. BK-3
Box 23444
Washington, D.C.
20026

Founded in 1966, RIF is a national, nonprofit organization with local projects run by volunteers in every state of the union.

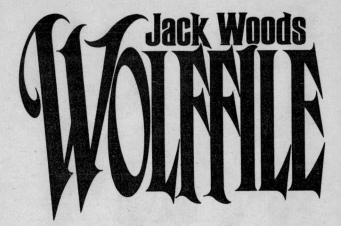